MW00978781

The Spirit of Kehillat Shalom

To Bob & Helen —
For our learning together
in especially music
Enjoy Boston
Shalom
Sandie

Rhoda Kaplan Pierce
& Sandie Bernstein

Sandie Bernstein

authorHOUSE®

AuthorHouse™
1663 Liberty Drive
Bloomington, IN 47403
www.authorhouse.com
Phone: 1-800-839-8640

Published by AuthorHouse   11/14/2014

ISBN: 978-1-4969-3895-4 (sc)
ISBN: 978-1-4969-3894-7 (e)

DEDICATION

To our amazing mutual friend, Amy Kaplan Moran, who brought us together one afternoon many years ago to see a film we cherished only for its title, ALL THE COLORS OF THE WORLD. For you, Amy, who have mutually imbued our worlds with the arts, with literature, with social conscience and with love, this endeavor would not have come to light without you.

"Every blade of grass has an angel
standing over it whispering 'grow."
The Talmud.

ACKNOWLEDGMENTS

To Phyllis Fitzpatrick who read this work with heart and mind using her editor's eye to make it more direct and poignant

To Mark Adam Kaplan who inspired the characterization of Serach

To Teme Ring for her profound consideration, ideas and patience while reading this manuscript

To Herschel Garfein for his musical expertise

To Neil Bernstein for his on-target recommendations and loving support

To Joel Moscowitz, an artist living in Sudbury, Massachusetts, for his wonderful cover art: Black Spiral.

To each other for inspiration and perspiration over easy and difficult times for the purpose of this mutual literary creation

PROLOGUE

*E*lijah confronted me in the Garden of Eden where I was happily planting the last of the bougainvillea, obtained from my recent trip to San Francisco. "Aviva Birman from the Kehillat synagogue near Boston, has been calling you for almost a year."

"Her voice was only a whisper."

"A year of whispers becomes very loud. She's worried about her mother."

I was aware of Ruchamah's obsession with her husband's death, but it did not concern me. "Two years ago I breathed a breath of life into that congregation," I said. "I brought them a new rabbi. Let Aviva talk to him."

"The rabbi has become distracted."

"So, we all have our problems," I answered glibly, but I was already packing my bag. When a rabbi is in trouble, a community suffers. And when a community suffers, I am obligated to do my best. I would have to return to Kehillat Shalom and whip the rabbi into shape.

"Serach, wait." Elijah called just as I was waving good-bye. He dropped some blank scrolls into the top of my satchel for record keeping and instructed me to put them out at night under the stars. "Shalom l'hitraot," he wished me bon voyage in the ancient language of our fathers.

"Three days is all this will take," I assured him. After all, I'm a fast worker with a speciality in synagogue repair. Elijah might not approve of my interventions, but at least I get results, which is more than I could say for the men in the Garden. They're responsible for monitoring world affairs and you know how well that has been going. It's a good thing they've been granted eternal life; at this rate they need it.

ONE

Dear Elijah,

I wasn't able to completely unfurl the scroll you shoved into my satchel just before I left the Garden, but surely you can read it. I'll place it outside under the stars as you requested. Since you insist I keep a record, I'll begin with the moment of my arrival as I plunked myself down on Ruchamah's stoop to rest from my journey. From this vantage point, I could see into her second floor windows. According to Jewish law, a person is supposed to mourn for one year. *Yahrzeit* candles glowed throughout the house. Fifteen years of mourning and a multiplicity of candles! No wonder Aviva was worried. Of course that's not my problem. I'm only here to help the rabbi. As long as I can assess his problem, come up with a solution and avoid the congregants, you will hardly have time to notice my absence.

It was an almost balmy night in Coolidge Corner, the early June weather reminiscent of the constant climate in our eternally perfect home. I reached into my satchel for my make-up, slipped synagogue clothes over my dusty traveling outfit and left for Kehillat Shalom.

As is the tradition on *Shavuot,* many congregants carried symbols of offerings from the first harvest, in this case fresh fruits and canned goods, which would later be given to those in need. Remember how we carried *bikkurim* to Jerusalem in baskets of silver and gold, Elijah? I had forgotten to eat before I left the Garden and was about to discretely pluck a juicy apple from someone's basket when I remembered how dangerous that had been for Eve.

Three stars appeared in the night sky before the doors finally opened. I thought I might catch a glimpse of the rabbi, but it was Marcia, the synagogue administrator, who let everyone in. Ruchamah seemed annoyed at something she said. She squeezed past Marcia without offering her a *Hag Samaiach,* quite unlike herself as I remember.

I took a seat near the front of the sanctuary. The pews had been replaced with upholstered stacking chairs the color of the eggplant we have in the Garden. Tonight, they were arranged in semi-circular rows. Time passed. Congregants glanced at their watches. Murmurs, sighs, whispers of exasperation echoed from one end of the room to the other. Unlike the first three stars, the rabbi was nowhere in sight.

I discovered Hillel in a Los Angeles synagogue when you sent me to find Kehillat Shalom a new rabbi. There had been no inkling of any problem. At the *Shabbat* service, he extended an invitation to the congregation to actively pursue *Tikkun Olam*. He indicated that the book he was writing would include sections written by members of the congregation on their efforts to make the world a better place. Congregants, both young and old gathered around Hillel and his wife, Beth, at the *oneg*. When I saw how much he inspired this diverse congregation, I thought he would be perfect for Kehillat Shalom. (I'm embarrassed to say I consider it almost a waste for this married rabbi to be so good looking.) Hillel is an earthly version of you, Elijah. He has a full head of hair, slightly graying and a muscular body, held so straight, it denies his slightly hooked nose. Unlike the piercing nature of your blue eyes, his are a warm brown that directly connected with me even from behind his rimless glasses.)

When Hillel finally arrived to begin the service, he offered no explanation as to what had kept him but began a passionate evocation concentrating on Moses as a baby, a rather unusual approach, I thought.

"*Shavuot* commemorates the night the Jewish people heard God speak, the night Moses was given the Torah at Sinai. The same Moses who, as a baby, had been placed in a basket and floated down a river to circumvent Pharoah's decree that all first born Jewish males be put to death. Imagine. A Jewish baby that was supposed to die, is found and raised by Pharoah's daughter. He grows up never knowing his real identity, but possessing a heart full of compassion for the Hebrew slaves. He intervenes on their behalf and is given a mandate by God to save his people. What could be more inspiring?" The congregation was rapt, his tardiness forgotten.

Hillel then asked a woman seated in the back of the sanctuary to come forward and help place us at the mountain on that fateful night.

"Look outside the window," Pam invited us. "It's getting dark, the 49th day of counting the *Omer* is ending; the moment is here, we are almost at Sinai.

"Even if you have questions about what really happened on the mountain, even if you have doubts, allow yourself for this one night at least to believe. Come tonight *b'lav shalom,* with a whole and complete heart: know that we met God at Sinai, know that we became one people at that moment, know that each of us was there." She motioned for all to rise as she continued.

"Moses has left us to climb the mountain. We know something big is about to happen but we are just waiting. Take a moment to think about what that feels like. Who are you right now? What are you thinking as you wait?"

I am transported back in time as she speaks. The anticipation was unbearable. Many became afraid Moses would not return and convinced his brother Aaron to allow them to make an image to worship. I watched helplessly as the men asked the women for their jewelry which they melted into a calf of gold. When Moses descended Sinai and saw the golden calf, he smashed it into a thousand pieces. Unable to contain his rage, he smashed the stone tablets inscribed with the Ten Commandments as well and had to return to the mountain. This time we waited without incident until Moses returned.

The congregants stood in silent meditation. The new cantor, Shoshanah, a woman to my surprise and pleasure, wrapped Kehillat Shalom in a ribbon of holiness with her luminous voice. The sanctuary vibrated with warmth.

The rest of the night was devoted to study. The sanctuary emptied, except for Ruchamah. And though I could detect nothing amiss with Hillel other than his being late, I decided to follow him to see what, if anything, I could discover, but I got caught up in the crowd heading for the door and had no idea where he might have gone. In search of him, I wandered the hallways, checking behind unmarked doors. Paint cans and ladders overflowed a storage closet. Volunteers from the congregation must have finished a first coat just in time for tonight; the institutional gray had been covered with enough white to render the walls almost silver, an effect I rather liked. I paid little attention to the workshops, glancing into classrooms only to assure myself Hillel wasn't there. Nor was he in his office, which was filled with pictures of children, obviously from Kehillat Shalom's preschool. On his desk a photo of Beth sat next to a tiny silver bird. The note pad in the center was clean. I thought it strange the office was so tidy, as if he sat quietly for hours each day, unable to do any work, his mind full of doubt, but perhaps he only put things away before leaving. I must have speculated about this for longer than I intended because classroom doors began opening. Congregants filled the synagogue hallways once again.

Beth was directly in front of me as I walked back to the sanctuary. She gave Ruchamah a quick hug as she sat down next to her. I took a chair directly behind them. As more and more congregants returned to the sanctuary, the noise level rose. I could hear them only intermittently and leaned closer. My forehead almost bumped the back of Beth's chair but I caught nothing until Ruchamah mentioned she was not herself tonight; she had fallen asleep unexpectedly before services and a crone had entered her dream of Daniel, obscuring her view. I must slipped into her dream on my way here though I had not consciously planned to do so. Beth attempted to reassure her but said nothing at all about the rabbi.

At midnight, Hillel re-entered the sanctuary and went to the ark to take out the Torah. Shoshanah removed its blue velvet vestments. The rabbi began to carry it down the three steps from the *bimah* when he suddenly stumbled. The two dowels parted and waved. The congregation gasped. Centuries flashed in milliseconds before my eyes. Walls crumbled. Synagogues burned. I focused all my energy; a congregant in the first row reached the rabbi just as the *Torah* began to fall. You were right, Elijah. The rabbi is clearly not himself. Had I ~~had~~ not been there I am sure this ancient scroll, considered so sacred it is buried as a person would be, would have hit the floor and I would have found myself at a funeral.

Hillel regained his balance, wrapped his arms around the top of the parchment, took a deep breath, nodded his thanks to the congregant and led us into the garden. Torches illuminated our way. A table, covered with a white damask cloth, held a delicate, silver *yad*. Hillel laid the sacred scrolls in the center and stood back as he spoke. "The giving of the *Torah* symbolizes the marriage between God and the Jewish people,"

I glanced at Ruchamah. Tears streamed down her face.

Although I never had a chance to marry or even to fall in love, I believe that if I had loved someone the way Ruchamah loved Daniel, I would have recalled a heart that had broken. I, too, might have grieved endlessly. My heart shifted slightly inside my breast. I straightened my body to escape this temporary perturbation and reminded myself that I hadn't come to involve myself in a congregant's personal angst. I was here to help the rabbi so that he could do that.

Hillel called Ruchamah to the Torah to recite the Ten Commandments. I watched as she pointed to each word of the sacred text with the handmade silver *yad,* her sadness much evident. "Tonight it is as if we are personally standing at Sinai to receive these words as new," Hillel said. "The *Midrash* tells us this was the moment the wombs of the women illuminated like fluoroscopes foretelling of generations yet to come." His voice broke. There was an uncomfortable silence until Shoshanah began a haunting *niggun.* I hummed along, quietly. You know how loudly I usually sing. Everyone in the Garden plugs his ears, except you. Somehow, Elijah, you always listen to me.

Aviva passed a basket filled with small white candles. Shoshanah lit the first one. Congregant to congregant, candle by candle, the flame was passed until the garden held a congregation of light.

The candles brightened the night sky. There had been no lights on Sinai. It was windy as well. Pam had already set the stage for re-enactment. I took a deep breath. Candles flickered; a few were extinguished, though they were immediately rekindled by someone whose flame had refused my invitation.

When we returned to the synagogue, I lingered outside Shoshanah's workshop on the Book of Ruth, tempted to listen to Ruth's declaration to Naomi. "Whither thou goest, I will go. Wherever thou lodgest, I will lodge. Thy people will be my people and thy God, my God." Ruchamah almost bumped into me in her haste to exit. Clearly, she did not want to be reminded that soon after Naomi sent Ruth to glean in a field, Boaz became her second husband.

Hunger overpowered me. I made my way to the kitchen and accepted a copy of the recipe for blintzes from Beth. I have not cooked a thing since I became an immortal and edged close to see how congregants measured out flour, eggs, milk and salt and tossed them into bowls. Aviva sprinkled cinnamon into the batter when no one was looking. Two men were already disagreeing as they pre-heated their fry pans. One wanted to make his shells like crepes, pouring only enough batter to cover the bottom of the pan. The other insisted on the technique his Aunt Ellie had taught him. Adding melted butter into the batter, he poured a small amount of it into an exceptionally hot pan and quickly transferred the excess back into the bowl to form a lip on the shell. A certain rhythm took hold as he banged out each of his finished products onto a dishtowel while the first showed off his flipping acumen.

My attention was caught by a spirited melody eclipsing this culinary tumult. The musician, Simon, entered the kitchen cranking out Klezmer music on his violin, his young son, Jacob, riding piggyback on his shoulders. As they passed Ruchamah and Aviva, Jacob reached out and tugged at Aviva's hair.

"Hi Jacob," Aviva said laughing.

"Sorry, Aviva," Simon smiled at both her and Ruchamah before circling around the kitchen serenading the cooks, stopping only to say, "I think my violin has become enriched from your cooking vapors. Perhaps molecules of butter flying into the air are landing on the wood and transforming the tone." Everyone laughed, including me. Congregants filtered in and out singing *Haveinu Shalom Aleichem*. I am ashamed to say I was so caught up in the festivities I completely forgot about

9

the rabbi, who, as I'm sure you have surmised, was not in the kitchen.

It was almost dawn by the time the blintzes had been safely settled onto cookie sheets and placed in the oven to keep them warm. Just as I found my seat for the morning service, Hillel entered from a small door behind the *bimah*. Next time I can't find him, I'll look there first.

During the *Shacharit* service, we blessed God who "removes the sleep from our eyes and slumber from our eyelids," this morning chanted before anyone even had a chance to go to sleep, ending with a poem by Miriam Weinstein, translated by Ruchamah.

WINGS OF THE DAWN

I had always imagined the wings of the
Shekhinah
were gray and white
until I woke early at sea.

A palette of color stretched before me
brilliance of red striated with subtler orange
to announce renewal, renewal of the day.

Pushing back slumber I prayed to God
who removes sleep from my eyes
and slumber from my eyelids
that I might catch the first point of light
so quickly followed by the brilliant arc of
incandescent orange.

I watched the orb rise from the horizon, elliptical
as though still lightly covered
by the wings of the Shekhinah
to gentle the awakening.

I wanted to run to that place in the sea
where ribbons of radiance fell upon the waters
to cup my hands
scoop up the light and pour it over my body
but the startling rays of dawn transformed
into white light so strong
I could not fix my gaze upon it.

Only when I turned my back
was its presence deeply known
the heat of its rays
wrapped 'round my shoulders
to penetrate my soul.

Lovely poem, but somewhat annoying as everyone always praises the *Shekhinah* and barely mentions me. I managed to set aside my resentment however, and joined the circle the congregants were forming to add my voice, (not too loudly) to the last verse of the Kaddish. "*Oseh shalom....* May God who makes peace in the high places make peace for us and all Israel."

You will be pleased to note that I did not jump the line when blintzes were served. They were, as I had suspected, delicious. I tried them with sour cream, with blueberries and strawberries and some with just plain cinnamon-sugar. I'll make some for you when I return.

Although I had intended to follow the rabbi home, I was too exhausted and much too full. I fell asleep in the sanctuary, waking only when the sun sent shadows across my ancient face.

Serach

TWO

"**M**om. You look so tired."

"Aren't you, Aviva? We've been up all night."

"I'm fine."

Ruchamah has to smile. They are on their way home from Kehillat Shalom and her beautiful daughter looks as refreshed as if she has had a good night's sleep. She checks the *yartzeit* candles as soon as they enter the house. Still burning. Good. Aviva's already on her cell phone. "Mom, do you mind if I go to Lori's?"

"Don't you want to rest a little first?"

"How about when I get back."

"Good enough." Aviva gives her a quick hug and is out the door. She's so like her father. Same red hair, same light heart spilling out joy. "I thank you,

Rhoda Kaplan Pierce & Sandie Bernstein

Daniel," Ruchamah says aloud, "for this wondrous child." She slips off her shoes, ignores the blinking message light. Her mother called just as she and Aviva left for services; she isn't ready to call her back. Her mother means well, but a few weeks ago she could hardly keep the excitement from her voice as she confessed she'd been in touch with Marcia, who informed her that Ruchamah had someone new in her life, a musician who attended Kehillat Shalom with his young son, much to Rucahamah's chagrin. "And why not," her mother went on. "Marcia and I are the world's best matchmakers. After all, aren't we the ones who found Daniel for you?"

"Marcia doesn't know what she's talking about," Ruchamah was unable to keep the anger from her voice. When her mother, usually a mainstay of support, accused her of refusing to take off her widow's cloak even for Aviva's sake, Ruchamah almost hung up. That phone call was followed by a note sending her a hug and a few presents in honor of *Shavuot*. For Aviva, a 60's outfit she had found in a local thrift shop, with peace signs embroidered on the blue denim vest and flowers strewn throughout the matching skirt, which she had worn to services. For Ruchamah, a rare edition of Bialik's poems, now sitting on the dining room table along with the translations she'd been working on before she left the house. There had been no mention of the phone call.

Ruchamah leafs through the translations, thumbs through the book of poems. Lassitude overcomes her. She stifles a yawn on the way to her room, removes her dress, lies down in her slip and throws an arm around Daniel's pillow. As she closes her eyes against the morning light, Shoshanah's words from the Book of Ruth, crowd her mind. "Entreat me not to leave you nor from following after you, for whither thou go, I will go and whither thou lodge, I will lodge. Thy people will be my people and thy God, my God." Entreat me not to leave you? If only there had been time to beg Daniel not to leave her. She tightens her arms around Daniel's pillow. She wants to sleep, but the sleep that brings dreams of Daniel, might bring the crone who had obscured her vision. Ruchamah gets up, goes into the bathroom to wash her face, straightens the picture of Daniel giving Aviva a bath a few weeks after she was born and leans against the sink. Distant memory washes over her.

"Ruchamah? Such a heavy name," Daniel commented the day they met. Marcia, who with her mother's help had insisted on this blind date, told her Daniel was a scholar. Obviously he was trying to impress her. "Based on the Yiddish *rachmonas,* for compassion and the Hebrew, *rechem,* for womb." He scowled. "You probably carry the weight of the world on your shoulders. If we ever have a daughter, we'll have to name her something lighter, something happier."

"Why don't you call me, Daisy, then," she told him flippantly. "You can think of me as the party girl in <u>The Great Gatsby</u>." What arrogance, to assume that they might have a daughter someday. Impossible since she was never going to see him again. But Marcia and her mother had gotten it right. They had been perfect for each other.

Who else but Daniel would have filled the house with helium balloons because he found her crying over a poem she was translating one day? Who else could have filled her heart with love whenever she looked at him? And who but she could have taken away his cynicism over the state of the world and taught him, scientist that he was, that God lives here, too. "Who made the atoms?" she would ask. "What Drum Major caused the 'Big Bang?'"

When she became pregnant, Ruchamah reminded Daniel of his desire to give their child a "happy" name.

"Daisy, of course, if she's a girl." he quipped.

"Let's make a list. We'll can start with Daisy and name all the flowers we know."

Daniel laughed. "We could name her after my grandmother, Annie," he said. "She was such a passionate gardener that from the first of spring a manic episode of flowers flooded her house."

"Aviva, for spring she shall be then," Ruchamah said. "And if our she, is a he?" But Daniel was convinced they would have their Aviva.

As soon as she was born, Ruchamah gave herself completely over to the routine of motherhood. Not one to quantify, she did not get caught up in watching the clock to determine feedings. Her only indicator, the feeling of milk entering her breasts, filling them almost beyond capacity. Daniel got up in the middle of the night to hand their daughter to her so she didn't have to leave their bed. His obvious pride in both of them touched her heart.

Sometimes, the three of them fell asleep together. As her body healed, she and Daniel slept in each other's arms, anticipating the time they could make love again. When *Erev Shavuot* arrived, Aviva was already sleeping almost four hours at a stretch. She and Daniel laughed, teasing each other all day, longing for the afternoon to be over. Some people still rang their bell before evening bearing gifts. Her mother and father, who couldn't get enough of their granddaughter, would often arrive unannounced to hold her in their arms.

They brought Aviva to *Shavuot* services. At the conclusion, when Rabbi Isaacs told the congregation that this holiday marked a new beginning, Daniel took her hand. "Come my love," he said as they left. "To our new beginning."

As soon as they opened their door, Daniel lit candles throughout the house while she nursed Aviva. He took the baby from her and sang her to sleep. Ruchamah took a leisurely bath scented with the Jean Nate that he loved. She washed her hair and barely dried it, letting it cascade over her shoulders. Daniel knocked gently on the bathroom door. "Guess what. Aviva hasn't stirred since I put her down. You have one contented baby, my love."

She had come out from the bathroom, wrapped only in a towel, her hair still damp. "Then it's time for one contented husband." Ruchamah dropped the towel to the floor and scooted under the sheets. "I confess I feel a little self-conscious."

"But it's my job to be conscious of you," Daniel grinned. He kissed her cheeks and pressed her hand against his face. "Please forgive me if I'm out of practice?"

She smiled. "Come to me, Daniel," she whispered.

He rained kisses all over her face and her neck. Ruchamah let the sheet fall so he could caress her breasts. A little milk trickled out. "Such a lucky baby," Daniel murmured. "Such a lucky me. You are so beautiful." Pleasure filled her entire body. Daniel embraced her with great tenderness, careful and patient, concerned about hurting her.

"Don't worry, Daniel. I'll yell if it hurts and I'll moan if it feels good." He burst out laughing and hugged her to him. They moved quickly past these gentle embraces as they found their way back to each other, caught in the tension between giving into the wildness and extending their lovemaking all night.

Daniel fell asleep first. As Ruchamah watched him, a smile never left her lips.

She slept until four when she heard Aviva wake. Rising quickly, Ruchamah changed and nursed her and placed her back in the crib. She took advantage of this quiet time for a leisurely shower.

Leaving the towel behind, she walked softly into their bedroom where Daniel lay fast asleep on his side, one arm around her pillow. She climbed into bed and planted little kisses all along on his back. No response, but then Daniel was no easy riser. Ruchamah placed her arms around his shoulders and rocked him towards her, laughing as she felt his resistance. She succeeded in turning him onto his back, found the spot between his ribs where he was most sensitive and began to tickle him. He must have been holding his breath so as not to laugh. "I love you," she whispered and lay her head on his chest. There was no heartbeat. "Daniel?"

Frantically she forced his mouth open and began breathing for him, in and out, tears streaming from her eyes. She had to remember: Open airway, check breathing and pulse, start compressions and mouth to mouth resuscitation on these lips, so responsive just a few hours before. She grabbed the phone to call 911.

The rest was a blur.

THREE

Mornings are never easy for Simon. He tries to make sure that Jacob is dressed and has eaten something before Tasha comes. Dressing is not a problem. Jacob can do everything but tie his shoes; Simon is unaware of the sneakers that fasten with Velcro. Even though the doctor has told him that Jacob is healthy, Simon worries because he doesn't eat properly. He prepares an elaborate breakfast of cereal, fruit, milk, toast and eggs every day, then has to throw most of it away.

Now he sits his son on his lap and assures him that he is coming back after work, a ritual they go through every day. He has taken him to the New England Conservatory of Music where he teaches and has gone so far as to draw a map to show him his travel route. Every day, they go over this. Jacob can point to the place on the page where Simon has drawn the subway logo: a T within a circle for the days he doesn't drive. He drew a clock with large round numbers with arrows that point to the time of day he will return. He makes copies and fills in the time each day. Today, for instance, he will be later than usual because of an appointment with the rabbi. Jacob nods, but Simon is never sure he understands. He questions him. "What time do I leave for work; what time do I have a class, when do I eat lunch?" Jacob points to the hours. "Yes, right, good. You eat lunch then, too." He points to the hour when he will be back. But there is always a look of surprise, coupled with relief, on Jacob's face when Simon walks in the door.

Simon glances at his watch. Tasha is late. His students will be waiting. Ordinarily he would take Jacob with him and leave her a note telling her to pick Jacob up at the Conservatory later, but this morning he can't. Simon is preparing for his concert at Jordan Hall and he won't be able to keep an eye on his son. His students will need all his attention.

On days like this Simon can barely tamp down his anger and resentment. If Karen were here he could simply kiss Jacob goodbye and leave. If she were working, they would have arranged for some kind of preschool. There would be the ritual of hugging him and dropping him off, of looking back to make sure he was all right before gaining the door. But Karen isn't there. Everything has been left to him.

Ever since his mother left, his perfectly normal son has not uttered a word. Simon is afraid to put Jacob in the Kehillat Shalom preschool; the other children might make fun of him or ignore him. His home is a protective cocoon. The two of them have been managing just fine with Tasha's babysitting. But even when he leaves Jacob with her, his son wears a worried look that Simon knows won't completely disappear until he returns. He glances at his watch. Now Tasha is a half-hour late and he is out of time.

Sometimes Ida looks after Jacob but with everything she has to do for Nathan he doesn't feel he can impose on her this morning. And then he remembers how Jacob had reached out for Aviva and Ruchamah on *Erev Shavuot*. He walks out of his house with Jacob, lifts him up so he can ride on his shoulders and takes him around the corner to Gibbs Street. Later he will wonder why he didn't look at the temple membership list for her phone number. He had gone impulsively, as if he had known she would be home, known she would not mind, aware that almost everyone in the neighborhood comes to her for one reason or another. She is helping Tasha with her English.

He presses the buzzer, says his name and is immediately let in. When he reaches the top of the stairs Ruchamah is standing there, a bathing suit over her arm, a gym bag at her feet.

"Oh," he says. "I'm sorry to barge in. You're on your way out?"

"I have a few minutes." She reaches her hand out to Jacob who shakes it. They both laugh.

"My baby sitter didn't show up."

"Do you need me to look after Jacob?"

"I do, only for a few minutes, but what about your swimming?"

"I can go any time. The pool is open well into evening."

"I'm sure Tasha's on her way." Simon says. "There was no answer when I called her house. I'll leave a note on my front door telling her Jacob is here. Here's my cell number in case there is a problem." He searches in his pocket for something to write on.

Ruchamah rummages through her gym bag and tears off a sheet of paper from a small notebook. Jacob is already holding her hand.

"Come, Jacob," Ruchamah is saying as Simon kisses him goodbye. "How would you like some breakfast?" Simon doesn't tell her that he fed him already because Jacob hardly ate anything. If Ruchamah can get him to eat something he will be greatly relieved. He stops at the doorway. "You translate some things for my babysitter," he says. "She has told me several times how kind you are." He thanks her profusely and leaves. He has no idea that what Ruchamah has been helping Tasha with is her resume'. Or that he will be probably be needing another babysitter soon.

FOUR

" Ida?"

She sets aside her tea and February's book club pick, Milton Steinberg's <u>As a Driven Leaf</u>. She's missed several meetings and is only on page 73. She had dragged herself out of bed, earlier, careful not to disturb Nathan, who was restless as usual throughout the night, wandering into the living room, turning on the lights and television set, turning them off again.

"Are you ready?" He means for their morning walk, one of the few things comforting to him since his Alzheimer's has progressed. A walker all his life, he often left his car at home and walked to work from Coolidge Corner to the Little Building in downtown Boston, even in the depth of winter. Now his walks are limited to the neighborhood.

Ida lives in fear that he will somehow escape her watchful eye and wander someplace where no one knows him, someplace they may regard him as a crazy old man who can't remember his own name. It takes him so long to collect his thoughts that sometimes he substitutes the first name that comes to him. He has referred to himself as their son, Martin, a few times in her presence.

Nathan dresses as carefully for this walk as if he were still going to work. He puts on a suit, a bow tie, perfectly knotted, which he can still accomplish, places his hat at a jaunty angle, peering into the mirror to make sure everything is exactly right before they leave the house. This procedure takes almost an hour and usually he forgets something. Oh? Today it's his suit jacket, which Ida hands him with a smile. He frowns as he puts it on, then grabs a sip of his coffee, the strong African roast, he prefers. Somewhat bitter, Ida thinks. She is tempted to make it half decaf; cutting down on caffeine is one of his doctor's recommendations but she is afraid he will notice and complain.

Nathan proceeds briskly down Beal Street. Ida catches hold of his arm and he slows down. He has retained his courtliness in spite of the rapidly advancing Alzheimer's.

"Oh, look, there's Simon." Ida points and waves as they pass John F. Kennedy's former homestead. Nathan nods, although Ida is pretty sure he doesn't remember who Simon is when he sees him outside his house. It is the house he recognizes. He rings the doorbell before Ida can stop him. Simon doesn't seem to mind. He and Nathan usually select something from his music library as Jacob settles himself on her lap. At times like this her husband seems like his old self. She's happy to linger, enjoying Jacob and the music and the tea Simon pours for her while the two men compare the version of the piece they are listening to with recordings by other conductors. Nathan's steps are jaunty as they leave. In a few minutes he won't recall having visited Simon and a querulous tone will creep into his voice as he asks Ida where she thinks she is taking him.

They walk steadily until they reach the S.S. Pierce building, which stands at the crossroads of Coolidge Corner. Given its distinctive Tudor architecture, and hexagonal turret, the store is a neighborhood landmark. He and Ida used to walk inside to select their favorite delicacies, many of which were German specialties. Although the outer shell is the same, one glance beneath the awnings shows signs for the many new retail operations housed within.

Nathan frowns. He's looking for Jack and Marion's Delicatessen with its Fresser's sandwich, but it too is gone. Although it was beneath his dignity to order and finish one of those huge creations, he would always marvel at the appetite of the young men who gorged themselves, then showed off their name featured on the "Fresser's Fraternity" wall to their girlfriends.

Since his Alzheimer's progressed, Nathan becomes annoyed in restaurants, even his favorites in the North End of Boston with their fabulous selection of Italian food. This is something Ida had been indifferent to and now misses. He forgets that he has to wait for the food they have ordered. Waiting sends him into a state of anxiety. He usually gets up from the table and heads for the door.

Soon they pass the synagogue. Nathan starts up the steps, intent on the early morning *minyan* he attended whenever he could. Years ago, the *minyan* met daily; now it meets only on Thursdays. Today is Wednesday. It's too early for the synagogue to be open. Nathan shakes the door handle. Marcia opens the door. "Poor thing," she whispers to Ida. Ida doesn't know if Marcia means Nathan or if she is the intended "poor thing." She has such a combination of pity and harshness in her eyes. Ida turns away from Marcia to indicate her annoyance and tightens her hold on Nathan's arm.

Rabbi Kramer, making his way up the street, smiles as he approaches. He reminds them that tomorrow is the morning *minyan* and that he will see Nathan there. Nathan nods agreement. He tips his hat as they leave, courteous as always. If Rabbi Isaacs had not retired, he and Nathan would have begun a conversation that continued as they walked inside the synagogue together discussing this board event or that commentary on the *Torah* portion of the week. Rabbi Isaacs appreciated Nathan's opinion. He would have called him up to the *Torah* for an *aliyah* despite his Alzheimer's. After all, Nathan retains the ability to recall sections of *Torah* portions the way others summon up the names of friends and family members. This rabbi has practically ignored her husband. Ida thinks the older congregants have always been last on his agenda, and lately they are not on his agenda at all. This morning she is determined to ask him to help Nathan. Perhaps he can start by resuming the daily morning services.

"We have so many more members since you came," she will tell him, "It's likely we could get a *minyan* more than once a week." She'll have to struggle to be polite; she's tempted to tell him he is here only because Nathan changed his mind.

Nathan had been a member of the Board of Director's when Rabbi Isaacs was ready to retire. He tried his best to convince him to stay, finding a way to offer him a raise, fewer hours, possibly even an assistant, to no avail. When the Search Committee selected Rabbi Kramer, they invited him to meet with the Board preceding the congregation's vote of approval. Nathan believed a rabbi should be an unquestioned leader, a figure of wisdom and authority. Hillel considered himself to be in partnership with the congregation. He used excerpts from a prayer book written by his former congregants and stepped down from the *bimah* while giving his sermon, not even a sermon, more like a discussion. Most appalling, he invited the congregation to call him by his first name.

"How can this committee propose to the Board that we hire a rabbi with ideas so different from our own?" Nathan was passionate in his objections on the way home.

"Kehillat Shalom is dying," Ida told him. "The new people in our neighborhood are younger. They leave us because they want a chance to have more of a say in their spiritual life."

"They don't have to have more of a say," Nathan declared. "The service should be up to the rabbi. I like knowing what to expect. I like our *Siddur.*"

She bustled about in the kitchen as soon as they reached their house. "Come, sit." She placed a piece of Nathan's favorite cherry cheesecake in front of him, and pulled her chair next to his.

"Why don't we give Rabbi Kramer a chance? He can't change everything right away. Our friends are here; this is where Martin became a *Bar Mitzvah.* Susan was married here and David loves the children's services. If we leave, we lose it all."

"I don't think he's going to work out," Nathan said.

"You finished your cheesecake. Let me get you some more."

And so Rabbi Kramer had come.

"Rabbi?" Ida calls, but Nathan has already started home. She hurries after her husband, without having a chance to speak to Hillel.

The hardest thing about these early morning walks is the return. Nathan can walk for hours. Ida's hope is to tire him out. On their way back he asks her when he can attend the *minyan.* "Tomorrow," she says. He repeats "tomorrow" right after she says it as if he understands. He will ask her again, many times today. As soon as they enter the house, Nathan sits down at the kitchen table to wait. He has had the same breakfast every day since their marriage, coffee first, followed by rye toast and a soft-boiled egg in an eggcup and a fruit of some kind. Ida tries to keep as many things the same as they have always been, hoping to ease Nathan's ever-growing anxiety. She pours him a fresh cup of coffee, then hands him the morning paper. He eats his egg and toast, then asks her for them again. She shakes her head no, telling him gently that he has just eaten and that lunch will be soon, but he's furious, so she gives him a little more toast in an effort to calm him. With all the extra food she has been feeding him, he has not gained one ounce.

From everything she has read about Alzheimer's, the days to come will be ones of deterioration rather than restoration. Things are not that bad, really. Not yet. But they will get worse.

As soon as she is assured that Nathan has dozed off while reading his paper, she picks up the phone to call her daughter. Lately she has had to ask Susan to shop for them because she is afraid to leave Nathan alone. Bringing him with her doesn't work as he begins to wander around and pick up things they never use. She has had to rely on both her children in a way she never expected. Martin has had to straighten out their very ragged finances, without indicating to his father in any way that he has done so.

Nathan retains the illusion that things are almost the same as ever, even though he is aware of being forgetful. Yes, Nathan can retain his illusions, but hers are gone. Only a few years ago she was preparing elegant dinners for his clients, embarrassed but pleased, when at the end of the meal, he raised his glass in a toast. "So," he asked the assemblage, "What do you think of my Ida?" She shopped in specialty shops like Gertrude

Frank's in Washington Square, selecting clothes he would admire, then sat for hours listening to his stories, heroic tales of a man doing legal battle in a pin-striped suit.

Although she has given herself over to Nathan and the children, she has done it in a way that managed, always, to preserve her independent and adventurous spirit, making rich experiences out of ordinary occasions. She was the mother dancing in the rain with her children, the hostess who surprised her guests by provoking scintillating conversations. Now there are no elegant dinners, no scintillating conversations, no plans for trips to exotic places. Nathan no longer gets up each morning to leave a delicate flower at her table setting reminding them of their pleasure of the night before. Her heroic husband is lost in the past; his Alzheimer's has made them both victims, something Ida rails against with all her strength.

Susan isn't answering. Ida leaves a message and hangs up the phone.

FIVE

Dear Elijah,

My three days expired last night and I have not yet discovered the source of the rabbi's problem. I've taken up temporary residence in the synagogue, sleeping in the little room off the kitchen where the old pews have been stored. They're not nearly as comfortable as my bed in the Garden, though that's only a straw pallet. I lie outside under the stars and the air is fresh and clean. The storage room has no windows and is therefore quite suffocating. But at least I can raid the refrigerator, which is full to being stuffed at all times. No matter what else they do, this congregation eats.

Early this morning I ransacked the closet where the sisterhood keeps the garments they collect for their twice annual rummage sales since the wardrobe I brought was somewhat limiting. I selected a dress, basic black. Hopefully none of the congregants will be able to identify their discard with certainty. Reaching into my satchel I brought out just the right accessory, thanks to an artist named Adele, who left the vibrant red scarf she had designed on a seat in a synagogue in Paris. I waited until I heard the front door open, left the basement, entered the synagogue through the front door and made my way to the main office.

Marcia, was on the phone with the editor of the temple Bulletin, complaining about mistakes in her daughter's wedding announcement. I adjusted the scarf to cover the original bead work on my borrowed dress and cleared my throat to announce my presence. She had already begun to read the corrected version of the announcement out loud just as Hillel came in, papers in hand.

"You seem to have reinterpreted my Friday night sermon," he said when she hung up. He spoke to her without preamble. Neither took notice of me.

"I copied what you gave me," Marcia countered.

"No, I have the original here." He handed her the sheaf of papers, asked her to redo the sermon, hesitated, then sat down on the chair at the side of her desk.

"I know you're busy with wedding preparations. If you'd like time off, I'll find a volunteer to cover for you."

"That's not necessary. I have everything under control," Marcia almost shouted. "Just like I did when Rabbi Isaacs was here."

I could tell from the way she emphasized Rabbi Isaacs' name that she had much preferred working for him.

"Very well," Hillel said. "If you change your mind, let me know." He was on his way out of the office when he turned back. "You must be so proud. Debby and Jeff's vows include not only a commitment to each other, but a pledge to enhance the lives of children through the literacy and art program they're developing for after school centers. His voice broke, just it had on *Erev Shavuot* when he mentioned that the wombs of the women had been illuminated. Whatever the rabbi's problem is, I think it must have something to do with children.

I cleared my throat to announce my presence, told them I was new in the area and wanted to look around Kehillat Shalom, as I might be interested in joining their congregation. I expected the rabbi to ask Marcia to escort me. Instead, he handed me a copy of the latest Bulletin and led me out of the office himself, probably relieved to escape further confrontation with his office manager.

He was quite animated as we walked, apologizing for the ladders and paint cans that were occasionally strewn on our path, commenting on how well these renovations were going, "thanks in large part to the teen group that did most of the painting."

I made no mention of having been at Shavuot services nor of my own tour, which included his disappearance for much of the night. He led me to the library that held so many books some were stacked in piles on the floor. Taking the Bulletin from my hand, he opened it to show me a list of activities, pointing out an artist group that had offered to hang their Judaica in the hallways and donate a portion of sales to the synagogue *tzedakah* program, a poetry seminar, several Torah workshops, a group called, If Not Us Who, which, he explained, focuses on current issues of genocide, such as in Darfur, and a discussion group on the Middle East. "And look," he pointed to one of the letters to the editor, "there was even a suggestion last month to develop a free medical clinic. So many members responded that the committee has already scheduled a first meeting."

So much is going on here, Elijah, just like in the Los Angeles synagogue. In fact, the rabbi stopped talking for a minute and stared at me, a slight smile creasing his face. "Forgive me," he said, "but I seem to have a recollection of you attending a service I led in a different synagogue." His gaze was intense. I was so taken aback it took me a minute to respond. "I was in Los Angeles," I finally said. "It's quite a coincidence to see you here."

"Indeed," he said. "Actually I never intended to leave there, but here I am." He frowned for a moment, then turned to continue our tour. "And of course we have an active pre-school, thanks in large part to my wife." He indicated the classrooms full of children, whose voices were raised in excitement. His own voice dropped. His enthusiasm seemed to wane. Determined to keep his attention, having overheard his offer to find a volunteer to assist Marcia, I offered my services saying that I found Kehillat Shalom to be a synagogue with which I was completely compatible. He was thanking me profusely just as Marcia approached us noting that she hadn't booked an appointment for me. "I'm so sorry I didn't catch your name," the rabbi said.

"Sara," I said, which was as close to Serach as I dared.

"Sara has offered to spend some of her extra time in the office," he said. "We can certainly use her help, Marcia." Without waiting for her response he asked when I could start. I told him immediately. He shook my hand vigorously and held it a moment. Of course the rabbi has no way of knowing that I was responsible for his appointment here. Still, I feel he senses we have a connection beyond coincidence. I wanted to tell him I was here to help him. The words, "You seem slightly unlike yourself. If you tell me what's wrong I can fix it," formed on my lips. I might have added, "Elijah sent me." I thought he might have believed me, but of course I said nothing at all.

Marcia brought me back to the office in a most unfriendly manner, threw some copies of the latest Bulletin along with two inserts down on a table in the back of the room and asked me to start collating.

The office was extremely busy. Congregants poured in and out all morning; many stopping to welcome me, curious as to who I was. Forced to think of a story for myself, I invented a family that had lived here years ago, a move to California, recent widowhood and children who hovered over me to the point where I had to get away. I told them I had decided to return on a trial basis to see if I could make a new life for myself, possibly to meet someone as well so my children wouldn't feel responsible for me. To my dismay, my goal is to avoid congregants and get on with the business of whipping the rabbi into shape, this tale evoked great interest and several dinner invitations which, of course, I hastily declined. The congregants also had requests I couldn't fill. I constantly had to interrupt Marcia to ask for her help. "I thought you were supposed to be helping me," she muttered under her breath, reluctantly getting up to show me files, supplies, old Bulletins. The phone rang constantly. I rushed around the office attempting to look competent. I was getting something for one of the *Shavuot* breakfast cooks, whose leftover blintzes I had discovered on one of my refrigerator raids, still so delicious, even reheated, when Ruchamah came in.

Marcia got up from behind her desk to hug her. "What a horrendous morning." She pointed to the Bulletin copies I had set at the side of her desk and reluctantly introduced me as the new volunteer. Ruchamah seemed to have no idea that I was the crone who had inhabited her dream *Erev Shavuot* as she welcomed me to Kehillat Shalom.

"Debby's announcement is completely messed up," Marcia told her.

"Let me give you a *Mazel Tov* anyway. I didn't realize the wedding was so close."

"Why Rabbi Kramer instituted management by committee is beyond me. Things were so easy when I could just slap the Bulletin together. Rabbi Isaacs used to be thrilled I got it out of the way."

"Then my timing is good. I came in to see if I could help with the mailing."

"I knew there was a reason I was happy to see you." Marcia smiled at her.

"I don't see the announcement for the *Rosh Hodesh* group," Ruchamah said, flipping through the pages. I hadn't seen it either and I would have certainly noticed a reference to our ancient tradition of honoring the moon's cycle. She handed her copy back to Marcia who appeared to peruse each page.

"It's that editor," she said quickly. "He's been leaving a lot of things out. Just as he did with Debby's announcement." But I had a feeling that Marcia didn't approve of the *Rosh Hodesh* group and had deliberately neglected to include it.

"I'll just sit down and add the information by hand," Ruchamah said, "and mail them on my way home."

After she left, there was a brief lull in the office. I took this down time to look through the Bulletin on my own and noted that although there were listings for many of the groups the rabbi had pointed out, there were also many cancellation announcements as well as several letters to the editor full of complaints, an indication that things were not going as smoothly as Hillel had suggested.

He remained in his office after my tour. I managed to wander in and out a few times, with questions Marcia hadn't answered. She had been emphatically striking the computer keys as she retyped the rabbi's sermon, reading every word aloud, leaving me to cope with the congregants.

After lunch she handed me the new version of the Friday night sermon and sent me to the rabbi to see if he approved. When I came back to the office, Simon was there.

"You're a half hour early," Marcia greeted him. "Sit down. Talk to me." She leaned forward and cocked her head as he took a seat. "Any new developments in your life? I told you there are at least three women in the congregation who would be happy to go out with you. Ruchamah for instance; you just missed her."

Simon laughed, but I could tell he was uncomfortable with this suggestion. Marcia handed me another collating job, which I did while they were chatting. After a while Simon got up. "I think I'll wait for the rabbi in the sanctuary," he told Marcia. I finished my task quickly and opened the door to the sanctuary to see him pull a prayer book from its holder, leaving it unopened. Rabbi Kramer walked past me to invite Simon into his office. I grabbed the folder of announcements from the lectern so I would have an excuse for being in the ante-room, where I stationed myself to listen.

When they settled themselves in the office, Simon didn't seem to know how to begin. After a few moments the rabbi asked about Jacob.

"Jacob's fine," Simon said. "He's the best thing in my life."

The rabbi nodded. "That's the most important thing, then."

"You probably know my wife left me about the time you took over for Rabbi Isaacs," Simon finally began. "It has taken me this long to realize that

Karen isn't coming back. She told me, over and over, but I couldn't seem to take it in."

"Perhaps your heart was too full of hope," Rabbi Kramer said kindly.

"I haven't changed a thing in the house, including our wedding photograph. It still hangs over the fireplace mantel. All I've managed to do is move out of our bedroom into the little den that serves as my music room. Simon leaned forward in his chair. "For almost two years I have felt like a robot. I've been going through the motions of living for Jacob's sake."

"How does Jacob cope without his mother?"

"Except for the fact that he doesn't talk, he seems like a perfectly normal little boy. Actually he's an extraordinary little boy. One day, a few months ago, he walked into the kitchen, a grin on his face and my much too large violin foisted under his chin. I laughed for the first time since Karen left. His fingers could barely reach the upper frets. His other hand held the bow loosely and sawed it back and forth over the strings, making high-pitched screeches. I put my arms around him. 'Let me tell you what we are going to do,' I said. 'I'm going to buy you your own violin, just your size.' That's how we began talking together, conversations with our violins."

"He always looks happy when I see him with you," Rabbi Kramer said. His voice sounding wistful. "Especially, the other night on *Shavuot,* perched on your shoulder, so proud."

"So tall," Simon laughed. "He didn't want to get off. Anyway I am here to say I think it's time I moved on with my life. I would like to apply for a *Get*."

"Do you think there is any possibility of Karen's return?"

"After two years? I don't think so. It seems clear she wants nothing more to do with us."

"It seems? Do I have your permission to contact her?"

"You can try," Simon gave the rabbi Karen's phone number.

"If she says she wants to come back, would you be willing to talk with her again?"

"I don't know. It seems so unlikely, her return, that is."

When Simon left, the rabbi sat in his chair staring out the window.

"Simon and I," he mused aloud. "We are both incomplete. A family of two that should be three. Simon lives for his child, but there is no wife. I have a wife but there is no child."

So that's the issue? The rabbi has no issue! If only you had told me, Elijah. I would have started looking for his child on my way to Kehillat Shalom.

Serach

SIX

Hillel stands in Shoshanah's doorway. There's a warmth and vibrancy about Kehillat Shalom's new cantor, a sense of non-judgement. If only he could unburden himself and seek her counsel. She has wisdom beyond her years, evident the day she applied for her job. She had been slightly nervous, clasping and unclasping her hands as she told him this would be her first position if she were fortunate enough to be hired. "My mother would have become a cantor had it not been for the prohibition placed on the role of women in those days," she added. Now she carries her mother's dreams along with her own. Hillel was sure Kehillat Shalom would be the fortunate ones. Here was a young woman with the ability to meld the past with the present, something he himself is unable to do.

After she was hired, Shoshanah invited her mother to help lead her first service. New congregants brought their parents. Older members invited their children. The synagogue was filled to capacity as the women's voices rose in joy and celebration. Perhaps if he speaks to her openly, as the congregants do, she might offer him the understanding he does not presently possess, a way out of the conflict that has begun to cause him to lose sight of himself, his wife and his congregation.

A slight breeze blows through her open window and lifts the myriad of papers on her desk, which also displays an assortment of silver pieces. Although Shoshanah gifted the synagogue with a delicately wrought *yad* before *Erev Shavuot,* he's sure she hasn't had enough time to attend her silversmithing class lately because of the work he's been piling on her during his self-imposed retreat. Not that he's on an actual retreat. He comes to the synagogue every day and practices avoidance, as his father would have told him had he known. But his father doesn't know. He doesn't accept Hillel's evolving approach to Judaism, his disregard for traditional ways of doing things, which includes his hiring of Shoshanah, although there is a *halachic* tradition for women cantors dating back to before the thirteenth century.

Hillel has been unable to continue working on the *Tikkun Olam* book he began in the Los Angeles synagogue. The only time he opens it is to borrow a few sections to use as sermons. He's not studying *halachic* texts nor even reading for pleasure, no

43

longer able to find solace in the stories of Isaac Bashevis Singer or Shalom Aleichem. His father's mandate that he is responsible for restoring the family blood line lost in the Holocaust absorbs him completely. Hillel tells the congregants that all human beings are interconnected, that "every person is designed in the image of God and is therefore sacred," extolling the work of Rabbi Michael Lerner. All children he constantly reminds himself, all children are sacred.

"Rabbi?"

He turns. "Stan," he says, relieved to have been called out of his thoughts, smiling in spite of himself at the sight of his friend in his usual baseball hat, the brim pulled over his eyes. "That was some catch you made *Erev Shavuot*. You saved two lives, the *Torah's* and mine."

"Ah," Stan says, "So now, you owe me one?"

Hillel laughs. Stan has been his closest friend since he became rabbi here, popping into the office the first day to tell him he was needed on the temple softball team. "You've missed the men's breakfast," he says. "You've missed four practices and one game. And of course you almost dropped the *Torah*. So I know something is bothering you, but if you'll come to a game, you won't have to make up a story about what it is."

"I've been thinking of taking a break from the team."

"What! Now we really have to talk. Let's go for coffee."

"I was looking for Shoshanah."

44

Stan peers into the office. "She's not here. This will only take fifteen minutes."

"A Jewish fifteen minutes?"

Stan grins.

"Okay, I'll leave a note for her."

In Starbucks, they get their coffee and sit down at one of the few empty tables near a window.

Stan's arrival had been fortuitous. Any earlier he would have found the office door closed and assumed his absence. "I appreciate your stopping by to check up on me, Stan," the rabbi says.

"You're the best shortstop we've got."

"I'm the only shortstop you've got."

Stan sips his coffee and stares out the window. "Isn't that Shoshanah?" He points to a blue Corolla stopped at the light.

Hillel looks, nods. "She's probably on her way to visit someone." He doesn't tell Stan that Shoshanah has taken on almost all congregants' visits unless it's an absolute emergency.

"Anyway," Stan says. "There's something I want to ask you."

Shoshanah hasn't noticed them as she passed. Early this morning she had come to the office to vocalize, a practice she has undertaken since she realized her early morning warm ups disturbed her neighbors, the walls of her apartment being far too thin. When she opened the window to let in some fresh air, she watched Ida start up the steps to say something to the rabbi, turning instead to hurry after Nathan.

Shoshanah pulls over at the next light. She wants to pick up some flowers for Ida and some cookies for Nathan. The three of them have formed a bond, a little community inside the larger community of Kehillat Shalom. It's hard now to believe that Nathan had been her nemesis before her interview with the Board, telling her he couldn't make the leap to having a woman lead him in prayer. She thought she was fired before she had a chance to be hired. When she began to sing he sat staring at her silently. A few weeks later when she returned to audition for the congregation, Nathan took her aside. "My grandfather was a cantor," he told her. "He taught me to love music and to know a woman's place in the synagogue. That was fine until I met you. When you sing your face becomes a countenance, enhanced by the spirit of the music and imbued by God. I want you to know I voted in your favor, and my wife, "he pointed her out in the audience, already loves you, without even hearing you sing." As soon as she saw Ida's smiling face, Shoshanah had loved her in turn. Ida's keen observations, her wisdom and perspective help Shoshanah achieve a sense of balance no matter how much work Hillel piles on her. It is to Shoshanah that Ida has confided her angst over the changes in Nathan, her feelings of helplessness and despair since his Alzheimer's has progressed, something Shoshanah is well aware of. Nathan loans her selections from his collection of liturgical and classical music, but doesn't remember having done so when she returns them.

Ida greets her with delight when she opens the door, finger to her lips. Nathan has fallen asleep in his chair in the living room. She ushers Shoshanah into the kitchen and takes the flowers from her. "You shouldn't have," she says, pleasure evident on her face, "but I'm so glad you did." Ida's heart is lighter whenever Shoshanah visits. The last time she came she brought her a little silver mouse charm. "I'm not quite sure why I made this mouse," Shoshanah says, "but I thought you'd like it." How Ida had laughed. The little mouse was adorable and besides, he was holding a tiny bouquet of flowers.

"You'll stay and have a late lunch with us, yes, Shoshanah?"

"I wish I could. I have to get back to the office."

"Then I'm packing some food for you. You never take enough time to eat," Ida says, "but never mind that right now. Tell me how you are?"

"I'm fine; I came to see how you are."

Ida sighed. "You know. Sometimes these days are hard. I miss my Nathan. The way he used to be, but I'm getting used to this one."

Shoshanah laughs.

"Ida?"

"He's up," Ida says. "Come, Shoshanah. He's always happy to see you. Maybe we'll sing some of the old Yiddish songs together. Nathan still knows every word."

By the time Shoshanah gets back to the office, Hillel is waiting. He pulls up a chair. They sit side by side. For a moment this shared space feels as it had when she first came to Kehillah Shalom. They spent hours talking about programs they wanted to develop, their hopes for transforming Kehillat Shalom from a typical conservative synagogue into one that encompassed a wider spectrum of Jewish tradition.

Shoshanah expresses concern about Ida and Nathan.

"We should do more," Hillel says quickly. Of course he should be doing more for the older congregants. He's not sure why he hasn't. "And speaking of more," he tells her that Stan has asked him to start a Yiddish class. "His parents spoke it at home so that he and his sister wouldn't understand what they were saying. Recently he went to a Yiddish film festival and felt a longing to do more than read subtitles. My parents spoke it as well," he adds. For a moment he's silent. Even if he and his father spoke Yiddish together they still wouldn't be able to communicate.

"The older residents might like that," Shoshanah says. This will be a good activity for Ida and Nathan. It won't lighten her work load but Hillel will, if not regain some of his previous tasks, at least begin something new again. Who knows what could happen after that. Perhaps she will offer one session of Yiddish songs. She smiles. This is the way things used to be. One would have an idea, the other come up with a complementary suggestion and they would begin to collaborate.

"I wish….," Hillel begins, stops abruptly and smiles, a smile that reminds her of Pagliacci, a clown hiding great sadness. His mind is already on something else, she realizes. When was it he became so distracted? She searches her mind for any clues he might have given her in the past few months. Beth left the preschool a few times for doctor visits. Perhaps she is ill and they haven't wanted anyone to know.

She waits for the rabbi to continue speaking, but Hillel has decided that he cannot confide in Shoshanah. She is taking care of the congregants. He can't expect her to take care of him as well.

I'll see you tomorrow, Shoshanah," he says. "You might want to close your window. That's a very strong breeze."

He's is on his way home with flowers for Beth when the breeze becomes a wind of great intensity, almost a whirlwind, and he is spun around. In his turning he hears a cry. Before him stands a woman holding a small child. The child holds out his arms. Hillel reaches towards them but is spun around again. The woman and child disappear. He picks up the bouquet of flowers he dropped in his astonishment and veers off in several directions looking for them. When he can't find them he decides the woman was most likely a spirit of some kind, a sign. Perhaps the child he and Beth have longed for will come after all. Hillel hurries his steps, as elated now as he had been despondent before.

SEVEN

By the time Marcia gets home she has a migraine. "I have to lie down," she tells Jack. He's in the kitchen making his famous *matzah* ball soup. Her Jack. Such an easy-going guy. He never gets that upset about anything, unless she's upset and, lately, she's been very upset. She gives him a quick kiss, goes into their bedroom and gets into bed. She won't be able to work on the seating arrangements for the wedding tonight and she can't count on Jack to do them. Jack doesn't care where anyone sits.

She pinches her forehead, the area just above her nose. Sometimes that relieves the pressure. No. Tonight, it doesn't help. She takes a washcloth from the linen closet in the master bath, drenches it with cold water, wrings it out, returns to bed and places it over her forehead. Today, besides having to cope with the rabbi, that stranger, Sara, had come in without an appointment. She had offered to volunteer in the office so quickly, Marcia thinks she might be after her job. The announcement for Debby's wedding had been a mishmash until she straightened it out with the Bulletin editor and then, Ruchamah had the audacity to scribble the *Rosh Hodesh* listing into the calendar. Why anyone chooses to belong to that fringy moon-worshiping group is beyond Marcia, which is why she deliberately left out the event listing in the first place.

If she says anything to Jack, he will just tell her to quit, something he's been saying ever since she stopped entertaining him with amusing stories about how over the top the new rabbi was. Hillel's excitement about his new program plans had been so contagious at first, she would nod agreement, even though she didn't completely understand what he meant. He spoke in parables, never seeming to come to a definitive point. He arrived early each day to begin implementing his ideas, providing her with handwritten notes expounding on the importance of Kehillat Shalom being part of the world interfaith community. He planned shared conversations with community leaders, including Christian and Moslem clerics. There would be visits to churches and mosques, joint meetings held at the synagogue. He was fixated on what the congregants wanted. Marcia couldn't seem to make him understand that he was the one in charge. She didn't bother telling him his ideas were out of sync with the way things used to be or that Rabbi Isaacs had focused solely on leading the congregation. Taking care of the world he considered beyond the scope of the synagogue.

She often turned Rabbi Kramer's words around to suit herself. If he had asked why, she would have said she couldn't read his notes, but since he rarely asked, she was free to give her own interpretations. Sometimes she took the papers he handed her and shoved them into the back of her desk drawer. There were always more papers, more new ideas.

Suddenly, something changed. The rabbi was no longer enthusiastic. There were no long explications, no more friendly chats. She began to feel excluded. This had never happened with Rabbi Isaacs. Now she has only the greatest appreciation for her old friend, even though she had complained about him constantly to Jack throughout his tenure. Rabbi Isaacs appreciated the way she arranged his schedule, edited his sermons, screened his calls and advised him about various congregants.

From time to time, lately, Hillel roused himself to greet a congregant, but Marcia was left to deal with the fall out. Their questions came, first in the form of puzzlement, then, finally complaints. "That's cancelled? But he asked me to head the committee. What about the trip to Israel? Pushed back indefinitely? What's going on?" If Rabbi Isaacs had been on the end of those complaints she would have made excuses for him, but she did not support Rabbi Kramer with an excuse. She came home every evening with a headache and told Jack she felt as if she no longer fit in at Kehillat Shalom.

"You're not that little girl whose parents made her move to Brookline, Marcia. You fit in anywhere. You always did," he reassured her.

Her Jack, who had captured her heart the first day they met with his bright smile and the look of admiration he gave her as he raced up the steps of her Dorchester home to meet her brother, just as she was running out to meet her friends. They started dating the following weekend. She told all her friends she had met her *'bashert'*. Jack doesn't understand how those feelings of not belonging had never really gone away. They lay under the surface waiting for something to remind her of how alone she had felt the first day she entered Brookline High. The girls, especially the cashmere sweater crowd, snubbed her. She longed to be back in Dorchester, sipping cream soda with her Jack and the gang at the G&G delicatessen. Most of those girls would marry doctors and lawyers, live in mansions, have nannies for their children, even if they didn't work. "But I," she had consoled herself, "will marry Jack. And be happier than any of them."

Those Brookline high school girls and their husbands were members of the temple now. When Rabbi Isaacs hired her to be his personal assistant, it was Marcia they had to come to when they needed something. Soon they began to sing her praises. Every night when she came home from work she would regale Jack with stories. Patti couldn't get over the way she held their *Bar Mitzvah* caterer to his contract. All Marcia had to do was remind the owner of "Ess, Ess, Mein Kind" that he might not get any more referrals from her. Then there were Yvette and Harry who were thrilled with suggestions on how to handle a temperamental bandleader. After her daughter's wedding, Paula called Marcia irreplaceable in front of Rabbi Isaacs, who readily agreed. But since the advent of Rabbi Kramer, with his new policies and procedures and committees for handling everything, Jack is the only person who would say this about her now.

The cloth she had placed on her head was not doing a thing. She got up to run fresh cold water over it and returned to the bedroom. Jack poked his head in to tell her dinner would be ready soon and that Debby had called. Debby, who managed to remain her usual happy-go-lucky self, leaving Marcia to rush around and make all these last minute arrangements. If her daughter would pitch in, Marcia would not be caught between trying to ensure that her job was safe and that every last detail of the wedding was in place.

Her daughter wanted a simple ceremony; simple was not Marcia's style. They have been arguing about this since she announced she and Jeff were getting married. Yes, they wanted a formal wedding ceremony, but a small one in the temple with the rabbi officiating. "I know you want our wedding to be The Wedding of Kehillat Shalom; Jeff and I just want family and friends. Please, Mom."

Jack agreed with Debby on this, but he also knew how important her wedding was to her mother. Neither Marcia nor Debby could count on him to take sides when they argued.

The other night Marcia had ratcheted herself up into full gear. "You are going to have the wedding I never had," she said. "You'll be glad for it later. Your dad and I were married in the rabbi's office. At the time it was all we could afford. I want more for you."

"You want more for you, Mom," Debby exploded. "You'll be off to Filene's to find God knows what for me to wear. You're treating me like a mannequin in a store window. You would probably be happy if I glided down the aisle with the price tag still hanging from the underarm of my gown."

"That's ridiculous," Marcia said, not admitting this held a certain appeal. The invited guests would not only know the magnitude of its price, they would appreciate the enormity of the bargain.

"My gown is only the beginning," Debby said. "There's the florist and the décor you've selected, complete with miniature evergreens strung with blinking white lights, no less. Jeff and I don't want that. We don't need the finest linens covering the tables and certainly can do without the caterer's heart-shaped chopped liver display."

"It's too late to change anything," Marcia said, a migraine beginning in the back of her head. "Everything's settled but you."

Debby would not be deterred. "And then there's the guest list," We want something small, intimate, but you are inviting everyone, people we don't even know."

"The invitations are going out tomorrow," Marcia told her. "Jack, please say something to your daughter." She rubbed her temples, hoping Debby would back off.

"We could pull some of them. You make me feel as if I don't have a say in my own wedding, Mom."

"You'll have your marriage, Debby. I will never interfere in that. Can't you just give me your wedding?"

Marcia's only consolation is the fact that at least Debby had not threatened to elope. She gets up to rinse out the washcloth again and places it over her eyes when she returns to bed. Ah, this helps a little.

After a while Jack calls her to supper. His *matzah* ball soup will do wonders for her headache, he assures her.

The only thing that will do wonders for her headache is if she can get things under control at the temple and convince her daughter that she knows what's best. She doesn't feel a bit hungry, but if she doesn't eat Jack will go into his harangue about how she should give up her job. This she does not intend to do.

"The soup is good," she tells Jack, her mind not on the soup at all.

EIGHT

Simon is on his way home from the conservatory after working with a student more enthusiastic than able. Still he has made remarkable progress, enough to keep Simon from having to suggest he try a major other than music.

Usually Tasha has supper started but nothing is simmering on the stove when he enters the house and Tasha looks upset. No, Jacob is fine, he's doing puzzles in Simon's study. She has to leave them, she tells him. She needs a full time job because of the health insurance.

Simon is taken aback. "I can try to give you a few more hours, Tasha," he tells her. "I can give you a raise. You certainly deserve one."

"It won't be enough, Simon. And I don't know how to tell Jacob I only have a few more days with him. My new job starts the first of July."

"We'll tell him together, Tasha. You have been so good to my son. If there is any other way I can help you, please let me know." He hopes his desperation isn't apparent. He's counted on her staying for a long time. He wonders if she had been out looking for another job the days she was late.

"Thank you Simon." She hugs him quickly, goes in to say good night to Jacob and thon she is gone. Simon prepares dinner for his silent son, which Jacob, as usual, doesn't really eat. Simon picks at his food. He wants to call someone and ask why the women in his life all leave. Sometimes he wishes he had listened to his father, who had taken one look at Karen and told him she was too self-absorbed to make either a good wife or mother, though how his father could have known that, he has no idea. But if he had listened, he wouldn't have had his son. Jacob is everything to him. He picks up the temple Bulletin, which is with the mail Tasha has placed on the kitchen table and looks through it. No one is advertising babysitting services.

The last time he needed someone to take care of his son, he'd thought of Ruchamah. Something about the way she brought his son into her kitchen reminded him of the easiness he associated with his own childhood. He had wanted to follow her in himself and sit with her as she gave Jacob something to eat. Perhaps she knows someone. When he calls, Ruchamah tells him Aviva was looking for a summer job. "The junior counselor slots at camp are filled." Greatly relieved he asks if he might come over with Jacob and talk to Aviva. Ruchamah suggests they come to his house so he won't have to disrupt Jacob's schedule. He's able to give Jacob a bath and lay out his pajamas by the time they arrive.

Aviva has crayons and a coloring book for Jacob. She spills the crayons into her hands. "What's your favorite color?" Jacob picks the blue one.

"His favorite stuffed animal is blue," Simon tells her, smiling at his son. "Jacob do you want to show your bear to Aviva?" Simon and Ruchamah stand in a somewhat awkward silence as Aviva and Jacob disappear into his bedroom before Simon thinks to offer her something to drink.

"Tea would be wonderful."

He takes out the basket with its variety of choices.

She selects orange-spice. Simon boils water, takes out the celadon teapot Karen bought, puts it back and pours the water directly from the aluminum kettle.

They sit at the table in Simon's small kitchen. Jacob's drawings cover the refrigerator and cabinet doors. On the kitchen counter is a miniature porcelain sculpture of two figures, one large, one small, each carrying a violin.

"That's you and me," Simon always tells his son. "Daddy and Jacob."

He excuses himself and goes to check on Jacob.

"He's engrossed in the coloring books Aviva brought," he says when he comes back, "he didn't notice me standing there."

Simon asks Ruchamah if she knows about Karen. Ruchamah tells him Marcia had mentioned something. She hopes he has no idea how relentless Marcia has been in her efforts to bring the two of them together.

As they drink their tea, Ruchamah realizes that there is a kind of energy and intensity about Simon that appeals to her, an intelligence that shines through even though they are just sitting, having a cup of tea. He's younger than she is; she can't tell by how much. Fine lines around his eyes and mouth render it impossible for her to judge.

Simon sets his cup down and begins wandering about the kitchen, aimlessly picking things up and setting them down. "I can never sit still," he confesses, concerned Ruchamah might find his pacing disquieting. "Why don't we go into the living room?"

A collection of family photos sits on the fireplace mantel. In one, a woman, obviously Jacob's mother, holds her tiny son on her lap. She looks as if she has been asked to pose and doesn't feel natural doing so. Above the mantel is a wedding portrait. Simon's wife is beautiful, ethereal, Ruchamah thinks. When Marcia indicated that Simon was available she gave no explanation as to why Karen left, clicking her tongue as if to say that wasn't important. What was important was that Simon was free. Free and unable to relax. He's now pacing the living room. Simon picks up his violin, puts it down. He tells Ruchamah that he's sorry for not being a very good host. He has a concert coming up at summer's end and he's not sure he will be properly prepared.

"Do you need time to practice? Aviva and I can leave anytime."

"Oh, no. No," he says. It's only that he's somewhat at a loss for small talk. He is inclined to explain that she is the first woman he has asked to his house since Karen left, but refrains.

"I'm not very good at small talk either," Ruchamah says. "Especially when I'm facing a translation deadline. I usually think I haven't gotten it quite right. I become obsessed." Simon laughs. "At least you still have the translation. When the last note of the piece I am playing fades, the music is gone.

"Not the music, only your performance, unless you've recorded it." Ruchamah smiles.

Such an open smile. He had been in such a hurry the day he left Jacob with her, he hadn't noticed how attractive she is. Her hazel eyes have flecks of green. Unlike Karen, she doesn't give the impression that she will fade away unless he looks after her. Ruchamah has a swimmer's litheness. He feels comfortable with her, one artist to another discussing craft. "Tell me," he asks. "What made you decide to become a translator?"

"Yehuda Amichai's poems about love and war captivated me when he gave a reading at Hebrew University my junior year. Later, when I looked at some English translations of his poetry, I had an idea for a different approach to one and attempted my own. On impulse, I sent him a copy and asked for his opinion. Amichai sent the poem back with a note saying he liked it and added that he thought I had a gift as a translator."

Ruchamah is animated. Her face glows as she speaks, her hands move in conjunction with her voice. Simon's living room seems to vibrate with waves of energy. Everything in his house has become brighter since she and Aviva arrived.

"What about you, Simon? Did you always want to be a violinist?"

"I wanted to be a chess champion. My dad and I played all the time. One night my mom turned the radio on during our game. My knight was in mid-air when I heard the opening of Bruch's First Violin Concerto. At that moment, I knew I would become a violinist. Jacob loves classical music, too. Most evenings we listen to something together." He pauses. Ruchamah's eyes are sparkling. She's enjoying their conversation as much as he is.

Simon takes a seat in a chair across from the sofa. Ruchamah racks her brain for something interesting to say. She's not used to talking about herself so much.

"Did you know that in 1929 an entire library in ancient Ugaritic, the root of the Hebrew language, was discovered intact in Northern Syria by the archeologist, Cyrus Gordon?" she says as she sits down on the sofa. So this is all she can think of? As if it's perfectly normal to discuss some obscure thing only another translator would be interested in. But 'in for a penny, in for a pound' as someone once said. "He went on to crack the Ugaritic code," she continues. "Translators have had a heyday ever since."

"That's like finding early manuscripts of a musical composition." Simon moves his chair closer. "Joel Cohen, the Director of the Boston Camerata, the group that performs early music on original instruments, does that kind of ~~the~~ research."

"Several years ago, I heard the Camerata play in the MFA courtyard. Since then, I wander down to the basement into the early instrument room whenever I am at the museum."

"It's a wonder we haven't seen each other. I often go there when I take a break from the Conservatory. Next time I'll look for you." He will definitely do that, he decides. He notices her empty cup and jumps up. "I'll get you more tea?"

"I'll come with you."

Aviva pops her head into the kitchen to ask Simon if she can take a walk with Jacob to buy him a Popsicle. "He's changing into his regular clothes."

"That sounds like fun," Simon tells her. "Let me give you some money."

"My treat today." Aviva moves further into the kitchen, revealing a dressed and grinning Jacob. When he goes out the door he does a little happy dance behind her.

"Look at them trotting out there, almost like brother and sister," Simon says before he realizes it.

"They get along very well," Ruchamah says. "Aviva wasn't meant to be an only child. but...." Her voice trails off.

"I wanted more children, too," Simon tells her and then he doesn't know how to continue. Ruchamah is holding onto the tea basket, a far-away look in her eyes. He could explain what happened with Karen, although she said Marcia had mentioned his situation, but knowing Marcia, she could have told her anything. He could tell Ruchamah that her presence tonight has filled his house with light.

I could tell him about Daniel, Ruchamah muses, but I would probably be inclined to add that I haven't dated anyone since he died. Although why she is thinking about this at this moment, she isn't sure. She's only here so Simon can decide whether or not he would like Aviva to help out with Jacob. She could tell Simon that she finds him easy to talk to.

"Orange-spice, right?" Simon asks her.

"Right," Ruchamah she sets their cups on the counter. Simon finds a tray in the cabinet and a little dish for their tea bags. The only treat he can offer her are some Fig Newtons he keeps around for Jacob.

"Do you write your own poetry?" he asks, sitting down next to her on the couch when they return to the living room. He sounds as if he's interviewing her. He doesn't want that.

"Nothing that I would take out of the drawer," Ruchamah answers quickly. "I keep a journal, though I haven't written in it for a long time."

She doesn't seem to mind his questions. He waits for her to offer something more about herself.

"How about you?" she asks. "Do you compose your own music?"

"Nothing that I would play for anyone," he grins. "Sometimes I improvise on a theme; occasionally I try for my own cadenza, if a composer leaves space for that. And of course I make up songs for Jacob. My variations on 'Pop Goes the Weasel' crack him up."

Ruchamah laughs, an easy, lilting laugh. Simon wants to hear her laugh again. Nothing amusing comes to his mind, however. He tells her he's been thinking of taking Shoshanah's course on learning trope. She tells him she took it last year..

"You know cantillation is a lot like recitative in opera, the way ordinary conversation is turned into a sort of sing-song. He demonstrates. "Would you like any more tea?"

"No thank you, I've had quite enough." She imitates him.

In his tenor voice, he continues, "It's such a lovely evening. How about waiting outside for the kids?"

In a trope style chant, she responds, "Very good. *Tov m'od.*"

"*Tov m'od.* Very good. Even I can translate that," he says as they go out of his house together and sit down on the top step. "I only know a few words in Hebrew. Don't try anything complicated or you'll lose me."

"I wouldn't want to do that, Simon," Ruchamah teases. She almost has to lean against him, so small is the space on the top step.

I wouldn't want to lose you either, Ruchamah, Simon is about to respond, when she moves so their bodies are no longer touching. "It's humid tonight," he says instead. She has clasped her hands together now. He senses her unease. "So," he says, hoping to make her feel less uncomfortable, "how do you do that anyway?"

"Do what?"

"Find the exact words in English that match the poet or writer's intention?"

"Oh, that," Ruchamah is grateful to talk about work again. She hopes she doesn't ramble, but it's so unusual to have someone with whom she can share her process. "Well, first, I try to get an overall sense of what the writer is saying. Then I concentrate on specific words." Simon nods his understanding.

"For example, knowing that *adam,* Hebrew for mankind, and *adamah,* which means earth, share the same root evoking an image of God forming mankind from the earth, extends the possibilities for translation." She looks as Simon intently. "As soon as I have a decent draft, I tape it to one of my kitchen cabinets and keep going back to it, as an artist would a painting, tweaking it here, revising it there. While Aviva was a baby I would carry her in my arms and walk around singing all the drafts to her to see if the sounds and rhythm come close to the original. I still walk around singing my wall drafts even though Aviva is old enough to make fun of my hardly melodious voice."

Simon laughs. "I find your voice soothing." Some of her hair has escaped its headband. He watches as she tucks it behind her ears.

"When I start a new piece," he adds, "I line up my scores to decide which edition to play. Something like your wall drafts. Then I have to determine the fingering for each note. Did you know that the degree of pressure and even the amount of flesh on your finger affects the tone? Fat and thin fingers give you different tones. My fingers are thin." He holds them up.

"Mine, too," she says as she holds her hands up. Then she giggles. "I feel a little silly, sitting here with my palms extended, like a kid showing her mom she's washed her hands thoroughly."

"Let's see," Simon says, eager to have a reason to touch her. He takes her hands in his and examines them closely. "Very clean," he says. He holds onto them until she pulls them gently away.

"The more you talk, the more I realize we are in a similar business, if my interpretation is correct, that is." Ruchamah winces at her bad pun.

"We might be kindred spirits. At the very least, we're workaholics."

"Robert Frost said, 'Poetry is what gets lost in translation.' His words haunt me. No matter how hard I work, I never feel I'm finished."

"Perhaps because ultimately we have to let go and send our work out into the world."

"And wait for the response," Ruchamah says. "Sometimes that's the hardest part. Speaking of waiting," she looks up the street, "our kids have been gone a long time."

"It's amazing that Jacob took off with Aviva like this. I think he'll have a terrific summer because of your daughter."

"Her father would have been very proud of her." When she doesn't say anything more, Simon asks, "Would you tell me about Daniel?"

Ruchamah hesitates for a moment and then nods assent. "The day Daniel died my joy turned to fear," she finishes softly. "That's not a good way to live. I depend on Aviva too much."

"Jacob hasn't spoken since his mother left. He laughs and cries, but words elude him."

Their situations are different, Ruchamah thinks, but the loneliness is the same.

"Here they come." Simon waves. Aviva and Jacob are laughing, their popsicles drizzling all over them. Jacob's shirt is off. The cold grape liquid running down his chest makes him laugh even more. Simon starts to laugh as well and runs inside for a washcloth.

NINE

Ida watches Nathan nodding off in his chair. It is an extremely hot afternoon for so early in July. The air conditioning unit isn't working and she is having trouble keeping her eyes open. She forces herself to sit up straight. Maybe she should have a cup of tea, a little caffeine wouldn't hurt. It's almost three o'clock. Too early to start supper. She yawns. Despite her best effort to stay awake, her eyes close. She should water the plants. Nathan used to do this on a weekly basis but he forgets lately. By the time Ida reminds him and he gets the watering can, he stares at it in his hand with a puzzled look, then asks her what he is supposed to be doing. Sometimes she helps him, but this takes over an hour and lately she hasn't felt like it. Occasionally, Nathan looks at his plants and waters them himself.

On those days she has hope again, hope that the Alzheimer's is not advancing. She knows this is not possible. Her children are appalled that she would even think this, but deep in Ida's heart everything is still possible, even a miracle such as this.

Suddenly the air in the living room cools, as if clouds have passed over the sun. It might rain soon. A drenching, cooling rain.

When Ida wakes the room is dark. Has it rained? No the air is still warm. She longs to sink back into sleep, but something doesn't feel quite right. She sits up. Nathan? She glances at his chair. He's not there. "Nathan?" She calls out to him but he doesn't answer. She searches the house, opens the front door and calls him again. Perhaps he has just gone for a little walk and is on his way back or perhaps he has bumped into someone and they are talking for a while.

She hurries onto the street in her house slippers, almost running, in the direction of the synagogue. Perhaps Nathan thought he should go to services. She begins calling his name with every other step. Aviva is walking towards her with Jacob, on their way to the playground. "I'll get my mother," she says holding Jacob tightly by the hand; the two of them race towards Ruchamah's house.

By the time Ida reaches Ruchamah's, a cadre of neighbors who have heard her calling, are leaving their homes to join the search for Nathan.

"Nathan," they call, a chant they repeat over and over, their voices a chorus of pleading. "Nathan come home." "Nathan turn back." "Nathan look carefully if you are crossing the street." "Nathan,

Ida is looking for you." But there is no sign of Nathan, no response to their chorus as they reach the synagogue.

"I haven't seen him," Marcia says. "I checked with the rabbi. He hasn't seen him either."

"We'll come with you," Rabbi Kramer says as he enters the office, cell phone in hand. Shoshanah is right behind him. "Marcia, I'll check in every few minutes to see if you've heard anything."

"I don't want to alarm you, Ida," Marcia says, "but just the other day I read that an Alzheimer's patient wandered away from his family, hopped a train and was found days later, eating garbage from dumpsters in a city hundreds of miles from his home. But he was found," Marcia adds hastily, looking at Ida's terrified face as she realizes she has made her afraid, which was not her intention at all. Marcia sighs. Lately everyone misunderstands her. She doesn't know why. All she has ever tried to do is be helpful.

Ruchamah puts her arm around Ida. "We'll find Nathan. There are so many of us and no one will stop looking until he's home again."

Ida nods and squeezes Ruchamah's hand.

"We used to walk through here in the winter to get out of the cold," she says as they take a quick look inside the arcade on Harvard Street. They stop and ask people ask if they can help. They give them the synagogue phone number. Some shoppers join them. The crowd grows larger; people disperse to cover more stores, to ask if anyone has seen a man, about 5'4", neatly dressed, wearing a steel gray fedora, which, unconsciously out of the habit of half a century, he must have placed on his head. There had been no sign of it in their house.

It's already after four. If only Ida hadn't fallen asleep. Usually she doesn't nap when Nathan does and even if she does, takes only a cat-nap except for the one time she slept for an entire hour and woke up in a panic only to find him still asleep. "Anything could happen to him," she tells Ruchamah. "He could have assumed he was supposed to go to work. Oh God forbid, he could be on the T. I think we should go to the Coolidge Corner stop. That's the one he would have used."

As soon as they find Nathan, she will find some way to alarm the house so she'll know if he leaves. Wind chimes by the doorway might work, and maybe she can get him to wear one of those Medic Alert bracelets in case he does go out. Even as she thinks this, she despairs about her inability to prevent this from happening. Her children have warned her repeatedly. Susan, in particular, has been begging her to read about her father's disease. "Sun-downing," she has repeatedly told her. "It means wandering. Mostly late afternoons and early evenings." But Ida has ignored her daughter, annoyed at the way Susan has suddenly begun to parent her.

In spite of the fact that both children have entreated her to get help with Nathan, Ida feels perfectly fine about her decision not to do so. She is fortunate to still have all her senses. She can take care of their father. They will find him soon and this incident will be over, never to be mentioned. But what was it Marcia said, someone was found hundreds of miles from his home. Oh, God. She hurries her steps as she nears the T and looks up in time to see Simon descending the subway car.

"I left the Conservatory early today," he says. "Why are all of you here?" He picks Jacob up and gives him a hug, then sets him down. He is alarmed when he hears that Nathan has left the house unexpectedly. He knows all too well what that's like.

"I thought he might be here," Ida says, "but there's no sign of him. He could be on his way to Boston by now. I think we should call the police."

"Have you tried the library?"

Ida tells him no.

"Let me check. If he's not there, I'll call the police immediately." Jacob tugs at his hand. "Don't worry, Jacob. We're going to find Nathan. Everybody's looking. He won't be lost for too long. Wait here with Aviva. Ruchamah, will you come with me?"

Ida tries to remain calm, as she sits down on a bench between Aviva and Jacob. Poor Nathan, she thinks. He has no idea what he is putting me through. Jacob looks very upset. Ida pats his hand. "They'll find him, Jacob. I remember a time when I was lost," she tells him. "Nathan thought I was lost for a long time. And here I am." Jacob's eyes widen.

"I was in Israel with a group from the temple, at a kibbutz in the Galilee, near the northern border. Nathan had fallen asleep in our room. I was on my way to the pool when Walter, our guide, came along and asked me if I would like to look for stone-age tools known to exist in the area. We came upon several specimens and lost track of time. Meanwhile, Nathan woke up and went to meet me at the pool. I wasn't there. No one had seen me. We weren't far from the Syrian border, a potentially dangerous place, even though it was well guarded. Nathan was nervous and began to check with other tourists on our trip. They formed a kind of posse and went looking for me. After two hours, Walter and I, who were on our way back, heard Nathan calling my name. As soon he saw me Nathan started yelling. 'Where were you? How could you get lost like this?' I was calm when I answered. 'Why are you upset, Nathan? I wasn't lost. I knew where I was all along.'"

Jacob is staring at her, still concerned. "So maybe Nathan knows where he is today," Ida says. "Like I did then. And maybe we're the ones who are lost."

Aviva laughs and hugs her. Jacob leans against her side.

"He used to spend hours here," Simon is saying.

Ruchamah has to run to keep pace with him. "I'll stay outside and keep an eye out in case you miss him," she says, as soon as they reach the building.

Simon races downstairs. And just as he had hoped, Nathan is in the music room, wearing a set of ear-phones, listening, as always, to a particular version of a piece that's not in his record library. Simon sits next to him for a minute but Nathan raises an index finger to indicate he hasn't finished. "I'll be right back." Simon takes the stairs two at a time. "He's just listening to music," he tells Ruchamah. He has no idea anyone thinks he's lost."

"I'll call Marcia." Simon hands her his cell phone. Downstairs in the library, Nathan is still completely engrossed in the music. Simon picks up the CD case lying on the table. *"The Best of Fritz Kreisler."* Short pieces. The wait won't be long.

Nathan removes his earphones, offering them to Simon so he can listen.

"I have to get back to Jacob," Simon says. "But if you come with me now, I'll return with you tomorrow so we can listen together."

When they go outside Nathan greets Ruchamah affectionately. "The two of you are such a lovely couple," he tells them.

"Thank you, Nathan," she says gently and takes his arm.

Ida, who has been keeping a constant look-out, jumps up and runs to Nathan as he comes into view walking between Ruchamah and Simon. She hugs him so tightly he has to tell her to let go.

"I told you we'd find him." Simon kisses Jacob and hoists him up onto his shoulders for a piggy-back ride all the way to Ida's. "Aviva?" he turns his head. "Can you stay a while longer tomorrow? I promised Nathan I'd go back to the library with him."

"So you were at the library." Ida is still holding her husband's arm "I was worried, but of course," she winked, "you knew where you were all along."

As they pass the arcade, a voice in the distance is still calling out, "Nathan come home. Nathan, Ida is looking for you."

"She found him," Aviva calls back.

Soon Ida and Nathan are surrounded by friends, neighbors and shoppers who had been searching for him. When they reach the house, Rabbi Kramer and Marcia are waiting on the front steps.

"Come in. Come in." Nathan says to the crowd. "Ida, everyone's coming for coffee."

TEN

The phone rings just as Shoshanah is getting ready to leave her apartment. If she answers, there's a good chance she'll be late to the first of the two make up classes the DeCordova is offering before the end of June. She listens as the voice comes in on her answering machine. It's Hillel. She picks up the phone. He has to make a meeting with the Coolidge Corner Peace and Justice Coalition but a congregant urgently needs to speak with him. Is there any possibility that she can visit the congregant? "I'm sorry to give you such short notice."

"Can you ask someone from the *Hevra Mishpachah* to go? Or have Manny handle the meeting? He's the committee chair." Shoshanah winces as she says this. She can't help worrying about the congregants and she has a hard time saying no to Hillel, but she hasn't gotten home before ten o'clock any night this week and she will need both classes to be able to finish her bracelet before the museum's session ends.

"Go to your class, Shoshanah. I'm sorry to be asking so much of you. It isn't fair."

"If you can't get anyone else, call me on my cell."

"Beth said she would visit the congregant if you were busy. It's okay Shoshanah. See you tomorrow."

She grabs the tiny silk purse filled to the brim with her bracelet pieces which she had set on her kitchen table as she gulped down a fast ~~cup of~~ glass of cranberry juice and took a few bites of the *bubke* she had picked up on her way home. It's hard for her to keep weight on and the sugar she's consuming only gives her quick energy, just enough for her class. She promises herself she'll eat something more substantial later, but even as she inserts the key into the ignition of her car she considers calling Hillel back. She hadn't asked which congregant. If it's Nathan or Ida, she should go. Hillel doesn't communicate well with either of them and Beth has enough to do with the pre-school. Torn between wanting to finish her bracelet and feeling she should make sure the congregant is cared for, she sits in her driveway unable to start the car. If only Hillel was doing his share or even spending time with some of the congregants who had volunteered to participate in recently established committees. She's going to have to tell him he needs to stop leaving everything to her, but tonight, she turns on the ignition and backs onto the street. Tonight she is safely on her way to class.

She's more than a half hour late as she races into the DeCordova and goes directly to the silversmithing workshop. Setting her canvas bag on a worktable, Shoshanah takes out her stones, bezel wire, sandpaper, round file and safety glasses. The pickle pot in which she will clean her pieces is already heating up. Tonight she hopes to set a golden citrine in the center of each of her perfectly designed flowers, the edges of which took her hours to file. She glances at her table mate. Noah, she reminds herself. She can't remember if he's a pediatrician or an internist. He often has to stand in the doorway to answer his pager; sometimes that's the last she sees of him for the evening.

She has hardly spoken to him or anyone else in the class because this is her refuge, the only place she has besides the sanctuary in Kehillat Shalom to both meditate and create. Her apartment is small; the phone rings constantly with either Hillel or congregants on the line. It's hard to get anything done there other than to file the edges of her pieces in order to save time from class, forcing herself to wear a mask so as not to breathe in any of the silver dust. Noah places a paper template on a sheet of silver and begins cutting out what looks to be a baby cup. Perhaps it's for his child although he's not wearing a wedding ring. Her mother keeps reminding her that she's getting older. "Older and older," her mother said the last time they spoke. "When am I going to give you a wedding?"

Noah is tall and thin, with a shock of black hair that he pushes impatiently out of his eyes. Perhaps, like her, he's had no time to have it cut. Shoshanah has wrapped her own dark hair in a scrunchy to keep it out her way. The room feels hot even though the air conditioner is on; her hands are sweating. She wipes them on a paper towel. The Coalition for Peace and Justice has begun organizing interfaith meetings throughout the Boston area and Hillel is scheduled to speak on *Tikkun Olam* in a few weeks. Perhaps she should have gone to the meeting to give him time to work on his speech. Not that he would have used it. She frowns, reminds herself she's in class, not at work and attempts to shake off her concern and focus on her bracelet.

"I've never heard that exact melody before," Noah says, startling her. She must be humming under her breath. Probably she had interfered with his concentration. She's about to apologize when one of the citrines rolls to the floor. He smiles as he picks it up and lays it on their worktable. She thanks him and glances at her watch. If she doesn't finish the bezels tonight she will never be able to set these stones. She reaches for the wire and cuts slowly and carefully. When she's done, she fits them around each piece of golden stone. She waits for her soldering iron to heat up, then solders the centers in place, picks up a copper tong and carefully inserts them into the pickle pot.

Noah is using different size hammers to raise his cup and moves a small torch over its surface to anneal it. The sound of his hammer hitting the silver is comforting in its steadiness. His hands are strong; his grip on the hammers gentle but firm. There is no danger of anything flying away from him. She cuts tiny pieces of wire for the jump rings which will connect each flower and picks up her soldering iron again.

She is almost finished by the time Linda announces that there are only five minutes left to class. Next week all she will have to do is toss the rings into the pickle pot and attach the bracelet together. Noah hasn't finished his cup either, although he has soldered the sides and attached the handle.

Shoshanah puts back her tools, wipes her side of the table, then gathers the bejeweled flowers in her hand. The citrine stones shine in their bed of silver just as she had hoped. She folds her fingers around them instead of putting them back in the silk purse as she walks to her car.

She probably should have asked Hillel which congregant he was calling about; Shoshanah rummages through her pocketbook for her cell to call him at home, still holding the stone.

"I'm sorry I couldn't visit the congregant," she tells Beth when she answers.

"Mrs. Siegel is fine," Beth says. "She's just a little lonely."

"I was just going out the door when Hillel called."

"You do so much more than your share. Shoshanah, while Hillel..." she stops.

Board members as well as congregants have become disenchanted with the rabbi lately. Shoshanah hopes that it is not true for Beth as well. Beth assures her that everything is fine before she hangs up.

"I think you dropped these" her classmate says, bending to retrieve a few sections of her bracelet.

"That's twice tonight you've rescued my work," Shoshanah says.

"Surely that's worth a cup of coffee," he grins.

"Another time perhaps," she says as she gets into her car. And immediately steps out. "Wait," she hails him. "May I change my mind?" At least this way she can tell her mother she's finally been on a date.

ELEVEN

D ear Elijah,
     More than a month has passed since my arrival here. So much time gone with so few results. I thought I had figured how to solve the rabbi's problem a few weeks ago, but Hillel completely misinterpreted my appearance holding a child in the whirlwind and begged Beth to keep trying in-vitro, even though she has apparently told him over and over that her body can no longer tolerate those treatments. I'm beginning to wonder if I'll have to stay here for the rest of this rabbi's life before he can accept the fact that any child of his will not be one of his loins.

Not that I'm interested in speaking of the rabbi's loins. Nor in the amount of time I'm spending with congregants because I'm volunteering in the office.

This is how I ended up looking for Nathan the other day. So many people joined in the search I suddenly felt very alone. The only time I ever belonged to a community was as a child. I began to wonder who would look for me if I were lost. Who, besides you, even knows where I am? If anyone asks, you might tell them I'm behind the synagogue kitchen door waiting for the *Rosh Hodesh* group to begin.

I was getting a little snack for myself just as Beth came into the kitchen, which accounts for my having to hide so she doesn't wonder what Sara the volunteer is still doing here.

Beth is walking in and out to bring candles and candleholders, small vases filled with flowers for the table, but she forgot the cloth. Now she's standing in the middle of the kitchen shaking her head at her apparent distraction. She sighs, opens a cupboard drawer, withdraws a white satin covering and walks into the main room. She removes everything she has already put on the table just as Ruchamah pushes opens the door; she takes a quick look behind her, as if she's afraid someone has followed her, before letting the door close.

She hasn't even waited to dry her hair. Elijah, I just couldn't help it. I made a little intervention earlier this evening while she was swimming. Did you know Ruchamah does meditative laps, 18 for, *chai,* wishing life for someone in need of healing and 36, double *chai,* for the world at large? In my opinion she should be swimming one for herself.

"What happened?" Beth exclaims noting Ruchamah's pallor. She sets down the tablecloth, takes a chair from the circle of chairs that have been set up for the meeting and urges her friend to sit.

Ruchamah takes several deep breaths before blurting out her story, which I'm sure is about me. "When I was swimming the 12th lap, the one I do for Daniel because we met on the 12th of May," she begins, "a strange woman started swimming along side of me, even though the next lane was empty. Even worse, she would not get out of my way. I couldn't see her clearly until we came to the end of the lap. We turned at the same time. She was wearing a woolen knit bathing suit from the twenties! I swam as fast as I could, but she kept pace. All of a sudden I realized she was the crone from my dream, *Erev Shavuot*." Ruchamah put her hands over her face. "Am I going crazy?"

I had no intention of frightening her again, Elijah. I was merely trying to show her that if an ancient crone like myself can still swim laps, she can find a way to get on with her own life. A metaphorical intervention. Next time I will be more direct.

"Hillel saw a stranger as well," Beth begins. "A woman, holding a child. In a rush of wind, he heard the child cry. He came home elated, thinking his vision meant I would somehow be able to conceive. I don't know whether or not he thought he saw someone in order to convince himself of this, but if he did, I'm sure his stranger was up to no good." Can you believe that Elijah? Both Ruchamah and Beth think I am trying to harm them!

More women come bearing refreshments now: a fruit salad loaded with kiwi fruits, a cake with raspberries spilling over the sides, an entire tray of brownies topped with confectionary sugar, all kinds of cookies and a tray of clementines. I'm so hungry I feel faint.

The women mill around chatting until Beth asks everyone to take a seat.

"It's difficult, even impossible," she tells the gathering "to imagine what life was like in the beginnings of Judaism, before electricity and our scientific awareness of the cosmos, what it must have felt like each month when the moon waned to the point of no moon at all. Faith that the light would return was the most that one could hope for. "Like the women of old, we gather each month with faith that the light will return. We are less afraid of the dark as we support each other with hope and prayer."

That's exactly the way it was, wasn't it Elijah? When my mother and I were in the Red Tent, we were afraid, but being together gave us courage.

Beth opens a *tallit* someone has embroidered with all their names. The women make a circle to lift it high over their heads, chant a prayer to create a sacred space, fold the *tallit* and regain their seats.

"Tonight is the new moon of *Tammuz*," Beth continues, "which begins the month of omens and portents, marking the time the first brick was removed from the holy temple in Jerusalem. If our ancestors had perceived this as a warning, could they have done anything to prepare for the destruction and their exile? Could they have determined what they should do to ensure their future?

I could have answered her. We did not realize we were being warned. In retrospect we went about our normal lives rather blindly.

Ruchamah cranes her neck, peering deeply into each corner, probably looking for a crone in a bathing suit, but I'm still in the kitchen, taking notes for you.

When Beth asks the women to consider the omens and portents in their own lives, there is a brief silence. The women shift positions in their chairs. If this group is anything like the ones in the tent, everyone will share their most personal stories.

"My grandmother Rose died of breast cancer," Carole offers. "She used to call me her '*zeezen madele*' and come to my house to make *challah*. Whenever she hugged me, the flour from her apron wafted up. A few years ago as I made *challah* for the first time, she suddenly appeared next to me. 'But you're dead,' I said, then instantly remembered I had ignored my doctor's instruction to schedule a mammogram. When I learned I had breast cancer, like my grandmother I blamed the *challah* and couldn't make it for months until I realized it was the warning that saved my life. Now I bake it every *Shabbat,* however, my grandmother has never visited me again."

More stories follow. One of the women says "there were early warnings of the Holocaust. Some people risked their lives to get messages out to the rest of the world, but they were ignored by leaders, even at the highest levels."

She's right, Elijah. People didn't pay attention then. People don't pay attention now. Take the rabbi for instance. Since I've been in the office I'm very aware of the members' dissatisfaction, but the rabbi can't seem to hear what they're trying to tell him. Beth speaks but he doesn't listen. I didn't pay attention when I was a child. My mother used to warn me not to talk so much. "No one has to know that you know things they don't," she said, but I thought everyone would want to be informed. As it turns out, she was right.

Nancy tells the group the group that talking about omens and portents terrifies her. "When I dream something is going to happen, it's usually does. I had a dream a few weeks before my father died and when he died, exactly as it happened in the dream, I became afraid to go to sleep."

Although I sometimes appear in dreams Elijah, this wasn't me, I promise. You know I don't foretell death.

"What would make you less afraid?" This from Ruchamah.

"A guarantee that a sign means something good is going to happen. A promise from the universe."

"I'm not sure this could be considered a promise," Beth offers, "but we do have a biblical ancestor who is considered to be a portent of things to come. We said earlier that the removal of the first brick was a sign that the Temple would be destroyed. Not many people know that in 9th Century Poland there was a pogrom in which all the synagogues in one community were burnt to the ground, except for one, the synagogue, Serach bat Asher."

"Serach? Isn't she the stranger who appears in different guises over time?" Gail asks.

"*Midrashim* tell us Serach has often appeared throughout history to indicate a time of change," Beth adds. "She is considered a comforting portent. Ruchamah's friend, Miriam Weinstein, who will be coming to Kehillat Shalom for the scholar's program in the fall, brought these ancient rabbinical stories together in her poem, Serach,"

They're speaking of me, Elijah! I open the kitchen door as wide as possible so I don't miss a word as Ruchamah reads Miriam's poem aloud.

SERACH

Serach
She was number 70, the perfect number
this sole woman in an all-male census of the
Jews who entered Egypt.

Serach
Beautiful and wise, faithful and pious
daughter of Asher, she brought hope to her
distraught grandfather
the patriarch Jacob
when she was the first to prophesy that her
uncle Joseph yet lived.

Serach
Only woman among the seven
granted eternal life, according to the Rabbis
in their *Midrashim*.

Serach
Key to the redemption of Israel from Egypt
four centuries after his burial
she located the bones of Joseph
for Moses, so he could keep the vow our people made
to carry his remains to the promised land.

Serach
Convinced the leaders of the people to follow Moses
from slavery in Egypt to freedom in Canaan.

Serach
Watched over the parting of the sea
the parting of our people from *Mitzrayim*
she came as an eagle
dipping low between the walls of the sea
then soaring above
gleaming sunlight reflecting off her wings
a golden beacon to all.

Serach
Woman of mystery
you who sweep down into our lives
whenever we need your help
bless us with redemption.

"The last verse is like a prayer," Carole says, almost in a whisper.

"She's a magical figure." Nancy adds. "A protector of sorts."

"I think of her as a guide," Julie says. "In the poem, when she watches the Israelites cross the Red Sea, she becomes a beacon, providing light to lead their way."

So many compliments! I'm a magical figure, a beacon. And best of all I'm a good luck omen. You can imagine how much I long to reveal myself, Elijah. Miriam indicated that I was beautiful as well as wise. Not that I'm becoming vain, but there aren't any mirrors in the Garden. Of course, we do have those lovely reflecting pools. I'll have to start taking an occasional peek as soon as I return. The discussion continued for a few more minutes. Sadly, it was no longer all about me.

"We've traveled back in time, from the removal of the first brick in the temple and forward to our *Rosh Hodesh* group here tonight to welcome the new moon of *Tammuz,*" Beth begins to wrap up the meeting. "I hope this new moon helps us look at omens in our lives in a new way. Signs that appear frightening at first can help us when we have the courage to pay attention. And I want to thank all of you for sharing such personal stories. We are not so different from the women who shared their stories in the Red Tent."

The group disbands to gather around the refreshment table. "This is my grandmother's favorite putterkuchen," Carole says as she cuts a slice for everyone.

"Now there's a sign I can totally relate to," Julie hugs her, smiling. Beth opens the door leading to the synagogue garden and everyone takes seats outside. I'm leaving the kitchen now to grab a bite.

"The ancients used to find omens and portents in the stars," Nancy says. "This is the perfect place to watch for the arrival of the new moon."

"Can you see her yet?" Carole asks.

"Not even a sliver."

"Oh, look. There she is."

I stand in the synagogue doorway, Elijah, and suddenly I see myself as a little girl, my mother's arms around me. We wait in the Red Tent's opening to go outside when that tiny silver sliver appears. I don't like it when we gather our belongings. The camaraderie we share by being together will be gone until the following month. Life was easier when we had no responsibilities for fathers, sons or husbands. My mother used to let me stay up as late as I wanted. And I had so many friends, Elijah. Just like the women in this *Rosh Hodesh* group.

I hurry back to my hiding place as soon as the women pick up their now empty plates and get ready to leave. Beth and Ruchamah remain behind and come back to the kitchen together. Beth pours two steaming cups of tea.

"I was greatly relieved when that woman who's haunting me didn't show up." Ruchamah tells her. They lean against the table in the middle of the kitchen.

"Don't be offended but I was sort of hoping she would."

"Maybe Serach will drop in on you," Ruchamah says. "I certainly don't wish you my stranger."

Beth laughs.

"I almost told the group about her," Ruchamah says. "Perhaps someone would have a good idea about how to banish her."

Not yet, I could have told her. I have a job to do and I always do it. I'm just usually faster. I found myself staring at Beth. Her face has the same shape as my mother's. Oval. And her hair is almost the same honey color. Images of my mother rushed at me. Elijah, I had to hold on to the door for support. I hope you didn't send me here to regain memories of my life before I came to the Garden, as well as to help the rabbi. I don't want to remember. I don't want to know that I miss my mother or that, like Beth and Hillel, I once longed for a child of my own. I used to hold the women's babies in the Red Tent. I used to think that being a wife and mother would be my life. I never dreamed of becoming an immortal. No one asked me, Elijah. You know that.

I wake from this reverie in time to hear Ruchamah tell Beth that she is worried about her. "It is hard to miss the tension between you and Hillel. I don't want to pry, but please know I care about you."

Beth hugs her and nods her head. "I could hardly bring myself to lead the meeting tonight. I"'m so angry at Hillel I want to shake him until he turns back into who he used to be."

"Maybe he wishes he could."

Beth laughs a little. "I was a tomboy when I was a child, always running around chasing my brothers, begging them to let me play with them. I never thought I would grow up to marry a rabbi, but Hillel was so evolved, so open minded, so compassionate when I met him. He was non-judgmental. This Hillel bears hardly any resemblance to the man I married. I'm now the wife of a very stubborn man who can hold only one idea in his head. He's obsessed with having his own child. His own. When we always said, even if we had our own children we would give other children a home. I don't understand what's come over him; I blame his father though I shouldn't be blaming anyone. I should be trying to understand, but I can't."

"Is there anything I can do?" Ruchamah asks.

Ask me, I want to say, though I am beginning to feel that this situation is more complicated than I realized. I feel myself inclined toward the congregants though I don't want to care about them. The first time I was here, I did become a little attached to Ida. And I admired Aviva for trying so hard to take care of her mother, but I never involved myself in their affairs. Of course I was never here or anywhere longer than 3 days. At least it seemed like 3 days to me. I did linger in that synagogue in Hawaii, but that was because Hawaii reminded me of the Garden.

More later, Elijah. Beth and Ruchamah have finished cleaning up. I'm tired from thinking about all of this. As soon as I figure out the right intervention for the rabbi, I'll be on my way home. Then perhaps you can consider giving me a sabbatical. Five thousand years is a long time without a vacation.

Serach.

TWELVE

Beth closes the door after Hillel leaves. When he kissed her goodbye, he seemed unaware that her body stiffened. He can't stop talking about the spirit that came to him holding a child; their mornings are fraught with tension. They eat breakfast quickly, he at the kitchen table, she at the counter, then leave for Kehillat Shalom. As soon as they arrive they go their separate ways. Although Kehillat Shalom is the first place they've worked together, they no longer seek each other out at lunch time or walk down the hall to share a funny story. She stays in the preschool and he stays in his office. Tonight the preschool is hosting a children's book fair featuring the author of *Hannah Rachael and the Sabbath Queen* and she doesn't have to be in until mid-afternoon. Maybe Hillel will drop in to see the children today. She's told him how they wait, eager to forsake what they're doing and rush to hug him yelling "rabbi time." They want him to swing them up in his arms and set them down as gently as if they were eggs. The last time he came was on Israeli Independence Day. They tugged him through every classroom to show him the *kibbutz* they were creating. He ate cookies in *Kitah Aleph* where they had set up a kitchen and spent a half hour in *Kitah Bet* making a clay pot. He hasn't been back since.

When Beth first told Hillel that the doctor said they had to stop the in-vitro, he took her in his arms and promised that they would figure out what to do together. All he seems to have figured out is how to avoid her. He locks himself in his study, always with an excuse. He has a deadline. He's working on a program. He started coming to bed after she had fallen asleep.

"You're hiding," she accused him one day.

"I can't seem to get over this," he admitted. The doctor had assured them it was neither of their faults. It was just one of those things. "Not being able to have a child is not just one of those things," Hillel told the doctor that day, as angry as she had ever seen him.

Getting up from the kitchen table, she gathers the breakfast dishes and takes them to the sink. She's not the only woman unable to conceive, but because she's the rabbi's wife she doesn't feel she can burden the women in the *Rosh Hodesh* group with her personal travail, except for Ruchamah. They had become instant friends the minute she and Hillel walked into the synagogue office their first day. Ruchamah, who had been helping Marcia with the pre-school mailing, put her work down immediately to greet her and invite her to her home. A few days later Beth walked into a dining room filled with women from both the sisterhood and the *Rosh Hodesh* group.

Her heart had gone out to her friend last night when Ruchamah rushed into the meeting, so terrified of the crone she feared was following her, she was trembling. Thinking to reassure her, Beth had indicated she would not be adverse to seeing this spirit herself.

"I certainly don't wish you my spirit," Ruchamah replied. "Maybe Serach will come to you."

If only you would come, Serach. Maybe you would have some advice for me, even some magic.

She washes the dishes, goes into the bedroom to get dressed and returns to the kitchen for a second cup of coffee. She stands at the sink again staring out the window. Ordinarily she works in the garden on mornings like this. It's cool enough for early July. And her roses are already in full bloom, but she's not the mood. Perhaps she'll go to the study and straighten up. Setting things in order always soothes her. Beth climbs the steps and pauses at the second floor landing facing the open door of the room that had been intended for the baby. Her footsteps resound in the empty space.

Hillel thought their little boy would like walls as blue as the sky, or perhaps, even if their baby was a girl, she would like blue just as much. "We'll paint the walls a soft, soft blue with clouds, and birds of all colors," Beth told him. They had almost decided to begin when the doctor told them in-vitro was no longer a possibility. Perhaps it would have been harder if they had gone ahead anyway. "Empty room, empty womb," she says aloud. Her words reverberate as she closes the door and continues climbing the stairs until she reaches the study.

All the rooms in the house are cozy but this third floor hideaway with its skylight is what sold them on it the minute they saw it. They had stopped listening to the realtor's expansive description of this home as "one of the Victorian gems of Coolidge Corner" as soon as they reached the top floor and opened the door.

She sits down on the forest green velvet sofa covered with small pillows they have collected, and hugs one to her chest. Crafted by an Ethiopian woman, who had come to Israel on the Wings of Eagle's flight, symbolizing a world of mothers and children lifting their arms to the sky, it was given to her by the children from the pre-school in the Los Angeles synagogue when she and Hillel came east.

The walls are lined with shelves crammed with books, the top displaying mementos of trips they have taken. Beth's glance falls on a photo from their honeymoon in Hawaii. They are in a restaurant, the waiter having covered them in flowers. How grand was that trip, pre-planned so they could relax after the hectic days of the wedding. So organized, except that in the rush of packing she had forgotten her birth control pills. Both she and Hillel had agreed there would be no harm if she had become pregnant right away. When that didn't happen she found herself relieved that they could just be a couple for a while. After a year, they began to long for a child, a gift they had not been fortunate enough to receive. On the night they moved into the house, they brought drinks upstairs and ended up making love on the sofa as the colors of twilight deepened before them through the windows and skylight. A few months later, they began their round of failed in-vitros.

Don't go there, she tells herself. Think of the happy times. Next month people will be coming to their semi-annual Shabbat open house, a tradition they started right after they moved to Coolidge Corner.

"Leave everything to me, Beth," Hillel had insisted. I want to do this to show how much I appreciate you. This will be the party I throw, not even pot luck brought by congregants. Certainly, no cooking by you. I'll do everything."

"So this is really a catered affair," she had laughed, after lugging in the ingredients she had shopped for, setting up cooking pots and pans, pulling mixers out of the cabinets, and putting away some of the cookware left in the dish drainer.

Hillel used his mother's recipes for *tzimmis,* fish, noodle pudding along with veggie platters. The former owners had left a swing set and the beginnings of a tree house in their back yard. The latter part of the day was reserved for congregants who wanted to stay and discuss the weekly *Torah* portion. Some would remain until *Havdalah* so they should share wishes for a sweet week with the rabbi and Beth.

This is a good time to start a list for our summer *Shabbaton,* Beth thinks. She walks over to the desk for some paper. The new Bulletin is sitting on top of the blotter. Hillel must have brought it home last night. Usually she proofs them, the way she does portions of the *Tikkun Olam* book, but lately he hadn't asked her to do that. She picks it up. A notice at the top of the front page reads: SHABBAT OPEN HOUSE AT THE RABBI'S CANCELLED. Cancelled? She checks again. He couldn't have cancelled it without telling her. The *Shabbaton* is a mutually conceived event. One person in a marriage does not cancel these kinds of plans alone and certainly one person does not have the right to decide on the only way to have a baby. Is this what their marriage has come to? Something so screwed up and one-sided. And the side is all his!

This man who believes that the world would be a better place if people work together is deciding everything himself. The *Tikkun Olam* book must have a passage about that. She tosses the Bulletin aside and reaches across the desk for the notebook in which Hillel stores copies of his essays and flips past the introduction written when he arrived at the synagogue in Los Angeles. Essays about *Shabbat,* Israel and Palestine, How to Perform a *Mitzvah,* the meaning of *Tikkun Olam* fly through her hands as she turns page after page. Nothing about working together during times of great disagreement. Of course, nothing had gone wrong then. She scans quickly until she reaches the essays begun at

Kehillat Shalom. The very first essay starts with a quote from Martin Buber's *The Way of Man*. God asks Adam, "Where are you?" Adam hides himself to avoid rendering accounts, to escape responsibility for his way of living. "Every man hides for this purpose, for every man is Adam and finds himself in Adam's situation." A perfect description of Hillel these days, Beth thinks. Such significant and on-target writing. Obviously Hillel has not reread this recently. The essays come to a halt January 2, 2005, the day she forced herself to tell Hillel the doctor told her she should not continue the in-vitro treatments.

All these hours he's been spending in this room since then with the door closed, and he's written nothing. Not even a few notes. Except for canceling the *Shabbaton*. He seems to have had no trouble writing that.

THIRTEEN

It's the crack of dawn. Marcia has no problem finding a seat on the T. By the time she gets back she'll be schlepping Debby's wedding gown on an almost empty subway car. As long as she is first in the store, spots a gown and hits the cash register, she can make it to the synagogue within a half-hour of her normal starting time.

Ordinarily a trip to Filene's Basement would inspire eager anticipation, but she's so agitated, she can hardly bring herself to get on the train. Yesterday Debby suggested she temporarily borrow one of the gowns being brought to the temple to donate to the *Rabbanit B'racher Kupach* in Israel and had the nerve to say that Marcia should donate the one she insisted on buying her as well.

"Mom I'm joking," she finally said taking a look at Marcia's beet red face, but Marcia wasn't sure. The gowns never should have been in the office in the first place. It annoys her that no one read the sign she posted asking that they be taken to the cloakroom. Instead, the donors, most of them her friends from the Sisterhood who had been invited to the wedding, pile the gowns on the table that volunteer used for collating and shoved their boxes underneath. When they asked her how things were going and what Debby's gown was like; she gave them a rather vague answer. She doesn't want them to know that she was planning to shop for her daughter's wedding gown in the Filene's Basement extravaganza or that Debby had refused to come. That girl doesn't have the sense she was born with. What could be more important than her wedding gown? How she had raised a daughter who cared more about the preservation of the earth than her own appearance, Marcia will never know. Debby has a mother who knows weddings inside-out, but who does she insist on consulting with? Jeffrey. Her daughter hasn't learned one thing from her. How many times has she said, "Get this straight before you're married. You don't discuss everything with your husband."

Oh, Park Street. She's here already. Marcia takes the escalator up to the street and walks the few blocks to Filenes. The annual Bridal Gown Sale, better known as "The Running of the Brides" is one of the store's most anticipated events. At six-thirty, she's at the entrance waiting to storm the doors the minute they open at eight. Although she enjoys *kibbitzing* with fellow bargain hunters, nothing deters her competitive spirit. The moment the doors open, she's a New England Patriots running back, elbows poised, pushing through for a touchdown.

To the uninitiated, this, the original and unique Filene's Basement in downtown crossing, is the most confounding of stores. Bins holding sportswear, leather goods and intimate apparel display their wares in a tangled array, with items cascading down the sides. Hangers on the dress racks are intertwined, causing them to resemble the "before" pictures in closet organizer ads. You have to be a pro to shop here.

Marcia knows all the tricks of a consummate Basement shopper. She relies on simple strategies like moving a size 16 dress to a size 10 rack as she continues on her shopping spree. She doesn't consider this unethical since she always returns the dress to its home rack before leaving. The big problem with shopping the Basement is that the dressing rooms are only for men, who hardly need the privacy. It's not unusual to see a woman with a skirt slipped over her jeans consulting a fellow shopper about the fit. Given that the basement is known for selling irregular goods, although Marcia might be tempted by the low price of a dress, she never fails to inspect it with the eye of a quality control engineer in an aviation manufacturing facility. Nothing gives her greater pleasure than hastening back to Kehillat Shalom where few can avoid hearing her boast about her latest coup.

In a flash she spots the perfect wedding gown for Debby. Someone yanks it from the rack just as her fingertips make contact with the luxurious silk. Marcia watches the bride-to-be pull it over her head and smooth it over her hips. Fortunately the-bride's friend hands her another dress and lays the one she had tried on over the rack. Marcia seizes it. When the bride's friend catches her, she grabs the other end and yanks. After a moment's struggle, Marcia dashes off victorious to the cashier where she quickly pulls out the cash to pay for the gown, which, fortunately, is still in one piece. The bride-to-be rushes over to complain, only to hear the cashier say, "I'm not a referee. First person to reach the cash register with the merchandise gets it." Marcia quickly inspects the gown one last time or once again for any rips resulting from the struggle before it's packaged in a plastic cover.

Holding the gown like a waltz partner, she waits for the Beacon Street car in the subway and heads back to the office. Like all the other wedding arrangements, she has accomplished this purchase in record time. Marcia works fast when she works alone. No need to confer with others over details. She sits down and shifts the huge dress bag with Debby's wedding gown to a more comfortable position. Now she has taken care of everything for the wedding; she mentally ticks off the items on her list just to make sure. Yes, the gown was the last thing. Mission accomplished. She closes her eyes. She knows these stops by heart.

The other day one of the congregants came into the office to organize a "Meaningful Conversations" program so members could share their passions and thereby strengthen a sense of community within the synagogue. Marcia sees no need for anyone to arrange to have such a conversation. But if that congregant insists on turning them into special occasions, maybe after Debby's wedding, she'll sign up for one with the rabbi and tell him how nosy that new volunteer is. She'll ask him if he's noticed that Sara finds reasons to be in his office Or if he's aware that she talks to the congregants as if she's in charge, writing down their complaints so she can bring them to his attention. Marcia never bothers him with things like that. She might not mention that Sara has a soothing effect on some of them, as she points out the programs that are working and asks them if they want to become involved in those while waiting for their requests to come to fruition. No. Marcia doesn't trust her. Her clothes look as if they have come out of the rummage sale closet. The sisterhood has received so many contributions, she can't remember them all.

She would like to have a meaningful conversation with Ruchamah and Beth as well. The other night the *Rosh Hodesh* group left candle wax on the floor. Sometimes, just before the meeting, they rush in to Xerox something Marcia never gets a chance to look at and they often leave unlabeled food in the refrigerator and forget about it, although lately the refrigerator seems emptier than usual. She drums her fingers against the plastic covering

Debby's gown. As soon as the wedding is over, she is going to make sure Sara knows her place and that the *Rosh Hodesh* group cleans up after itself.

When she reaches her stop, she walks the few blocks to Kehillat Shalom. "Thanks for coming in to open the office," she greets Beth, making it clear she's back and the one in-charge, as usual.

She puts the gown on the desk covering whatever it was Beth had been working on.

"Is that Debby's gown?" Beth ignored Marcia's dismissive tone.

Marcia nods.

"I'd love to see it."

"I don't want to disturb the beading on the bodice." She hesitates. "But, you can inch the plastic up from the bottom and take a peek."

It's later than usual by the time she gets home. There's a note from Jack that he has taken Debby and Jeff on a little outing. She scans it again. He must have forgotten to mention where they were going. Marcia walks down the hall in the empty house, hangs the gown on Debby's closet door and lies down on her daughter's bed just as Jack arrives at Debby's apartment.

"I have a surprise for you and Jeff," he says when she opens the door. This is the first time he'll be alone with the couple in months. Marcia is doing everything else, much of which he doesn't agree with. This surprise, however, is completely his idea. He ushers them out to his car and drives them to the store. They follow him into the small back room where bottles of wine, a pitcher of water, a medium size bowl and a line of glasses have been set up. This is his daughter's wedding and he wants nothing but the best. He's selected the Cabernet Sauvignon 2000 from Segal's Galilee Heights Vineyards in Israel, touted to be a superior vintage, good directly out of the bottle even before it hits the air and Herzog's Special Reserve, Russian River Valley Chardonnay 2000 from California, a wine that changed his mind about Kosher Chardonnays. Of course he has other bottles there as well to give them a real choice.

"Try these and tell me your favorites. Remember to rinse out your mouth after each taste and spit the water out in the bowl between samples." Debbie wrinkles up her face and Jeff laughs. They pour small amounts of wine and begin taking sips. Jack sticks his cigar in his mouth but doesn't light it. After a while Jeff tells him he likes the sweet white wine. Debby chooses the dry Herzog. They decide on the Segal's for the red.

"I'll be right back." Jack goes to the car, returns with a package and opens it. He takes out two wine goblets. "Hand blown by a local artist. Look at the gold stem. I picked these out myself at The Wild Goose Chase." He hands one to each of them and makes a toast, prefacing it with: "I wanted to do this before the wedding so I could say what I really want in privacy to each of you." He chokes a little and closes his eyes against the tears that have begun to form. "You're my baby," he tells Deb. "For you, I want only the best." He glances at Jeff to see if this seemingly lackadaisical young man knows the treasure he is getting, not that anyone else but he would completely appreciate his daughter, so like him in so many ways. He surmises that Jeff is more selective in his taste in women than he is in wines. "This wine is a symbol of all the blessings you deserve to receive. I want you to know you two can count on me for anything. You're a little broke, come to Jack. You're a little stressed, come to Jack.

"And this is my advice about marriage. Your mother and I have been happy. True, we argue a lot, but it's just our way. We both have big mouths and we don't hold anything back. But after we fight, it's over. We don't hold grudges. This is what has made our marriage work. Fight all you want. No two people can agree on everything. But then, forget it. Love and cherish each other." He leans over and kisses his daughter's cheek and gives Jeff a bear hug. "Drink up." He pours himself a full glass of wine.

"*L'chaim.* To life. To your life together."

FOURTEEN

"Lori, are you awake? Lori?"

"What!" Lori wakes with a start.

"Sorry. Sorry. Go back to sleep."

"I'm awake now. What, Aviva?" She snaps on the light beside her bed in the cabin and smothers a yawn. "Where were you anyway?"

"I took a walk with Ari."

"I wish I had warned you about him."

"Nothing happened. Well almost nothing."

"Almost nothing?"

"He kissed me."

"And left it at that?"

"There are counselors all over the place. One of them told me to go to bed."

"Good. My cousin is big flirt. He thinks he can do anything now just because he's going to Israel."

"He's thinking of making *aliyah.* I might not ever see him again."

" Don't be silly. His parents are against it and if he does make *aliyah*, he'll have to join the Israeli defense force."

"I think he's very brave."

"I wish he hadn't decided to come to the retreat with us. He's really got it down."

"He's got what down?"

"You know, the gentle but strong approach girls just can't resist. He was like this before we moved, too. Coming over on weekends just to meet my friends."

"I like him."

"I know. Even girls who have boyfriends bat their eyelashes at him. His Israeli girlfriend writes every day begging him to return. He showed me her letters when he came back from his last trip."

"He's very handsome."

"I can't believe you, Aviva. You're a peacenik. You have no business with a guy like my cousin."

"He doesn't want to kill anyone. I asked him."

"Well he might have to if he makes *aliyah.* What do you think they do in the Israeli army?"

"Maybe he won't go."

"What would your mother say if she knew you had a crush on him?"

"I have no idea. My mother has been asleep ever since my father died. She'd probably say, "Use your best judgment, Aviva. Think about what you are doing and what it means.""

"I think this just might wake her up."

FIFTEEN

Aviva isn't back from her weekend retreat with Lori yet. Ruchamah's taking care of Jacob, something she's been looking forward to ever since Aviva asked her. The minute his father left, Jacob climbed onto her lap while she read some stories to him. He cut out pictures of trucks and cars to paste onto sheets of construction paper. He's been willing to get down to help her make cookies but climbs right back onto her lap to finish pasting until it's time to clean up and make pizza for lunch.

Ruchamah sets out the pizza dough and pan. Jacob spreads pizza sauce over the dough, his version of finger-painting, and laughs as she carries him into the bathroom to wash his hands. Jacob has a full throttle laugh; his eyes shine with mischief. Ruchamah is laughing too. "If you do any more painting, we might never get to eat lunch. How about making a happy face out of olives on top of the cheese before we bake it?"

When lunch is over, she packs up two of the monster size cookies they'd made earlier. "One for you and one for me, for when we get to the playground," she tells Jacob.

She watches him swing, climb and slide to his heart's content. Ruchamah has no idea how his mother could have left this precious little boy.

As they return from the playground, Aviva comes towards them smiling and waving. She looks older from a distance and when she comes closer, Ruchamah sees that she's wearing makeup. She's jolted by this futuristic image of her daughter. Aviva's closer to womanhood than Ruchamah had realized.

"Do I look like a clown?" Aviva asked laughing, as she reaches them. "My eyelashes are almost stuck together from all this mascara."

Ruchamah feels herself relax. This is still her Aviva, au natural.

"You look beautiful," she says. "And very grown-up."

Aviva takes Jacob's hand and the three of them walk back to Simon's house.

Jacob points to Aviva's eyes, then to his.

"Shall I paint your face, too?" Aviva opens her make up kit and carefully draws a clown face with eyeliner on this eager four-year old.

"Hold still, Jacob. I don't want to smudge you." She rings his eyes with blue eye shadow, fills in the lips she has outlined, dabs his nose with bright red lipstick, paints his cheeks with deep rose blush and walks him to the bathroom so he can see himself in the mirror. Ruchamah can hear him jumping up and down with excitement.

As soon as Simon comes home, Jacob throws himself into his arms.

"Has anyone here seen my Jacob?" Simon looks over his son's head. "Maybe I have the wrong house. This house has a clown in it." Jacob giggles. Simon sets him on his shoulders. "I think we have a Jacob clown here." The little clown leans his elbows on his father's head. "Do clowns eat dinner?" Jacob tugs at his father's hair. "Is that a yes? Can we all eat together?" he looks expectantly at Ruchamah and Aviva. "I can get take-out."

"Why don't you go with Simon, Mom. I'll stay with Jacob. You know what I like." She grins knowingly at her mother.

It's time to have a little chat with Aviva when we get home, Ruchamah decides. There is nothing but friendship between herself and Simon; she doesn't want Aviva to get any wrong ideas.

"How was Jacob today?" Simon asks when they were outside. "He's usually good."

"We were having so much fun I forgot to leave when Aviva came back," she admits.

"You have something on your nose," Simon offers her his handkerchief.

"Oh, my gosh. I forgot. After Aviva turned Jacob into a clown, he gave me a clown nose." She rubs at the red makeup. "Is it off?"

Simon takes the handkerchief from her, rubs a little more. "It is now." He puts it back in his pocket. "I never even asked if you were hungry."

"I'm starving. I tried the pizza with Jacob, but my real meal was one of the cookies."

Simon laughs. "I looked in the cookie jar before I left. You made a lot. They're really good. I guess that's a give-away. Caught with my hands in the cookie jar."

Ruchamah laughs. "I used Aviva's special recipe."

"Chocolate chip with peanut butter and marshmallow pieces?" It would have felt so natural to take Ruchamah's hand, but he shoves his hand in his pockets instead. He isn't sure she would like walking up the street hand in hand with him. When he left the house this morning, he had been thinking that he would like to be alone with her somewhere. He would ask her out to dinner, but he's not sure she would accept his invitation. Eating "en famille" will be a fine substitute.

Simon tells her he'd been thinking about what she said the night she came over with Aviva, the connection between musical interpretation and translation. "There are so many links between the two art forms I never considered before. I think we're both interpreters. Perhaps after my concert, you might come one day and speak to my students about this. It would provide an interesting perspective. That is if you have time?"

"I'll make time for your students, Simon. I'd like to hear what they have to say." Every day, since Aviva began babysitting, Simon and Jacob walk her home and linger for a while. Aviva and Jacob usually make ice cream cones while she and Simon talk over the day's happenings with a cup of coffee in hand. Being together in this way has become a kind of ritual. But this evening is different. They're without their children, outside the boundaries of their homes and Ruchamah is self-conscious. Don't be silly, she tells herself. You're just taking a walk with a friend. You do that often. Yes, she also tells herself, but I don't usually want to hold my friend's hand.

By the time they reach Harvard Street, their strides are totally in sync. They stand for a few minutes considering where to go.

"Let's start with hors d'ouevres," Simon suggests. "Of course that means Rami's for hummus and babaganoush."

"No argument here. I once told Rami that his hummus was the second best I had ever eaten. Rami took offense, demanding to know where I had eaten the best. I told him. 'Many years ago in a luncheonette on Shamai Street in Jerusalem.' He just grinned and nodded."

Simon takes her elbow as they cross the street.

As they're about to leave Rami's, Simon turns back. "How about potato barakas. Jacob doesn't eat a wide range of foods, but these Israeli turnovers, he loves."

"Why don't we choose a main dish at Ruth's Kitchen?" Ruchamah asks when they're outside again. "Whenever I bring my out of town friends here, they're surprised that a Korean woman runs a kosher restaurant. Her husband is Jewish and served in Korea. When he brought Ruth back as his bride, she became a gift to ethnic dining on Harvard Street."

Ruchamah carries the oriental chicken from Ruth's Kitchen as they continue their walk.

"If we're going oriental," Simon says, "how about sushi from Takeshima? It's the best."

"We usually go to Zathany's for sushi," Ruchamah tells him. "Aviva's addicted to their California rolls."

"Let's go to both. We can call our walk 'A Taste of Coolidge Corner.'"

Entering Zathany's after Takeshimi's, Ruchamah asks for her California rolls and orders grape leaves and ratatouille along with it. Simon wanders over to the bakery case. "I forgot that they carry specialty desserts from Rosie's Bakery, my favorite for chocolate. Let's get four Boom Bars."

Ruchamah nods agreement. She has been staring at her personal favorite, Chocolate Orgasms. There was no way she can suggest getting them. She stifles a giggle. "What about *kichel?*" she asks him quickly. Pastry Lane has the best."

"Not Pastry Lane. Kupel's kichel is crisper." Simon can't believe he's arguing with her over a pastry, and with such passion. They are like an old married couple, disagreeing over a grocery list. "You know what," he says "we'll get both."

Ruchamah looks into Kupel's window. She's about to go in when she notices Marcia's daughter inside. Debby is nothing like her mother, but just to be on the safe side she says, "Let's go to Pastry Lane first. We're not in a big hurry."

As they stand outside juggling their bags and food containers, Simon takes Ruchamah's from her, and gives her back the kichel. "Carry this one. It's the lightest."

"That's all right," Ruchamah laughs. "Between cookies with Jacob and this taste of Coolidge Corner, I'll be sinking instead of swimming. But who cares. I think we should top things off with some candy."

"Jacob's mainstay. What kind?"

"Chocolate. My mainstay. I still yearn for the taste of Art's Candy but they closed years ago. My mother never failed to buy a box from them for every occasion. Their chocolate was so dark and creamy. Now I wait for my aunt to bring Charles' Chocolate back from Paris."

"I can't take you to Paris," Simon grins. "At least not today. Since anything less would be a comedown, how about penny candy? We can go to Irving's."

"I used to take Aviva there all the time. Irving's wife, Ethel, would do 'candy math' with her. Aviva would place a bunch of coins from her piggy bank onto the counter. Together they would figure out how many 'Mary Janes' Aviva could buy for a penny-a-piece and have change enough left over for a couple of packages of the higher priced tootsie rolls."

"That's it. Tootsie rolls will be our chocolate." They walk into Irving's and fill a bag with an assortment of their favorite childhood treats.

"We'd better hide these for a while when we get back or this will be the only part of dinner that will interest Jacob, barakas included. However, I don't think I can wait till we get back." He reaches into the bag. "Aviva and Jacob will never know the difference."

"I don't think they'll miss just one, or two." Ruchamah reaches into the bag of Mary Janes.

"Give me the wrappers and I'll throw them into the next trash barrel. Now I feel like a kid again, sneaking cookies and candy so my son won't know, just like I used to."

Aviva and Jacob are sitting on the front steps when they get back.

"Let's see what you got." Aviva reaches for most of the packages. Jacob holds the door open. She places everything on the table that has already been set.

"Look what Jacob did. He put everything in the right place, too." Aviva ruffles his hair.

"Good job, Jacob," Simon says.

"Good job, Mom and Simon," Aviva quips as she empties the bags. "You got lots of my favorites." They seat themselves and dig in, sampling something from every container. Aviva fills Jacob's plate with tiny portions. He makes a face. "Clowns are supposed to smile," Aviva says." Jacob takes a bite and shakes his head. He points to the barakas.

"Okay," Aviva said. "At least you're trying. Let me know if there's anything else you do like."

Without thinking, Simon leans over and takes some food from Ruchamah's plate and then realizes what he's done. "Oh, sorry," he said, but she pushes her plate across the table, laughing at him.

Later that night, as Ruchamah gets ready for bed, she looks in her mirror. Maybe she should ask Aviva to color the gray in her hair. And show her how to make herself up. Mascara might be nice. She walks into the dining room in her nightgown. Aviva's makeup bag lies open on the dining room table. She picks it up, ignoring the translation she is supposed to be working on and carries the makeup bag into the bathroom where she applies a little mascara, staring into the mirror as she does so. It imparts a beguiling quality. She wanders back into her bedroom. The moon shines brightly through her window and beckons her. The stranger from her dream is dancing in her backyard. Ruchamah draws in her breath. As the stranger turns in the moonlight she begins removing layers of clothing until she's wearing only a very sheer top and a skirt that swirls as she moves. Ruchamah can see her face clearly now. It's not the face of a crone, but rather that of a much younger woman, a woman free to dance in the moonlight. Ruchamah lifts the screen and leans her face in the direction of the moon. The stranger removes her blouse and slips off her skirt. Filled with a sense of freedom and sensuality Ruchamah begins to dance around her room in her nightgown, and then, on impulse, removes it.

SIXTEEN

As soon as Aviva arrives the next morning, Simon heads to Starbucks and buys two croissants, two brioches and two sesame bagels to go with his coffee order. He gathers up assorted sweeteners and creamers, dashes to Ruchamah's and buzzes her apartment. When she doesn't answer, he places the bags down on the stoop and leans over to find some pebbles to throw at her dining room window. Pebbles in hand, he hears the window open and waves.

"Simon?" Ruchamah says. "I'll let you in."

He can't help smiling. She stands in the doorway, clutching her robe; her hair is disheveled and she appears to be wearing mascara. He hands her the coffee and bakery assortments. "I didn't know how you like your coffee, so I brought everything."

She's just staring at him. And smiling in return.

"I'll be right back." She sets what he's given her on the dining room table and disappears down the hall.

In the bathroom Ruchamah glances in the mirror. The mascara she had put on the night before has stained her face. She closes her eyes and gently rubs her lashes with a washcloth. The stains disappear. Her hands shake slightly as she hangs her bathrobe on the hook behind the door and dresses quickly. Simon's visit is completely unexpected. But they're friends and friends can visit each other early in the morning, can't they. And bring coffee. It was a thoughtful thing to do.

"I don't usually sleep so late," she says when she returns. She has thrown on jeans and a tee shirt that reads SHALOM. Strands of hair escape the ponytail she has hastily fashioned. Washed clean, her face glows.

Simon removes the coffees from their bag. "I, uh, just wanted to see you before I left for the Conservatory," he says. He had been unable to sleep. At dawn he turned on the radio in his study only to hear the opening bars of Beethoven's Third, and almost changed the station. The last time he listened to the Eroica was right after Karen left. Every movement in that work seemed to echo his life. The first, the allegro con brio, was as full of promise as his childhood had been. His parents believed he could accomplish anything. They held the world out to him encouraging him to choose. He had believed in that promise until his marriage to Karen crumbled. The second movement, the

March Funebre, echoed his deep sense of pain as he lay alone in his study, unable to tolerate the bed where Karen and he had slept together. The sudden frenzy of the third movement jarred him. He lived this scherzo. Caring for Jacob. Rushing to work. Racing home to Jacob. When he went for a run he almost flew in his attempt to escape his thoughts. But this morning the finale of the Eroica, the allegro molto, with its resolute statement of life inspires him to leap out of bed, filled with thoughts of Ruchamah.

He wants to ask her to spend the day with him, to walk around looking in shops holding his hand as he asks her to choose something. He had rushed over with this in mind, but he doesn't know whether or not she reciprocates his growing feelings of attraction.

"I brought espresso and Colombian Roast," is all he can bring himself to say. "Which do you prefer?"

"Columbian Roast."

"How do you take it?"

"Just a little milk. No sugar, thank you."

They sit down at the kitchen table. Simon tells Ruchamah how relieved he is that Aviva is babysitting, how attached Jacob is to her. He asks if the coffee is okay.

"It's perfect," she answers him.

"I hope I didn't come by too early."

"Your timing is as perfect as the coffee."

"Great," Simon says. "Great. I wish I didn't have to leave so quickly but I'm teaching this morning."

"I have translations to do," Ruchamah says quickly. "My friend, Miriam, is coming in a few week.. I'm helping her with her latest book of poems."

"I hope your translations come easily."

"By the time I'm done the walls will probably...."

"Be covered in drafts." He grins as he picks up the empty coffee cups and heads to the kitchen. Ruchamah opens the cabinet under the sink and Simon tosses them into the recyclable container. He manages to exit her apartment without having told her she has changed his life.

Immersed in his thoughts, he's hardly aware that he has arrived at the Conservatory until he drives into the parking garage. He better hurry. Jonathan Chin will be ready for his private lesson.

"You came through the door like Baryshnikov making an entrance in Swan Lake." Jonathan says. "Maybe you won't notice my mistakes."

"Maybe I'll be more aware of them than ever."

Jonathan laughs and begins to warm up.

"This was a lesson extraordinaire," he says when they finish.

Extraordinaire. Yes. Ruchamah, Simon thinks.

All three of his students play with an exuberance that matches his own. This morning, life is good.

Baryshnikov once again, Simon leaps down the stairs from the office to enjoy some of this summer day. He stops short when he reaches the steps of Jordan Hall.

When he flew up from Houston five years ago to interview for a teaching position at the New England Conservatory of Music, he was enthralled with the possibility of making music in this turn of the century concert hall, newly restored to its original splendor and immediately accepted the appointment.

Tonight he will rehearse Bruch's Violin Concerto Number One on the very stage that Isaac Stern once stood. Simon bounds up the steps and walks into the empty hall. The carved wind gods always delight him. This hall, intimate enough for chamber music can hold the richness of a full orchestra. He can already imagine Ruchamah sitting in one of its 1,500 seats.

He retrieves his violin from his office and in no time is standing center stage of Jordan Hall playing the brief opening cadenza from the Bruch. There is a new dimension to the sound, a brilliance he attributes to Ruchamah.

Unable to restrain himself, he picks up his cell phone only to get her answering machine. "Ruchamah. It's Simon. I realize that this is last minute, but would you like to come to the rehearsal tonight? I can pick you up at six-thirty if Aviva can come back to look after Jacob."

"We don't have much time, Mom," Aviva calls, as she flies into the house. "It's already 6 o'clock. Ruchamah is pulling dresses out of her bedroom closet.

"How about the dark blue, or the black linen. But they could make you look pale." She gets her makeup bag.

"Careful, Aviva. Not too much. I don't want to look like a clown."

"Not to worry, Mom. I'll take it easy. Just this subtle shade of lipstick and I'll apply a hint of mascara." Ruchamah will have to make sure to wash it off thoroughly before she goes to bed this time. Aviva has more expertise with makeup than Ruchamah had expected. More than she could have acquired at the retreat.

Simon calls just as Aviva finishes. He's running a bit late and asks if the two of them can walk over together. "No problem," Aviva assures him as she hangs up.

"What do you mean 'no problem?' I don't even have my clothes on."

"You will. I really like the black linen. Sophisticated, not too dressy." Aviva unzips it and carefully helps Ruchamah put it on without smearing her makeup. "You look super, mom, but you could use an accessory."

Ruchamah opens the top drawer of her dresser. "Unfortunately, this is all I have." She holds up two flowery scarves. Aviva leaves the room and returns carrying a piece of African batik that she drapes artistically around her mother's neck. "This looks good," she says. "Hurry before we have to run all the way to Simon's."

In the car, Simon can't stop staring at Ruchamah. He hopes the sparkle in her eyes is because she's looking forward to spending time with him. As he glances in the rearview mirror, he catches a glimpse of the enticing stranger who had suddenly appeared at his kitchen table holding a glass of wine just as he gave Jacob dinner tonight. He sat transfixed as she took a sip, smiled, then vanished. He thought he had imagined her. Now she's sitting in the back seat of his car, sipping champagne as if she's ensconced in a chauffeured limousine. Startled, he almost swerves into the oncoming lane of traffic and immediately pulls over to the curb.

"Is something wrong? "Ruchamah asks.

"I thought I saw someone I knew." Another glance in the mirror proves him mistaken. No one is there.

"Jacob was so excited Aviva was coming for the second time today to stay with him this evening," he tells her when they are underway again. "He's not the only one. I'm excited,too, that you could come to the rehearsal with me." His feelings are contagious. Ruchamah has butterflies of her own by the time they enter the concert hall.

Simon escorts her to a seat in the center section, about ten rows back from the stage. "From here you get a perfect balance of sound," he tells her. "You'll hear the fullness of music and catch the on-stage conversation as well."

Stephen Larsen, the conductor, welcomes the players, then turns their attention to Simon, who sets his violin down to talk to the orchestra.

"For me, this is the realization of a dream. I was a kid when I first heard the Bruch concerto on the radio. I'm a violinist because of it, but I have never had the opportunity to play it until now. Bruch was a composer with soul. You've mastered the notes. Together we'll bring his spirit to our performance." He almost says more, tells them that, for him the orchestra and soloist are a community. He wants to wax rhapsodic about how the orchestra provides context and frame and lifts a solo the way a thermocline lifts a bird. He could go on and on; his joy is two-fold. Bruch and Ruchamah. But this is not a night for words. He lifts his violin to his chin and begins to play.

When the rehearsal is over, several students flock to Simon. It takes more than fifteen minutes before he's free to get to Ruchamah. "I'm sorry it took me so long," he says, as he sits down next to her.

"I didn't mind waiting. During the rehearsal, every time the conductor stopped the orchestra, I could hear how he encouraged the students to play first one passage and then another, over and over. He was very clear when he explained what he wanted. You and Bruch. What a pair!"

No, he thinks. You and I are the perfect pair. "Shall we walk across the street for coffee?"

"Isn't that how we started our day?" Ruchamah laughs.

"I'll order," Simon says as they choose a table. "Columbian Roast, right?"

"Right."

"De-caf or regular?"

"At this hour, half of each. Thanks." She checks her reflection in the compact mirror Aviva slipped into her purse. Everything is *b'seder.* Even her lipstick hasn't faded.

Simon sets the tray down. "I got biscotti. I didn't have a chance to eat beforehand. Did you?"

"No."

"Maybe we should go out to dinner."

"This is fine, Simon. I can still hear the Bruch in my mind, still see you playing. There was such energy, a union between you and the orchestra."

"They were doing a competent job before, but tonight they did Bruch proud. They're only students. I didn't expect that."

"I didn't expect anyone to eat during the rehearsal. One of the students had an orange, which he slowly peeled. Then he hunted around for something to wipe his hand as the scent of that orange wafted over the auditorium."

Simon laughs. "Henry, our percussionist. He has to wait so long for his turn, he sometime brings his entire dinner and munches discretely, not always discretely, through every rehearsal." Simon's stomach growls. Ruchamah laughs. "I think you're hungry."

He's starving, but he wants to talk to Ruchamah about the way he feels, not food, not the rehearsal. He's just not quite sure how to do that. He could tell her she looks amazing, but that might seem as if he doesn't appreciate how she usually looks, which wouldn't be true. There are only a few other customers in the café. He leans across the table and takes her hand.

"All night, while I was playing, I felt exhilarated. It wasn't just the orchestra or how well everything was going. My playing was inspired because you were there, because I knew that we were going to spend time together afterwards."

"I was happy too," Ruchamah says.

"For the same reason?"

"For the same reason."

"I hope we can do more of this."

"Do you have other rehearsals coming up?"

"I do," he says, "but I don't just mean that."

"Do you mean we should go out, on a date?

"Yes.

"As in what Marcia is always insisting on."

"Yes," he says, "only we won't tell her."

Date Simon? Her body is already inclined towards his, only the café table an obstacle between them. She hesitates. She could decline Simon's invitation and her life would continue as usual. The table presses against her chest and "Yes," she says. "Yes, Simon. I would like that."

"I was afraid to ask you. I have this tendency to go overboard, yet from the moment we met I felt a special connection. When we were talking about our work, I felt such kinship I could hardly believe it. Now, each time I see you, my life is enriched. This morning when I brought you coffee, I almost said something, but I felt it might be too risky, because you haven't indicated that you regard me as any more than a friend, and that of course I hope I am and always will be, no matter what else happens."

"Of course," Ruchamah says.

"I'm beginning to feel dizzy," Simon says.

"You haven't eaten anything except biscotti. We should get something more filling."

"I'm dizzy because you have agreed to go out with me." He pretends to fall on the floor.

Ruchamah laughs. "She reaches out her hand to help him straighten up.

He clutches her hand to his heart. The darkened café brightens and time slows. Heat flows through her body. Simon kisses her hand and releases it. "We'll do many things together, with the kids and without. Is that all right?"

"More than all right." Ruchamah leans on her elbows and smiles at Simon. "Do you like movies? We can go to Coolidge Corner Theatre to see the latest independent films."

"Have you ever been to Tanglewood? Yo Ya Ma is playing in late August. I can check the calendar."

"More coffee or biscotti?" Their waitress looks tired and slightly bored.

"We probably should go," Ruchamah says, after they decline. "It's late. Besides, Aviva might wonder what's happening to us."

Simon takes her hand to help her up, then brushes his lips across her forehead.

SEVENTEEN

S cattered among the brochures Susan and Martin have brought over for their mother is Kehillat Shalom's latest Bulletin, with its request for *Mitzvah Corps* volunteers. As soon as she gets Nathan back on his feet Ida plans to rejoin her friends and lend a helping hand to others. After all she's one of their founders. Right now though her children are trying desperately to convince her to put Nathan into a day care center for Alzheimer's patients. She intends to look through the brochures, reassure her children she will consider them and toss them in the wastebasket. "You know this one," Susan is saying, as she passes one to her mother. "The Hebrew Rehabilitation Center?"

"Your father doesn't need a nursing home."

"Now they have a day care program, Mom, 'Great Days for Seniors'." Dad could go there and transfer to the nursing home when he needs it. This she does not say aloud.

"I'll watch him more closely. It was the heat, such a hot day when he got lost. I fell asleep." Ida cannot wait until her over-concerned children go home.

In the living room, Martin's son is sitting on the floor with Nathan, playing trains. Both voices are high pitched with excitement as they watch an engine rounding a corner of the tracks. It's embarrassing to see his father down on the floor like this, his shouts of glee not much different from his son's. Martin hopes Simon will understand when he brings Jacob over later to play with David. But of course he will. Simon talks to Nathan as if there's nothing wrong with him. When Jacob arrives, there will be three children playing with the train. Who would have ever guessed that his elegant and rather aloof father would be down on his hands and knees playing with four-year-olds? David always wants to visit "Pop Pop." Pop Pop is making noises like a train-whistle now.

Susan struggles to keep the exasperation out of her voice. Her mother is not really listening to her. "You could go with him for one day to see what it's like. Their van will pick you up. If you don't approve, you can drop the idea of the Hebrew Rehab altogether." Susan has always been the one to see where compromises can exist.

But Ida does not compromise. Not on promises. "I promised him," she keeps saying.

"You promised not to put him in a home. You never promised not to take him to look at a day care facility. Think of this the way you would a senior center. You never have to set foot in the nursing home part. So it's not as if you're breaking a promise."

"I'll take a look. But not with your father. You and I will go. I'll ask Simon if he can come over for a few hours next week."

"I'll stay with Pop," Martin tells his mother. He'll bring David with him for the day to act as a buffer. He promised Susan that if she could get Ida to agree to take a look at the Rehab, he would try and overcome his reluctance to be alone with his father. He will do this for his mother who has always tried to make peace between the two of them. "You can catch more flies with honey," she would tell him. "Your father loves you. He just wants the best for you."

But Martin had never been able to please Nathan. When he was a child and showed him his report card, Nathan criticized every grade that wasn't an A. When Martin preferred being on the basketball team to playing in the school orchestra, his father felt betrayed. And when he left his job at the upper level of management at IBM, his father had been irate. "How can you give up a top level job in a number one company to start a business out of a garage? You won't be able to afford to pay yourself for a long time, if ever. And if you don't succeed, then where will you be?"

"Dad, you and your partners built your law firm from scratch," Martin attempted to defend himself. "Look where you are now."

"Law is different; the times were different. How can you begin to know what you are facing? You're snatching failure from the jaws of success."

"I didn't go about this half-cocked. I have a business plan, a Board of Directors, who are actively involved, interested investors and a groundbreaking product. I have what I need. You don't. You need a son to brag about and a son who starts a business in a garage just doesn't cut it."

It doesn't help that Ida's credit card had been refused when she went to buy fish at Wulf's a few months ago because Nathan had forgotten to pay the VISA bill. After his mother called him, Martin knew he had to step in. When Nathan found out, he refused to speak to Martin for over a month. This is no longer an issue. His Alzheimer's has progressed to the point where his interest in financial matters is non-existent.

Susan hangs up the phone. "I spoke to the social worker. She can see us Tuesday morning at eleven."

"I don't need a social worker," Ida says.

Susan sighs. "Jan is the program manager and she also does tours. She can answer any questions we might have." Susan will have to come early on Tuesday. Her mother might change her mind about going and she will need the extra time to convince her.

And she is right. On Tuesday morning, Ida is getting ready to go for her usual walk with Nathan.

Susan has to remind her that Martin is on his way and will take him.

"He doesn't know the route," Ida says.

"We can write it down. Please, Mom."

Nathan comes out of the bathroom and smiles when he sees his daughter. She hugs him. "Hi, Dad."

"What are you doing here?" His voice is fretful, worried.

"I have the day off from work," she tells him. "Mom and I are going shopping." The lie rolls off her lips with unexpected ease. Ida winces.

The doorbell rings. Nathan frowns at Martin and grins widely at David. "No school today," David says gleefully.

"It feels cold in here," Martin says. Isn't it too cold for Pop?"

"He likes it this way," Ida says. "He wears a sweater. Please, don't adjust the air conditioning."

"Mom?" Susan picks up her pocketbook.

"Have a nice time with Martin and David," Ida says, unable to keep herself from buttoning and re-buttoning Nathan's sweater. "Susan and I will be back soon." She gives him another hug and kiss.

Ida points out the Arnold Arboretum as they drive up the hill to the Hebrew Rehab. "Your father and I used to come here every year for Lilac Sunday. I always dressed up, except for putting on low heels. We started this tradition when we were dating. Considering that your father was in Law School then, it was something we could easily afford. You probably don't remember coming with us. We stopped going when you developed an allergy to lilacs."

When they sign in, the receptionist buzzes Jan. In a few minutes the social worker sees them into a small conference room.

Jan explains how the day care center operates and Susan feels an immediate connection to her. "My mother just told me she used to come here to the Arboretum with my father." Jan looks at Ida for confirmation. Ida purses her lips. This is her story to tell isn't it? But she doesn't say a word. She will not give Susan one iota of help.

"My dad loves to be outside," Susan says.

"A group just came back from a walk in the Arboretum about an hour ago. We had only one problem. One of the women couldn't resist smelling the one variety of lilacs that blooms late. She's so allergic we almost ran out of Kleenex." Jan gives a little laugh. Susan is tempted to tell her that she, too, is allergic to lilacs as an attempt to encourage Ida to talk to Jan, but her mother just sits there, arms crossed, still mute.

"You must have some questions for me." Susan nudges her mother.

"This is a nice thing you are doing here," Ida finally says, "but it's not for Nathan. His Alzheimer's is not that bad."

"Actually, this may be the best time to take advantage of our program, when he can still fit in easily and enjoy the activities. It might even help to slow the progression of the disease. Come with me. You'll see for yourself."

They follow her into the music room where a group of men and women accompany the pianist with maracas and tambourines. "Jane, at the piano, and her husband, Al, on the accordion have been volunteering here for ten years. See Samuel over there." A wiry gentleman in the blue tee-shirt belts out words to the songs with abandon. "He speaks to no one, but give him some music, his voice soars. He used to be a member of a barbershop quartot."

"My husband is an aficionado of classical music." Ida can hardly bring herself to be civil to Jan. As soon as she gets home she will give Susan a piece of her mind. She should never have agreed to come.

"He might enjoy our classical music programs then. Judith plays segments of concerts on video and leads a discussion about the composer, genre and other points of interest." Jan says as they continue their tour. "It's scheduled every other week.

"And this is the art room." They stop at the doorway. "Hi, Ruth." Jan waves to the activities specialist. A woman places a picture of miniature seascape on top of a bar of soap and begins to apply layers of shellac. Another asks for help. Ruth holds the paper as she dips a paintbrush in and out of the shellac and across her picture of flowers.

"Can you see your father doing this?" Ida pulls Susan away. "Tell me the truth. Can you see your father cutting out pictures from magazines?" She shakes her head.

They walk through the lobby area that features murals of Blue Hill Avenue, a neighborhood in Dorchester when it was a thriving Jewish community.

"The G&G Delicatessen is the hands-down favorite," Jan tells them. "Lots of our participants end an activity by joking, 'Meet you at the G&G.'" They reach a circle of people engaged in a game of Trivial Pursuit. "Nostalgia games promote long-term memory. They're a strong suit for many with Alzheimer's," Jan says, "even though there might not be anyone in this room who could tell you what they had for lunch."

"This is not for my husband," Ida says when they return to Jan's office. "He wouldn't enjoy one thing here. He's not going to decorate soap. He's not going to sit in a group like a child and play games. It's a nice place and people seem happy, but it's not for Nathan."

"I understand," Jan says. "Most people would rather be anywhere else than here. I hope you can still manage completely at home. But if the time ever comes to consider a day care situation, we can start on a trial basis. Two or three days a week. Just to see if things work out. For both Nathan and ourselves. We gear our activities to each individual. From everything you've told me I can tell your husband is an extremely intelligent man."

Ida nods agreement.

"We also take trips to museums, like the Museum of Fine Arts and the Gardner. He might enjoy studying the *Torah* portion of the week. Every

Friday morning, two students from Maimonides School come to lead a group."

"He can study *Torah* at our synagogue," Ida tells her. "And I can take him to museums. We've been doing that all our married lives. Besides," she adds, "what would he do all day without me?"

The real question, Susan thinks, is what would you do all day without him?

When she gets home, Nathan is asleep in his chair. Martin tells her he has been napping for about an hour, "but earlier," he says, "when I went into the kitchen to make something for David, I heard the front door open. 'Pop Pop's taking me for ice cream,' David shouted. When I told them I would go with them, Dad said he didn't need me. I had to struggle with him to come back into the house. David was very upset. Later I offered to take him for a walk," Martin continues, looking at Ida's stricken face, "but he pushed me away and went to lie down." Ida looks over at her grandson. His eyes are huge.

When they leave, she leans against the table for a minute and then sinks into one of the chairs and tries to think. She was not exactly truthful with Jan. She and Nathan have not been doing any of their usual activities lately. She's afraid to leave him alone. There is no way they can go to a museum because he would wander away from her. But that doesn't really matter. There is always a slim possibility that Nathan will get better, in spite of what everyone thinks. They are fine, just as they are. Aren't they?

EIGHTEEN

The congregations of Kehillat Shalom and Temple Beth Chaim are joining together for a music service featuring both of their cantors this *Shabbat;* Hillel and Beth no longer have an excuse to avoid making the trip to Brooklyn. They pack and start the drive early on Friday for the visit to his parents.

The anticipation of his father's criticism and his mother's attempt to diminish its effect renders them both silent as Beth begins the drive. Hillel closes his eyes, the rhythm of the car lulling him into a light sleep for which Beth is grateful. If he's awake, the baby issue is bound to come up. It will only get worse when they reach Brooklyn.

She turns on the radio. A talk show. The host is a woman who asks people to call in to talk about their relationships. Several callers, as distressed as she has been lately, speak about leaving their significant others. She turns the volume up a bit. One woman says her children are all that's keeping her marriage together. Another is considering leaving her husband for the sake of their children, since all they do is argue. Beth is inclined to call in to say she and Hillel just want a child. She glances at him as he dozes off, his head leaning on the window. He hasn't been sleeping much; this will probably be his only real rest the entire weekend.

When she pulls off the highway, she drives through Brooklyn and around his parent's block a few times before telling her husband they have arrived. He wakes with a sweet smile; he might have been dreaming. She returns this smile and once again they are as usual, Hillel and Beth, a team, a unit, a barrier his father cannot penetrate, for they have brought their own spirit of *Shabbat* with them. Then reason returns, along with the stress of the past few months, the finality of the useless in-vitros and their *Shabbat* peace vanishes.

"If only it wasn't *Shabbat.*" Hillel says ruefully. "We could check into a hotel in Manhattan and drive in to visit them tomorrow."

"We'll be fine," Beth tells him. As long as no one asks when we're having a baby, she tells herself.

His mother's already on the front stoop as she pulls into a parking space directly across the street in this all too familiar orthodox section of Park Slope. She hugs them as soon as they reach her, hanging on to each of them for longer than necessary, long enough for them to feel the strength of her love as they enter the house.

"It is so good to have you here, until Monday no less." The pleasure in her voice warms them as much as her hugs. "Dad's in his study reviewing his *Shabbos* sermon." She doesn't have to add that he won't emerge until dinner. He never greets them until he enters the dining room; then he will hold out his hand to his son and nod hello to Beth.

Esther goes up stairs with them. They bring their luggage into Hillel's old room. She smoothes the bed, looking around to make sure everything is all right. "I put extra towels in the bathroom for you and extra pillows on the bed."

"You always give us exactly what we need," Beth puts her arm around her mother-in-law as they walk out of the room and head downstairs, leaving Hillel sitting on his old bed. He removes his *kippah* from his jacket pocket and sets it on his head, then walks downstairs himself to wander about his childhood home.

He stops in front of the bookcases that line the walls of the living room, full to the brim with his father's books and family photos. He hardly recognizes this little boy with long *peasahs* falling down his cheeks and *tzitzes* hanging from under his shirt, this boy who once was himself. And how can he be that little boy, holding an open book, mimicking exactly the father who sits across the desk from him in the study? There's his father with his arm around him, a loving father who dotes on Hillel's every word of *Torah,* so proud of this son, born to fulfill his rabbinical dream. "There will be six generations of rabbis in the Kramer family," he always would say. And so there are, Dad. You just refuse to recognize that.

On impulse he knocks at his father's study door and hears the familiar, "Come in, Hillel," as if his father had been expecting him. Other fathers would have come out from behind their desk to embrace a son whom he hasn't seen in four months, but Hillel's father remains seated, watching him stand there awkwardly. "*Gut Shabbos,* Hillel. Sit down." He indicates the chair at the side of the desk.

"*Gut Shabbos,*" Hillel says in turn.

"So how was the trip?" his father looks up from his book for a minute and then down at the page. His father is not interested in the trip. He is waiting, Hillel knows, for a sign of capitulation, for the words, "Papa, you are right. Without the traditional way of observing *Torah,* people are in danger of losing their Jewish heritage, only that is not the case at Kehillat Shalom. People come to services; they form study groups, they want to learn. They want more than he is capable of giving them at the moment. That's what he would like to tell his father, as if they were two rabbis with contradictory opinions, sharing their ideas like the rabbis of old, as if differences were discussions for the sake of heaven, interpretations that were all considered valuable. But the differences between his father and himself divide them. There will be no conversation that does not lead to an argument, no argument for the sake of heaven, only a discussion about who is right, and that can never be Hillel. So he rises now, as if his main purpose in coming into the study has been accomplished, and turns toward the door without an awareness that his father watches him leave, his eyes no longer on his books, a look of yearning in them that matches Hillel's own.

He walks through the living room, swings open the door to the kitchen and perches on a counter stool. Beth and his mother bustle about in tandem, anticipating each other's movements as they weave back and forth, almost like a dance. They are alike, he realizes. When he met Beth at a symposium on *Tikkun Olam,* he was in rabbinical school, struggling to define himself. She was a free spirit, laughter spilling from her lips as she told him stories about the pre-school children she taught and their responses to her lessons on *Tikkun Olam.* One child insisted *Tikkun* sounded like tickle. He didn't want to be tickled so he ran around the room enticing Beth to chase him. For Beth, Judaism was both a spiritual practice and a delight. She taught Hillel that really what mattered was honoring God according to one's most authentic self.

Both Beth and his mother have the ability to find happiness within themselves, something he's afraid he might be taking away from his wife, eclipsing her joy with a kind of dullness. But her usual warmth is concentrated into a kind of radiant energy as she bustles about the kitchen. She pushes her honey colored hair back from her face, laughing, as she consults with his mother about when to turn off the soup, what dishes to use for the salad. His mother feeds him little tastes of the soup, as she passes to get yet another spoon or pot holder. "Delicious," he says. Beth grins. She does the same for Hillel at home, each *Erev Shabbat,* accompanying every taste with a gentle kiss. That is, she used to.

The wine they will use for *Kiddush* is still on the kitchen counter. Hillel carries it into the dining room and sits down in his father's chair. For a moment he sees himself as his father must see him. A tall, somewhat awkward man, unable to fully express himself. In striving to achieve a balance between his father's certainty and his own doubt, he is often rendered speechless before his father, dumbstruck, although Hillel is a remarkable scholar, known for his ability to consider every opinion with an open mind and create a resolution combining the best of each.

He sighs, then stands as his mother and Beth come to light the candles. Each adds her own prayer. His mother's, he knows, is for peace to be restored between father and son, and Beth's, for a resolution between herself and Hillel. Almost the same prayer. Returning to the kitchen, they carry out the sumptuous dinner of soup and roast chicken with all the trimmings, fresh vegetables and a garden salad. Beth sits beside Hillel and leans her head against his shoulder. He puts his arm around her. He wants to tell her how sorry he is that he is making her unhappy. In his mother's house he finds these words, but they remain unsaid as his father enters the room to say the prayer over the wine and challah.

Everyone keeps the conversation on the light side throughout the meal, discussing the recent balmy weather, the unusual absence of humidity.

Esther tops off the meal with a rich non-dairy chocolate pie. She will give Beth the recipe before they leave.

When the men depart for *shul,* Beth helps Esther clean up. Her mother-in-law glances at her. There is a sense of unease about Beth. A tentativeness she has not seen before. Hopefully, her usually confident daughter-in-law will be able to share whatever is bothering her during the visit. Shortly after the men return, Beth and Hillel excuse themselves and go up to his old room, tired from the long day of driving and the release of the tension they have been holding since they entered the house. Hillel tells Beth that some of his old friends from the neighborhood had accompanied his father and himself home, clapping him on the shoulder, their shouts of "*Gut Shabbos*" ringing through the air.

They are up early the next morning. Beth makes the bed and straightens up a little before they go down to breakfast, then all four leave the house to go to services together. Together, but not totally. It always feels strange to Beth to look down at her husband from the balcony to which the women are relegated. Occasionally, Hillel turns towards his wife and mother, smiles and turns back to his book. Hillel is *davening* in the traditional way, his body swaying back and forth in rhythm with the words; his father places his hand on his shoulder. It is the only time his father will show him affection during the visit. Beth aches for Hillel. He has refused to explain himself to his father, and Asher has no idea that every *Shabbat* at Kehillat Shalom, Hillel dons his *tallit* and *davens* exactly like this.

A boy begins chanting his *Bar Mitzvah maftir.* One day their son will do the same. We might have a girl Beth tells herself. And she will become a *Bat Mitzvah* in the same way Beth had. Wouldn't Asher have a fit about that? She's somewhat ashamed of wanting to appall her father-in-law, but then again he is so disapproving of Hillel she feels justified. Esther knots her forehead concentrating on the text in front of her. Neither are relaxed as they go downstairs for the *kiddish* of bagels, New York lox, noodle kugel and *ruggelach* in honor of the *Bar Mitzvah* boy.

When they leave the synagogue, Esther suggests a walk through Prospect Park, which means passing by the many playgrounds, watching parents pushing swings and holding on for concern for their little ones balanced on jungle gyms. Someday this will be Hillel and me, Beth thinks, ignoring the pang in her heart.

"You're very quiet," her mother-in-law says.

Beth links her arm through Esther's.

"Hillel looks lost. You are upset. What can I do to help?"

"Maybe you can explain to me why Hillel refuses to consider having a child other than one of his own. His work suffers, our marriage suffers. I did not expect my husband to become as rigid as his father."

"Look at them walking ahead of us. Two poles with no sway. We're the ones who bend. I know that you will find a way to convince Hillel to change his mind, but maybe not the usual way." Her mother-in-law stops where she is and looks into Beth's eyes. "What we can't overcome, we have to go around."

She wants to ask Esther how one goes around a man who's entrenched in his desire to do what he thinks will win his father's love. She wants to ask how his father can be so rejecting.

"Asher's father," Esther says, almost as if she has heard her, "was a survivor of the German camps. He made Asher promise to carry on the traditions in which he had been raised and for which so many died. Although I became pregnant easily with Hillel, there were many miscarriages after him. The doctor finally ordered me to stop trying. When I wanted to adopt more children, Asher would not allow it. He told me his promise to his father meant he could only accept a child that carried on the family's blood line. My sister tried for years to become pregnant. When she finally conceived, she only carried the child until the fourth month. Ultimately she decided to adopt. If I wanted Hillel to play with his cousins, we had to go there without Asher's blessing. The irony is that her children are *frum* and Hillel goes his own way."

"That doesn't any make sense to me," Beth says. "There are so many children who are unwanted or whose mothers can't keep them. I didn't tell Hillel, but I made an appointment with the adoption staff at Jewish Family Service. The counselors were incredibly supportive; it was obvious I am not alone in this. They told me it usually takes longer, a lot longer, for the husband to accept the idea of adoption. Considering Hillel's attitude, I have no choice other than to explore this without him but I wish I didn't have to resort to subterfuge."

"I have no intention of being deprived of the joy of holding my grandchild in my arms no matter how he or she arrives," Esther says. "Don't give up. You will get through this. And you can count on me 200%, half for me and half for Asher. He won't know."

"Do you know how much I love you?" Beth says, hugging her mother-in-law.

By the time the women reach the lion guarded gates, the men are standing at the entrance to the park, arms folded, shared gestures of both father and son. "See. Two poles," Esther whispers as they join them for the walk home.

When they return to the brownstone on Sixth Avenue, the women take turns raiding the refrigerator, taking out herring filets in sour cream, humus, tuna and egg salad to add to the challah and pumpernickel from the metal bread box on the kitchen counter. His mom's prized black-out cake, a near-exact copy of the now departed Ebinger's Bakery specialty, graces the table for dessert. He and his father had always loved this *Shabbat* smorgasbord. They would circle the table picking and choosing so their stomachs would be full before having their usual chess game. But today, as soon as the food is served, his father comments, "it's too bad there are no children to carry on this family tradition."

"Not yet, but one day," Esther says.

"Please God." He is about to add something more, but Esther suggests it's time to take his

Shabbos nap. Asher hesitates for a minute, then gets up, bows slightly to his wife and leaves the table.

"Thank you," Beth says to Esther. "I do not want to discuss this."

Esther nods. "It's still *Shabbos.* I think I'll clean up and then read. I have a novel I can't seem to put down."

"We'll clean up," Hillel says. "Want to take another walk?" he asks Beth when they're done.

"No, I think I'll read, too."

"All right, I won't be long."

Hillel strolls through the streets of his childhood. Many of his friends have never left this neighborhood. Most married and continued on as they had been taught. A few became rabbis. He does not feel estranged from them. There has always been something comforting about the orthodox way of life, its structure that provides an unalterable routine. It is written, it is written, he tells himself. So many things have been written. Many orthodox rabbis would not be opposed to adoption; the most important thing being to have children and to teach them Judaism. It was in this neighborhood, as a child, that he first felt a sense of God. He had been walking, as he is now, when he felt incredibly energized, lifted up somehow, though his feet were clearly on the ground, and filled with an unaccountable joy. God, he thought. God is here. He ran home to tell his father.

"Understanding God," said his father, "is not such a simple thing, Hillel." And in that moment, there began the division between them, a division that had become a chasm. It had occurred to Hillel back then that perhaps his father did not feel God in the way he did. Perhaps his father's God had a heaviness that wore him down. He remembers now his own clarity on that day. His father might be wrong, he thought, however, later on he was no longer certain. His father had never been wrong before.

"God?" Hillel calls now. That simple act of calling does not result in feeling he is in the presence of something sacred, something holy. Perhaps the spirit he had seen that day, holding a child out to him, will come then. But there is only the sidewalk and his feet, firmly rooted, and the cars that pass and a few birds flitting about. It is with a sense of regret that he walks back through the Brooklyn streets into the house of his father. It's also my mother's house he thinks; strange how I only think of it as belonging to my father.

Beth, who has gone upstairs to read while Hillel was out, has decided that in the evening, as soon as *Shabbos* is over, she will ask Esther to go shopping with her. The entire neighborhood will be alive with people after *Havdalah*. Perhaps they can go to La Cafe for coffee and listen to Israeli music. All they have to do is stay out until his father goes to bed. So when Hillel returns and tells her he intends to reassure his father that they are continuing the in-vitro, she gathers all the patience she has, all the love she feels to beg him not to do that.

"I have such a hard time talking with you, about this, Hillel. Perhaps you really don't understand. For you these treatments are just donations yet my body so well knows the stress of preparation and hormone injections from the times we've tried, I can hear it screaming. 'No more!'"

"I see myself placing my son in my father's arms," he tells her. "It's my own child, Beth, I'm sure, because when I try to envision an adopted child, a child we might find in an orphanage somewhere, a Jewish orphanage, I don't feel a thing." No, it is only his own child that fills both him and his father with joy. He can see the love in father's eyes, the love passing from the baby to Hillel. This then is what he craves. If only he says, if only this can be. He will pray for this, he, who prays for the community as a whole, for wisdom and guidance, will pray now for what he wants.

"If you intend to bring this up with your father, and I beg you not to do so, you must tell him the truth."

"He won't accept anything other than a child of my own."

"Where is his compassion, then, his sense of justice? Where is yours? It is yourself you speak of, as well as your father."

"I want to give him hope."

"It will be false hope." Her stomach is in knots when they go for the supper of *cholent* which precedes *Havdalah*.

And true to her expectations, her father-in-law begins. "Most women your age have at least three children already, Beth," followed by Hillel's answer that they are attempting more in-vitro, which she immediately negates.

"Hillel and I will have a child one day. Three sounds good. Maybe we'll adopt triplets."

Asher shoves his chair away from the table. "I don't want to hear that, Beth."

"We're only discussing this because Hillel wants to please you," she raises her voice.

"Hillel wants to please me? Well there's a first time for everything. How is he planning to do that?"

"By continuing to believe the only child worthy of your love is one of his loins. That didn't work for him so I'm pretty sure it won't work with your grandchild. Perhaps I should divorce him so he can try with someone else."

"Beth, stop," Hillel says, but there is no stopping her.

"I cannot come back to this house," she says. "Your obsession about this is almost ruining our lives. I will not let you do that."

Esther puts her arms around her. "Shh, *madele.*" She wipes away Beth's tears with her hands. "We have been through all of this before," she says to Asher. "I want Beth and Hillel to have children any way they can. How long can we keep our family held to your ideas? Hillel is a rabbi. You refused to come to his ordination. He is childless, and you would keep him this way."

"Our inability to conceive is not a plot against you." Hillel gets up from the table. When his father doesn't respond, Hillel walks away. He has no idea how to make this up to Beth. He has no idea what to do.

NINETEEN

Dear Elijah,

Apparently, you've decided to honor my request for a sabbatical here at Kehillat Shalom or perhaps you don't care whether or not I return at all. You've given me no sign that you even read my scrolls. The congregants seem to think I'm a permanent fixture at Kehillat Shalom. They rely on me while you ignore me. The phone rings all day with people asking, "Sara, do you have this, Sara, could you look something up for me?" Once, Marcia yanked the phone right out of my hand, told the caller that I was busy and that she would take care of what they needed. I think she's jealous because I'm so popular. Some congregants even come specifically to talk to me. They want to know how I like it here, how my children are, whether or not I've met someone who could become a companion to me. Although reports of my widowhood are grossly exaggerated, my imaginary family is growing: three fabricated children, eight grandchildren and two on the way. Specific demands for my company are rising. Not only did Rose Horowitz invited me for dinner, she introduced me to her brother who was recently widowed. We had a most enjoyable dinner and I barely refrained from telling her I wasn't quite ready to meet anyone.

The other day someone came in to ask when the rabbi would get back to him regarding his essay "How I Performed A *Mitzvah* Under Adverse Circumstances" for the *Tikkun Olam* book. Marcia shrugged as if she didn't know. When I asked Hillel, he told me Marcia was supposed to be typing them up. She opened her desk drawer, handed me sheets and sheets of paper, some of them crumpled from being squirreled away there and told me to type them. I turned the computer on and pecked away at the letter, a totally unnecessary skill for life in the Garden. The congregant's essay was there as well as one by Aviva about standing a peace vigil and many that Hillel had completed before he became so distracted, which posed questions such as: What Does It Mean to be a Jew Today? Should Anti-Zionism Be Considered Anti-Semitism? There were assorted quotations from the *Talmud,* a treatise on how to conduct a discussion according to the teachings of Hillel, the Elder, who had such a love of learning that, as you know, when as a young man, he couldn't afford to enter the house of study, he would sit on top of the roof so he could listen. One day in the midst of a blizzard, he passed out from the cold and had to be rescued by the other students.

Marcia put my work on a disc that she tucked back into her drawer. I think she still intends to modify whatever the rabbi writes even though an awareness of her intention is the only thing that has pierced through the fog clouding his mind. I'm tempted to look in an orphanage, find a child and bring it home to Beth. "Surprise! Stop all this fussing. Here's your baby," I would say. As you can tell my patience as well as my prescience has deserted me.

This is all to say that that from time to time I have thrown on my traveling cloak and flitted around like a butterfly, making a brief intervention here, a particle of one there. A few days ago I attended Shoshanah's silversmithing class. She hardly has time to breathe what with all the extra work she does. Speaking of breathing, I leaned over her table a little too closely, my eyes aren't that good, to see what she was making, exhaled, and one of her stones fell on the floor. When her classmate picked it up, I had to pat myself on the back for this unexpected turn of events. Score one point for this quick fix up by Serach.

I stuck a few brochures from the Hebrew Rehab in Ida's daughter's mail box, hoping she would bring them to her mother. Ida deserves some time for herself, don't you think?

There were other things, hardly worth mentioning though I did borrow a deep blue satin dress, quite fetching, with shoes to match from the sisterhood rummage sale offerings, which I wore to Simon's house before the Bruch rehearsal. The alluring woman sitting across from him lifting a glass of wine was me. A bit later that evening, I drank champagne in the back seat of his car, which caused me to become quite tipsy.

Unfortunately, the Sisterhood collection held nothing I liked for Debby's wedding and I was forced to lift a gorgeous beige lace outfit from Filene's Basement. Don't worry, I will return it. Marcia insisted on putting the place cards around each table herself, and almost missed the family photo session. Annoyed that Jeff's grandmother was late, she told the rabbi to start the ceremony without her. I had to find Jeff's mother and asked her to accompany me to the lady's room pleading a torn slip, making sure we didn't come out until Jeff's grandmother had arrived. The wedding was perfect, although Marcia held onto her head as if it was coming apart.

All of this, however, shed no light on an intervention for the rabbi.

Hillel and Beth visited his family a few weeks ago. Not a good experience. At one point I stood right next to him on a Brooklyn Street corner just as he was hoping for me to appear, but he was unable to perceive my presence. His father's influence was too strong.

I felt as lost as Hillel then and tried to cheer myself up by thinking of home. Home conjured up, not an image of the Garden, but an image of my mother. The last time I saw her we had just left the Red Tent as the new moon appeared. Intrigued by the path the stars had made and reluctant to resume our regular life, I told her I would come in a minute, but of course I never did.

Even though you seem to have deserted me, I have a great longing to see you, Elijah. Fortunately I remembered that along with Passover, you manage to show up at baby namings so I decided to arrange one here. Instantly, I had the perfect plan for the rabbi! This baby naming would be for an adopted child. A couple from Kehillat Shalom has just returned from Russia with their daughter. As soon as the rabbi holds her in his arms to say the blessing, he will realize there is no difference between a child he and Beth adopt and a child of their own.

It's taken a little longer than usual for me to come up with this masterpiece for the rabbi, but now that I have, when you come for the baby naming, we can journey back to the Garden together.

Serach

TWENTY

J ack leaves for the store as if this is just an ordinary day. There's nothing ordinary about it. This is Marcia's second day of lying in bed waiting for someone from the synagogue to call her back to work. It's a shame she will miss the cookbook meeting the Sisterhood is planning. She had been looking forward to demonstrating her vegetarian lasagna with no-bake noodles. But she can't set foot in Kehillat Shalom until this misunderstanding has been straightened out.

She sits up in bed flipping through a bridal magazine and idly looks at the wedding gowns and flower arrangements. They don't compare with anything in Debby's wedding. Everything was perfect, from the hors d'oeuvres to the Viennese dessert table. The flowers were extraordinary: calla lilies, white roses and lavender, not the wildflower bouquets Debby preferred. She had given in to Debby on one thing. No one threw rice; the guests had miniature vials with wands so they could make bubbles, which they sent into the air as Debby and Jeff took off for their honeymoon in Hawaii. Her old friends from Brookline, who pride themselves on wearing the latest haute couture, came up to Marcia to tell her that Debby's gown was 'drop dead gorgeous.'

If she hadn't heard the rabbi talking to Beth a few days before the wedding, she would still be working at the synagogue. Thinking that he had already gone home, she had picked up the phone to call Jack to tell him she was leaving the office and overheard the rabbi and Beth talking about her. Marcia covered the mouthpiece with her hand so they couldn't hear her breathing.

"When Marcia handed me the printout of my *Shabbat* sermon, she deleted the section on the adaptation of the Jewish wedding ceremony for gay couples. Furthermore, she refused to give me a message from Joy Holden. When Joy came to the office to find out why I hadn't called her back, Marcia told her that I was too busy with the 'regular' temple members."

"We both know that's not true; you're ignoring everyone. That includes Marcia."

"Please Beth. Whenever Shoshanah or Sara aren't there, she sabotages my effort to create an atmosphere of acceptance for everyone."

Marcia nods agreement. Not everyone is acceptable. She sits down at her desk, slides her shoes off, crosses her ankles and picks up a pen and begins making notes on a scratch pad. This could be a long conversation.

"I'm sure you'll think of something," Beth says.

"You have a way of making things clear."

"I haven't been able to make them clear between us."

Marcia stopped doodling, her hand motionless on the paper.

"I'm working on that, Beth. Believe me, I am, but at the moment I have no idea what to do about Marcia."

There is a long silence before Beth speaks again.

"Remember Mr. Warofsky, from the Los Angeles synagogue. He insisted on coming to the *bimah* during every service to point out all your mistakes."

"I made him a *gabbai* so he could officially assist me."

"He was so happy to be validated he stopped criticizing me."

"I can't make Marcia a *gabbai,* even though she thinks she thinks she is the authority on Kehillat Shalom. Perhaps I'll ask her a Passover kind of question, *'Ma nish tanah?* Why is this office different from other offices?'* Then, I'll answer. 'Because this office is not just a business office. People count more than money. Everybody's ideas are respected. Feelings are valued.' Thank, you, Beth. Thank you."

You don't value my feelings, Marcia writes on her notepad with a heavy hand, following it with three exclamation points. It takes all her self-control not to break into the conversation and let them know she can hear everything they're saying. If she hadn't been so concerned with what the rabbi and Beth were saying about her, she would have made every effort to find out why Beth seemed so upset with Hillel.

"After the wedding," the rabbi continued, "I'll suggest that she take some time off to think about how she can best convey the spirit of Kehillat Shalom."

Beth doesn't respond. Marcia hears the click of a phone being hung up. Well, she'll have a little surprise in store for the rabbi after the wedding. She is not someone who can be manipulated or patronized. She is not someone who will take a little time off. She obsessed over this the entire time she was having her hair done and her make-up professionally applied. Her aggravation did not let up even when she helped Debby into her wedding gown. And when she and Jack walked down the aisle with Debby between them, she had such a severe migraine she was afraid she would pass out. It took a sheer act of will to let go of her daughter's hand and stand quietly on the side as the rabbi talked endlessly until he finally got around to the marriage vows. She could hardly bring herself to look at him when he leaned over to kiss her cheek and offer her a *Mazel Tov.* But then she reminded herself that she knew his plans but he didn't know hers and felt better at once.

Setting the magazine aside, Marcia gets out of bed, goes downstairs to the kitchen and opens the refrigerator door. There has been no need to go shopping. The remains of take-outs and leftovers from meals Jack had prepared, loom at her from the freezer.

Just before the wedding she would race home to find Jack pouring through old photograph albums, trying to find out how his little girl had managed to grow up so quickly. The fact that she no longer lived at home or that she had been dating Jeffrey since high school, seemed not to have registered. Jack was the one who cried at the wedding. Marcia was too busy formulating what she would say when the rabbi confronted her. And on Monday, as soon as the rabbi asked his rhetorical question she did not wait for his answer. She gave him one of her own. "This office is different from other offices because you are in it. I want the old rabbi and the way he did things."

Instead of intimidating Hillel and stunning him into silence, he had a suggestion of his own. "Why don't you call him in Florida see if he has a position for you there?" he said. There's no reason for you not to have what you want."

Marcia got out of her chair and without uttering a word, swept all the papers off the top of her desk into her tote bag, grabbed her coffee mug imprinted with the words "Just because you have a crisis doesn't mean I have an emergency" and left.

"I quit," Marcia told Jack Monday night. He made a ridiculous suggestion about going to work for Rabbi Isaacs in Florida.

"Pass the roast, please, Marcia," Jack looked at her skeptically. "And when you go back in the morning, forgive him. He's still green," he laughed.

Jack is not at all prepared to see her lying in bed after he gets up the next day. "Hey, Marcia. You're going to be late." When he comes home she's still in bed. At first he thinks that the exhaustion from all the wedding preparations has caught up with her. And then he realizes she hadn't selected her clothes the night before, she hasn't told him stories about who had come in and out of the office all day. She hasn't complained about the rabbi. She has not gone to the office at all. Maybe she is coming down with something. At the end of the third day he is convinced she really has quit. He makes dinner and brings it to her, tries to cheer her up with the old jokes that he always tells. She doesn't even say what she always says, that his jokes are terrible and laughs anyway.

Friday morning, he goes to the Kehillat Shalom. Marcia's chair is empty. No one is there to announce him, so he bursts into the rabbi's office. "Marcia told me she quit," he says, as he sits down unbidden. "I wish you would ask her back. You don't have to tell me what went wrong. She will make it right. I know my Marcia."

"I don't think she wants to come back," the rabbi says.

"She can't stay home all day," Jack continues. "She'll end up at the liquor store with me. I can't have that."

"I understand how you feel, Jack. Maybe you can help her find something to do. Something else," the rabbi says firmly.

"So you actually quit," Jack acknowledges as soon as he gets home. "I went to see the rabbi."

"What did he say?"

"That he didn't think you wanted to come back and that I should help you think of something to do."

"I don't have to do anything, "Marcia says. "In a few days he'll call me. Oh, perhaps they might hire someone else temporarily, but no one can do what I do. It's just a matter of time."

It's well past dawn when she finally falls asleep. She dreams that she has returned to the office. Sara is sitting at her desk working on a sophisticated computer spread sheet. The rabbi is thanking her for typing his sermon without leaving anything out. The phone rings. "Sure," Sara says. "Don't worry about that. Everyone is welcome here. Marcia wakes with a start. Her phone is ringing. It's Jack, checking to see if she is all right. "You were sleeping so soundly, I got dressed in the other room and left for work."

Marcia mutters something about being okay and hangs up. Her eyes close again. She falls back into her dream. Sara looks away from the computer and takes a sip from Marcia's mug. Marcia's eyes open. She propels herself out of bed and rushes to the kitchen. Her mug is not on the counter where she left it. She rifles through the cabinets. It's not there. She sits down at the kitchen table and takes a deep breath. She's been dreaming. The rabbi has not hired anyone else. Sara is not drinking from her coffee mug, which will turn up soon. She probably left it in the living room. Still it might be a good idea not to count on returning to work soon. She'll find something to do starting today until all this gets straightened out. She is a useful, competent person with more common sense than most people. Hadn't she run that entire office by herself before Rabbi Kramer came? Jack doesn't have to help her think of something. She's going to get dressed. She can be a phenomenal help to him. And won't he be surprised when he sees her working in his store?

But Jack is not at the store when she gets there. His assistant tells her that he doesn't know where Jack went, but that he's due back soon. She should wait. He ushers her into Jack's office, really just a cubby-hole in the back of the store where the surplus stock is kept. She sits down as his desk and leafs through the papers lying around in disarray. The first thing she will do is put everything in order. She'll create a filing system for him. She is sorting through his invoices when Jack's assistant knocks on the door.

"What is it?" she calls.

"There are a lot of customers in the store. Could you come out and help me wait on them?"

"Absolutely. Positively," Marcia says. Oh this is good. She wanted to help Jack and now she can. Starting right now. "Coming," she moves away from Jack's desk and opens the door.

TWENTY-ONE

Aviva has been babysitting for Jacob for much of the summer now. He is like the younger brother she always hoped for. They have this in common: both are only children growing up with only one parent. Two never feels like a family. The other day Jacob pointed to the picture of his mother on his bedside table and shook his head no.

"I don't have a father," she told him, surprised that those words flew out of her mouth. She has never said this in that exact way before. She took out the picture she always carries of her dad holding her in his arms and showed it to Jacob. "Look, Jacob. My father had freckles. And this is me as a baby. My mother said he held me so much she thought we were attached." Jacob nodded seriously. He walked across his room and opened the special box where he keeps crayons and scissors and, "glue," Aviva said aloud. Jacob smiled at her. Then he squeezed a little out rubbed it on his shirt and stuck his shirt to the one she was wearing. "Attached," Aviva said. "Very good, Jacob."

Attached is just how she feels about her almost little brother. There is something comforting about being with him. Jacob slips his hand into hers whenever she takes him to the playground. He jumps on a swing and pumps even though she is always ready to push him. Yesterday he stood up and pumped so hard, she was terrified he would fall. When she yelled at him to stop, he grinned and jumped off, straight into her waiting arms. He threw back his head and laughed as he swung his arms around her neck. She gave him a piggyback ride all the way to J. P. Licks for an ice cream. Then, they sat on his front steps reading the copy of *Mike Mulligan and his Steam Shovel* she bought for him from the library sale. Jacob placed his fingers under the words and followed along silently. He is such a smart little boy. He might almost be able to read. Although he refuses to mouth the words, he can whistle and imitate bird songs. Every so often she thinks they answer him.

Each day, when Simon returns from work, Aviva is full of praise for what Jacob has done. No mention is ever made of whether or not he has spoken, but Aviva knows that Simon is waiting to hear her say that he has. When Simon walks her home he holds Jacob's hand and Jacob holds hers, swinging himself between them. "One, two, three swing," she and Simon chant.

Today they're going to take the T into Boston to the Children's Museum. She has always wanted to go back, but the only cool way to pull it off at her age is to rent a kid. This is the perfect opportunity.

"He's ready, Aviva," Simon tells her. "I packed lunch for both of you. See if you can get him to eat something besides snacks."

Aviva opens the lunch bags when they sit down to eat in front of the museum near the sculpture of the giant glass milk bottle. "Let's have a race to see who finishes our peanut butter and jelly sandwich first," she says.

In the museum, Jacob pulls her from one exhibit to another, but when they reach the "Construction Site" that was created when Boston began its infamous Big Dig, Jacob runs over to the backhoe. He's fascinated by the jackhammer, the noise of which rings out in stark contrast to his own silence.

"Will you come to Grandma's Attic with me?" she asks. This has always been her favorite exhibit. She's not sure Jacob will like it and he shakes his head no.

"We can come back here before we leave."

Reluctantly he takes her hand. She is surprised when he starts rummaging through the piles of clothing and finds one costume after another to try on. He's a fireman, a policeman, a superhero and Bob the Builder all in one. She can hardly drag him away and after they revisit the Big Dig exhibit again, has to promise to read Mike Mulligan as soon as they get home.

Hot and tired from the ride on the T, Aviva heads straight into the kitchen for cookies and juice, only to find a half-filled glass of apple juice on the counter. Simon must have come home early and gone for a run while they were out.

When they come back into the living room she notices pictures of Jacob set up on the coffee table. She frowns. These are usually on the bookcase. It's not like Simon to move things out of place.

"Wait, Jacob," she calls, as he starts down the hallway to his room. They will get Mike Mulligan together. In Jacob's room, more things are out of their usual order. It's almost as if Simon had come home early and wandered around the house picking up things for close scrutiny, as if he had never seen them before. Several picture books are on top of Jacob's bookcase, his dresser drawers are slightly open, and Aviva is sure she shut them carefully. She's slightly afraid now. There are two more rooms to check. She would prefer that Jacob not go with her, but she can't let him out of her sight so she suggests they pretend they are characters in a storybook. "Let's be Goldilocks and the Three Bears."

In Jacob's room, Aviva asks, "Who's been sleeping in my bed?" in Papa Bear's bass voice. Jacob grins. They walk hand in hand into Simon's bedroom. Aviva begins again, "Who's been sleeping in my bed?" and stops abruptly. Someone is sleeping on Simon's bed. A woman with blonde hair. Jacob grabs Aviva's hand. She takes a careful look. It's Jacob's mother. For a minute Jacob stands perfectly still staring, then bolts from the room. "I'll call your dad, Jacob," she tells him, trying to keep her voice calm as she follows him into the kitchen. "He'll come right home." She is fully aware that sometimes, when people are divorced, one parent tries to kidnap a child from the other. Aviva has no idea whether this is the case but she is not about to take any chances. A moment later Karen is standing in the kitchen.

"I didn't mean to fall asleep. I must have startled you both. I'm Karen, Jacob's mother." She kneels down as she says this and holds her arms out to Jacob. "Hi, Jacob," she says gently. "I've missed you." Jacob clings to Aviva. "Don't you have a hug for Mommy?"

"How did you get in?" Aviva asks her, putting her arm around Jacob. Could she have left the door unlocked?

"I used my key. I never removed it from my key ring."

"I called Simon. He's on his way home. He asked me to stay until he gets here," Aviva adds, even though she had only been able to leave a message. Jacob looks relieved. She picks him up and holds him against her body. That evening the neighborhood buzzes with the news that Simon's wife has returned. People sitting on their front porches turn their heads in the direction of Simon's house but no one comes outside.

TWENTY-TWO

This is some way to mark 52 years of marriage, Ida thinks as she comes back inside after seeing Nathan off in the van that takes take him to the Hebrew Rehab. He hardly waved goodbye to her and he is totally unaware that today is their anniversary. Until two years ago he never missed the occasion, always walking over to Shreve's at lunchtime to select something precious for her. Even last year he had been able to buy her flowers. Ida retrieves the box that houses her anniversary treasures from her bureau drawer, takes the pile of cards wrapped in a ribbon next to it and sits down on her bed.

Holding the box on her lap, she extracts the jewelry from it piece by piece. Ida shakes her head when she pulls out his first anniversary gift, a colorful brocade purse. She had been trying to decide if she could tell him that it was far too gaudy, not her style, when he impatiently told her to open it. How was she to know that hidden within was a cultured pearl necklace? A most extravagant gift, given that his law practice was just developing. She puts the pearls on over her housecoat and as she smoothes her hand over them, she can almost hear Nathan laughing at the contrast they make.

When the phone rings, she stiffens. Nathan left only ten minutes ago, but what if there has been an incident with the van. So great is her relief that the caller is Ruchamah she doesn't at first register what she is saying, that she is on her way to pick her up.

"I thought the baby naming ceremony was next Saturday."

"It is. Today we're going to the Gardner."

"Oh, somehow I forgot. You should go on your own, Ruchamah. I wouldn't be good company."

"I'm not good company today, either. What if I come over and we decide when I get there?"

Ida loves Ruchamah like a second daughter, but she's exhausted from having succumbed to Susan's pressure to put Nathan into the day care program. She'll just have to convince Ruchamah that she can't go to the museum with her when she arrives.

As Ruchamah pulls into a space down the street from the Gardner, Ida says, "I'm glad you insisted I come. I haven't been doing much of anything since Nathan went into the Rehab."

"I haven't been here for years, myself," Ruchamah says. She gazes at the stone beasts that guard the entrance. "Aviva loves these lions. When she was little, I told her that Isabella Stewart Gardner, or, Mrs. Jack, as her husband dubbed her, took a real lion from the zoo for a walk on a leash one day. Of course that lion was so old, it probably didn't have any teeth." Ida laughs.

"'I would be braver,' she told me. 'I would take a lion with really big teeth. He'd listen to me and wouldn't bite anyone, like Francois in The Happy Lion book.' She petted one of these sculptures to demonstrate her fierce display of courage."

Ida nods. "Sound just like Aviva," she says. Do you know she called the other day just to see how I was doing?"

"She loves you," Ruchamah says as she purchases their tickets, despite her friend's protests. "Look at this courtyard garden. They change it every season."

"These lace hydrangeas have such a deep color. As do the yellow Asiatic lilies. Nathan brought them to me once in a floral arrangement. They were so beautiful I planted some bulbs."

"You gave me a few but I didn't have any luck with them. Maybe there wasn't enough sunlight in back; besides, you're the one with the green thumb."

"Well, Ruchamah, I'll have to start sending you Asiatic lily bouquets."

Ruchamah laughs and checks her watch. "It's eleven," she says. "We could start on the third floor, work our way down and break for lunch whenever we're hungry."

They wander from room to room, filled with Mrs. Gardner's eclectic art, porcelain and furniture collections from her European shopping sprees. Each room is unique in design and theme, with its sculpted mantle and embroidered fireplace screen stitched so long ago. Magnificent carved ceilings tower above. When they enter the Gothic Room, Ruchamah stops. "I always spend a moment with this portrait of Isabella. Ruchamah studies the canvas hanging in the Gothic Room. She looks demure and angelic. Of course she was neither."

"Sargeant must have made the tapestry brocade in the background look like a radiating halo on purpose," Ida says. I heard that when he painted this portrait, Isabella couldn't sit still. After eight sittings, Mrs. Jack told him that nine was Dante's mystical number, and voila, this is his ninth attempt. Mr. Jack told her, 'It looks like hell, but it looks like you,' and warned her not show it in public while he was alive. Just look at her waist. Do you think she ever ate?"

"But look at those hips," Ruchamah says. "She ate. Speaking of eating,though it's early, I'm starved. We can cover the second floor later. That way, we'll get our exercise after lunch." They take a quick tour through the rest of the third floor and descend to the Café. Having settled on the quiche, they find a table in a quiet corner.

"This entire place is so filled with beauty. It's ironic to think that it arose out of tragedy. Mrs. Gardner lost her only child when he was two,"

Ruchamah says, "After that, her art collection became her passion."

"I cannot imagine losing a child. Nathan and I have been fortunate in so many ways, at least until now. I just wish he had an illness that would get better over time." She touches her pearls. He gave these to me for our first anniversary. Today is our fifty-second, the first that Nathan didn't remember. I know he couldn't help it, but still I was feeling sorry for myself when you called this morning. The day Susan and I went to check out the 'Great Days for Seniors' program at the Rehab, Jan had two parakeets in her office. Yellow and blue, perched side by side, two love birds. Now, look at us."

"I still see two lovebirds," Ruchamah says. "Just the other day you and Nathan were walking hand in hand, like you always did."

"Not like we always did. Now I hold on so he won't get lost." Ruchamah reaches across the table and presses her hand.

"I can't stand myself when I become maudlin. Tell me what's happening with you."

"I've been feeling a bit maudlin myself, on the verge of tears, because Karen came back and Simon disappeared from my life. Even though Aviva's still babysitting, I have no idea what's going on with him, with us. I miss him. I'm only used to missing Daniel, not Daniel and Simon. It's like getting a present you really like and having the giver suddenly snatch it back."

"Or having a box full of presents from a giver who's no longer fully present," Ida says. "We're a fine pair today, aren't we," she continues with a slight laugh as the waitress brings their order. "I am a far cry from the girl I was when I lived in Berlin before the Second World War. I took off my armband, stuck it in my pocket and wandered the streets of the city as if I still owned them."

"Let's take a page from Mrs. Jack's life. Out of her sorrow, came this inspirational place."

"Even though it's a museum, I always feel as if she has invited us into her palazzo as her special guests. And of course," Ida adds, "if she were here she would serve dessert."

"Okay. One dessert, two forks coming up."

"Chocolate cake," Ruchamah announces as she returns. "Why not go wild? Mrs. Gardner did. She was an avid Red Sox fan. People might not think someone so cultured had such plebian appetites. When they won the World Series over the New York Giants, in 1912, she celebrated their victory by wearing a headband with the words, "Oh you Red Sox" in red letters when she went to Symphony Hall. A reporter described her as a woman gone crazy."

After lunch they climb the stairs to the second floor. "Come out here," Ida says. "We can peer down on the garden from this balcony just like Mrs. Jack. Sometimes I have imagined being her overnight guest and waking up in the morning to this view."

"In those days," Ruchamah says, "this was 'the' place to be. She held court for Henry James and the other intellectuals of the time. I would have liked to have been a fly on the wall."

They wander around until they reach the Tapestry Room. "Imagine how many shipping crates she would have needed to get everything here from Europe," Ruchamah says. "The tapestries alone took up more than their share of cargo space,"

One step into the Dutch Room and Ida is shocked into silence when she sees the empty frame that once held Rembrandt's masterpiece, "The Storm on the Galilee." She can't believe she had forgotten about this unsolved heist of art. When Mrs. Gardner left her palace to the city of Boston, it was with the immutable instruction: nothing was to be moved from its place. And now, this masterpiece is gone. "Mrs. Gardner was right. Nothing should be removed from its place." Ida puts her hand over her mouth and rushes from the room. Ruchamah hurries after her.

As soon as she gets home, Ida collapses into her chair, kicks off her shoes and puts her feet up on the matching ottoman. Her life hasn't been the same since this nightmare began. Three years ago. Passover.

Each spring, Nathan would begin to prepare weeks ahead for the *Seder.* He saw it as a mandate to impart his personal meaning to this festival. As a survivor of the Holocaust, Nathan had created a group at Kehillat Shalom concerned with continuing incidents of genocide throughout the world. That year he had written a piece for the group's "Passover Companion", a booklet for congregants to supplement their home *Seders.* He planned to read it aloud before the recitation of the ten plagues.

On *Erev Passover,* he took his seat at the head of the table, raised the cup of wine and began the Seder. As he chanted the *kiddush,* he winked at his grandchildren, who giggled as always when they downed their first of the four proscribed cups of wine. Here in the sanctity of the family home, an alcoholic beverage legally denied to them until they were 21, was not only allowed, but commanded.

Nathan reminded everyone that the word seder means order and led the family through the first part of the *Haggadah,* answering their questions as they went along. Before the recitation of the ten plagues, he began to read from the "Passover Companion".

"Many of us remember the delight we experienced when we were taught as children to dip our little finger into our cup of wine and remove one drop as we recited each of the ten plagues. As we grow older, and the world grows older with us, we see a world beset with modern day plagues. They echo the ancient ones – disease, ecological ills, and most difficult, the tenth plague, killing of the first born, tantamount to genocide. Today we grapple with those words of the *Torah* as have the rabbis before us. They remind us that God silenced the ministering angels when they began to sing praises at the liberation from slavery, as the Red Sea engulfed the Egyptians. 'My children perish. Cease your songs.'"

Suddenly he looked up. The Passover Companion slipped to the floor. "Songs?" he said, appearing confused. "Is it time to sing?"

"No, Pop. I don't think you finished reading." Martin checked as he handed the booklet back to his father. Nathan shook his head and stared at the words as if he had never seen them before. He seemed to be waiting for something.

Hiding her concern, Ida got up and walked over to him. "Why don't we continue," she said, rubbing his shoulder. "It's time for a new cup of wine and then we can name the plagues. Is that all right Nathan?"

"The plagues," Nathan said. "Yes, it's time for the plagues."

Ida pointed to the place in the *Haggadah* and resumed her seat. Nathan looked at the page but said nothing.

"Perhaps Martin can recite the plagues." She looked at her son and he began to read. Everyone dipped their little finger into the wine. Droplets fell on their plates.

"What are you doing?" Nathan asked. "You're going to mess up the tablecloth!"

"Remember, Pop Pop," David said, "We're supposed to spill the wine as we name the plagues."

For Ida, the rest of the Seder was a blur. Nathan remained at the head of the table, while Martin finished the service. Despite the injunction of Passover being that all should remember, Nathan was steeped in forgetfulness. Tears fell down his cheeks and landed on the *matzah* that he held in his hands until it became soaked like the parsley, they had dipped earlier into salt water to remind them of the tears of the Jewish people when they were slaves in Egypt.

She glances at her watch. The bus should have been here fifteen minutes ago. She grabs the phone when it rings. "It's Jan. Sorry we're late. Nathan wandered away from the group as they were boarding the van. They got to him quickly, but it took a long time to convince him to go back with them." She pauses a moment, then says, "It might be a good idea for us to meet in the next few days."

TWENTY-THREE

"The baby naming ceremony was beautiful, Hillel." Beth says as they get ready for bed. She smiles at him; warmth and trust having returned to her eyes. He knows Beth's happiness is fraught with the hope that, having named this child he will come to realize there is no difference between a child they bring into the world naturally and one they might adopt. Hillel is reluctant to admit that Shira Hannah had already begun to resemble her adoptive parents in some mysterious way, as if she really was their own. Well, of course, she is their own.

Beth slips on that gossamer nightgown he loves; her bare arms and neck gleam as she bends over to brush her hair. He rubs her neck and smiles as she lifts her mouth to his. Nectar sweet as honey fills him. He can't imagine loving another woman as he loves his wife. His barren wife. This is Beth, my partner, my soul mate, he immediately tells himself. How is it that I can reduce her to a vessel for my seed? He has prayed so many times to stop this obsession. It should be simple. A disappointment, yes. Not the matter of life and death that it has become to him. Please, he asks. Let me stop this craziness before I lose my wife.

"I love that the adoption forum was your idea," Beth says. He doesn't tell her that he found tho sponsoring agency's flyer on his desk one day and called to ask them to present a similar forum at Kehillat Shalom only so she might believe in the possibility that he might change his mind. She has hardly spoken to him since their return from Brooklyn.

"This makes me feel as if you're going to be able to get back to your book soon, too," she says. "And this time Marcia won't be there to misinterpret every word."

He almost wishes Marcia were still there. He would have someone to blame for how illogical his thoughts have become. But the heart is without logic, he reminds himself.

"I cleared my calendar," she says. "I had a meeting scheduled that night but I've already called to cancel it."

"Good," he says, as he lies down beside her. And even as he agrees, he knows he will find himself in another place that particular evening. There is always a congregant who might need to talk, a new family he can visit, although he hasn't been able to do any of this lately.

Beth curls up alongside him. They haven't made love since they returned from Brooklyn. After the scene with his father, they have been unable to even lie close together. He gathers her in his arms and shuts off all thought of how disappointed she will be with him once again.

TWENTY-FOUR

Dear Elijah,
   How could you leave without me! I was completely packed; I left a note for Marcia explaining that I had been called away. I was looking forward to seeing all my good work unfold from Eden, knowing the rabbi would now be happy in his life and effective in his community. I was not expecting to stay and watch events unfold from here.

   You didn't explain. You never said you accepted my proposal to go back with you, but you didn't say otherwise. You stood on the *bimah* with the rabbi as he held the child in his arms. You watched Beth come to tears upon seeing him with this adopted child. And then you were gone, without a word to me.

I thought you would at least stay for the party. There was so much good food, especially the chocolate ganache and blueberry cheesecake and I counted as least six different kinds of ruggaleh. The one with walnuts and figs was the most delicious. Truthfully I thought you might be too busy to eat because you were somewhere about giving blessings to people sorely in need of them, including the rabbi.

Upon reflection, something I don't often do, I did notice you frowning as you indicated the scrolls I've been sending when I came outside to greet you. And you did mention something about my interfering in the lives of the congregants. I didn't interfere exactly. I made a few interventions. Well, it took so long for me to come up with this marvelous idea for the rabbi, I couldn't just sit around. You might consider that my efforts to help the congregants as having been made on the rabbi's behalf. Shoshanah can't do everything.

Sometimes, I find you quite annoying, Elijah, and difficult to understand as well. You constantly quote sayings from the *Talmud* to me. You do not take into account my impatient nature. I did remember that saying about angels, whispers and blades of grass Ah yes, your exact words: "Every blade of grass has an angel bending over it whispering grow."

It's true, I never actually whisper, but here's what I think: Every blade of grass is unique and deserves to grow, which goes with my theory and Beth's, into which an adopted child fits so beautifully. There are many different grasses in the world Elijah: Egyptian mint, chicory, lemon grass, bitter herbs to name only a few, the list is infinite. Besides, those angels bending over those blades of grass might need a little help.

And yes, I played a few tricks on Ruchamah, but my intentions were honorable. How could I have known that Karen would come back, although I was aware one of the few times the rabbi responded to a congregant's request was to ask Karen to return. So what? She left once, she'll probably leave again. As far as Marcia is concerned, I did not threaten her job security. I just did a better job than she does. Did I think the rabbi would fire her? Of course not. Despite your opinion, I only tried to comfort Ida by arranging for those brochures. I didn't realize she cared so much about Nathan. I considered him to be a pain in her neck; evidently she did not. These mortals take ages, and I do mean ages to make meaningful changes in their lives if no one intervenes.

I was tempted to follow you, but I stopped myself. Life in Eden is predictable. And frankly, very lonely. You were my only friend. No one else talked to me. Or sought my opinion. Or thought me intelligent, creative and persistent. No. I take that back. The other immortals know I'm persistent. They came right out and said they found me extremely irritating, which is why I no longer speak to them. Remember when I first arrived? I was so young, around Aviva's age, actually, having just left my mother, who was grieving my loss, as Jacob grieved the loss of Joseph. I was able to reassure my grandfather that his son was alive in Egypt.

No one could reassure my mother that I had been granted immortal life.

As soon as I got to the Garden, everyone attempted to take me under his wing. I didn't want to be under a wing. I wanted to do what I wanted, when I wanted. You said I would become disoriented without guidelines. There was too much space in the Garden. I could get lost. You meant without you at my side. Well, you have not been at my side here. You offered no guidance. It's true, some of my interventions have gone wrong. Things go wrong in the real world, Elijah. And what's a spirit to do but try and fix them. Once the adoption forum is over, the rabbi and Beth will regard me as an angel, though they will never know I was the one to help them. And it won't matter that I didn't whisper!

Serach

TWENTY-FIVE

Shoshanah's leaving for the day when Sara buzzes her. "It's Rose Horowitz." She's sure this is Oscar's time. The rabbi is already there."

When Shoshanah arrives Rose tells her the rabbi is talking with Oscar in the bedroom. "Could you sit with me?"

"Of course," Shoshanah says.

"I made a raspberry torte." Rose moves about the kitchen with nervous energy and sets a plate with the torte in front of Shoshanah, pours them both a cup of tea and sits down. "I really appreciate how much you've been visiting lately. It's just that Oscar has been keeping you to himself and although that's great for Oscar I'm going crazy out here. I wanted a chance to talk to you." She jumps up then sits back down. "I'm so confused I don't know whether I'm coming or going, that is whether Oscar is coming or going. One day he's at death's door and the next day he says he feels so good he could make love. This I can't do. I don't want Oscar to die like that or any other way. Do you know what I mean, Shoshanah?"

"I"..., Shoshanah begins, but Rose interrupts so quickly she can't get out another word.

"And here's the worst thing, I'm so mad at him for doing this, for pretending to die and not dying, even though he's not pretending. I just don't know. Is he dying, Shoshanah? You've been here twice this week already. Tell me so I can be prepared."

Before Shoshanah can respond the phone rings. Rose tells whoever is on the other end that she can't talk, "because the rabbi and the cantor are here and Oscar is, or may be dying in the other room for the fourteenth time and Shoshanah is saying so many things that are comforting to me," and hangs up. "Oh you finished your torte and the tea," she addresses Shoshanah. "I'll get you some more." She sits down again.

"This is plenty," Shoshanah says.

"No, no. She jumps up, brings another plate and the teapot to the table and sits down again. "You see, Shoshanah, you're just a young girl with your whole life ahead of you and you have no idea what this is like. We've been together for over fifty years. I am Oscar and he is me, except he's ten years older and now I'm going to be alone. One of these days, maybe even tomorrow, he won't be here and I have never been alone. I went from my parents' house straight to Oscar. In those days we didn't live together first and then decide whether or not we liked it. We got married. I wasn't the most beautiful girl on the block, but Oscar said I had a lot of pizzazz. Even today he called for his 'Razzle Dazzle Rose. 'Razzle Dazzle Rose,' he says. 'Never let your razzle dazzle go out.' But when Oscar goes, it goes.

"It's going to be 51 years this fall that we've been married." She's close to tears, but does not allow them to fall. Rose recites the history of their marriage briefly, four children, daughter in Texas, one in Denver and one is Chicago. "You know our son who lives closest, in Springfield. The professor. The professor at Amherst.

"Oscar's been been trying to teach me about our finances but I can't understand a thing he says. I've been pretending to pay attention. A lot of pretense is going on here.

"We did everything together, not like those modern couples where one goes here, the other there. No. We've been all over the world. Israel three times." She gets up, then sits down again.

"Oscar is dying in the other room and I'm worried about being a widow." She covers her face. "Worse than that," she says, "I'm angry at him for dying first. I always knew it would be me. Oscar has never been sick before. Imagine. A man, so strong at 79 he still plays tennis, just switched to doubles two years ago. I'm the one with the aches and pains. My back gives out, my allergies never stop. Especially in the spring. All that pollen. See this bandage on my wrist. I fell the other day. I constantly fall. Who will pick me up if Oscar's not here?" She tries to smile.

"I'm not going to move. I love this neighborhood, but we've been a couple so long I'm not sure how everyone will feel about inviting me by myself. I don't want anyone to abandon me. Especially Oscar." Now she is crying and wiping her eyes with a napkin. "The doctors told me there's no hope at all. They've operated twice; he recovered. Now the cancer has spread to the liver. They can't operate again. There are new treatments. But they're not available yet or Oscar doesn't qualify. Anyhow, he says he doesn't want to continue living this way. Last night I came in to the bedroom and looked at Oscar, the oxygen mask. His breath was shallow. I lay down and held onto him; both of us reached morning alive. When you're here he rallies. On bad days he asks me to send for you; today he asked for Hillel."

Shoshanah listens quietly. If Oscar dies while she's here, it will be the second time she has been present at someone's death during the year she has been at Kehillat Shalom. Last year, a young man, Peter Jonas, only 23, afflicted with a long illness, passed away while she was sitting in his room. He loved astronomy; they had been talking about new stars that had recently been discovered. She offered to go to the library to pick up some books for him. When she came back, she walked into the room announcing the titles she had selected for him not realizing he had fallen asleep. She sat by his bed for a while. He looks so peaceful she thought and decided to leave the books on his night table. The hospice nurse who had been attending him came in just as Shoshanah was on her way out and called her back into the room.

She thinks of him as Rose is talking. As a child she had been afraid of death. Nightmares of pets and people dying plagued her and only her mother's singing had been able to calm her. On nights of very bad dreams her mother slept in bed with her. "Shhh, shhh. Don't be afraid," her mother put her arms around her. "You're all right; you'll be all right." It is this that she wishes she could tell Rose.

"I married the right man," Rose is saying, "kind, understanding, not to mention a good dancer. After chemo, he bought a hairpiece so he could still take me out dancing in style. It fell off the first night when were doing a tango. He picked it up, put it in his pocket, smiled and said, 'So, Rose, let's pretend I still have all my hair.'

Hillel comes out of the bedroom and leaves the door open. He takes Rose's hand. I'll come back whenever you need me," he says. She looks distressed. "Are you leaving too, Shoshanah? I called my son from Springfield. He'll be here in a few hours.. He'll stay the night."

It's almost midnight when Shoshanah finally gets home. She parks in front of her apartment building, gathers her notes and shoulder bag from the car, and trips over the curb. Her things fly up and lie scattered all over the street. The desk clerk, who is just finishing his evening shift, sees her lying there and rushes out to help her up. She shakes her head. She can't move. Pain shoots up and down her entire body. He calls an ambulance and waits with her. She's in the emergency room until the early the next morning. X-rays are taken of her back and the attending physician orders her to bed, "preferably your floor," he says, "if your mattress is soft. You'll heal faster that way."

As soon the taxi drops her off, she calls Hillel at home and explains that she has injured herself.

"Beth and I will be right there."

"I left the door unlocked," she tells him.

As soon as they arrive, Beth asks if she has called her mother as she sets containers of food in Shoshanah's refrigerator. Shoshanah says she hasn't; she'll be all right. "I might be able to make it in tomorrow. Could you cover for me today?"

"What did the doctor say?"

"A week of bed rest, make that floor rest," she says, "but I'm sure I don't really need it."

"I'm sure you do," Beth says. "Don't worry, Shoshanah. Hillel and I will take care of everything."

"I'll talk to Sara, too," Hillel says. She's been coming in every day. I offered to pay her for her time, but she says this is part of her contribution to *Tikkun Olam*. She's even typing some of my old essays that Marcia never got to do."

"I'll call and ask her to cancel my appointments."

"We'll take a look at your calendar and try to keep as many as possible."

"How is Oscar?"

"He passed away peacefully during the night," Hillel says. "His funeral is tomorrow afternoon."

"I'll be there."

"That's not a good idea," Beth says. "I'm sure you'll be able to pay a condolence call by the end of *shiva* week, Shoshanah. Please stay put so you can heal properly."

"We're going to leave now so you can get some rest," Hillel says.

"Call your mother, Shoshanah," Beth says over her shoulder as she reaches the door. "She would want to know."

"She'll worry for nothing. I'm perfectly fine."

"Good," Beth says. "As long as you rest."

An hour later Ida arrives. "What are you doing on the floor?"

"And what are you doing here?"

"Funny you should ask. Beth called me to see if I could round up a few members of the *hevra mishpachah* to help you out. You know I was a founding member?" When Shoshanah shakes her head, Ida continues. "Well I was. I used to set up visitors for other people. It occurred to me that I could visit you since Nathan is now in the rehab's nursing home. They keep telling me I should do other things so he can adjust to his program. So here I am. What happened to you?"

"I didn't look where I was going?"

"I told you to take it easy, Shoshanah," Ida says as she sits down on the side of Shoshanah's bed. "By the way, how's that young man you told me about, from your silversmithing class?"

"I haven't seen him for a while. He calls. I haven't had a chance to call him back. But he's busy too. He's a doctor."

"In that case you need him more than you need me. If you give me his number I'll tell him to come by and check up on you." She smiles. Shoshanah laughs.

"Ouch," she says. "Oh, it hurts to laugh."

"Is your mother coming?"

"Oy," Shoshanah says. "If I tell her I'm laid up she'll stop everything to be here. Then, what is she going to do. Sit around my house?" She doesn't tell Ida that her mother warned her just the other day that she was doing too many things. "Too much multi-tasking means you can't pay attention to any one thing, Shoshanah, and please, you have to protect your voice."

She reassured her mother that she gargled with salt water every day and sprayed her throat before singing, then ran into the bathroom and gargled for the first time in a week after she hung up. Besides, her voice is just fine.

"Why are you sighing like that," Ida asks.

"Now that I have time to call Noah back," she says, "I'm laid up"

"A perfect time," Ida quips. "You just cleared your calendar. This is very beautiful," she says as she picks up the silver bracelet Shoshanah finally had finished which is lying on the coffee table. "Nathan used to give me so much jewelry when he was well." She hands it to Shoshanah. "Put it on. Try to remember you have a life outside your job." She leans over and kisses Shoshanah's cheek gently. "Now I'm getting you some lunch. You eat like a bird. And maybe I can help you up so you can go to the bathroom at least once, before I leave? Don't worry. I may be old, but I'm still strong."

TWENTY-SIX

Simon paces the living room while Karen cooks dinner. He attempts to entertain Jacob with funny stories, but his independent and happy son has been clinging to him the way he did when his mother first left and Simon is unable to reassure him that things will be okay. He feels confused himself and has begun to relive the emptiness he felt when Karen first left.

The ebullience he felt with Ruchamah, the plans they've made together disintegrated the moment he walked into his house and saw Karen standing there. Unable even to formulate a response, he took a very protective Aviva home, carrying Jacob, who would not allow his father to set him down all the way to Ruchamah's where he could not even bring himself to say the words, "Karen is in my house," let alone "Karen has returned."

Karen has roasted a chicken with potatoes and steamed fresh corn and broccoli. She sits next to her son to encourage him to eat; Jacob won't even look at her. When she lifts her hand to smooth his hair; he jerks away. Neither Simon nor Jacob eat a thing.

Karen clears the table while Simon gives Jacob a bath. Only a few weeks ago, she was in Chicago clearing her one dish and glass off the table when the rabbi called her with what he said was his last message, the others she had erased from her machine as soon as she came home from work. This message mentioned something about Simon wanting a *Get*. She had quickly called him back.

"I think that's the best thing," she said when she reached him. "Of course he wants some kind of closure." She doesn't say she had assumed they had closure the day Simon brought Jacob to see her in Chicago right after she left them. He tried everything he knew to change her mind. Jacob cried and cried for her. It broke her heart to refuse him. She explained to Simon that she had panic attacks because she couldn't take care of their son. She told him that, once when she couldn't get Jacob to stop crying, she threw him down in his crib so hard he almost cracked his head. She had to leave.

"Simon is a wonderful father," she said. "Jacob will grow up to be healthier and happier without me."

"Jacob seems very happy," the rabbi said. "And except for the fact that he doesn't talk, he's a well-adjusted child."

"Doesn't talk? Jacob had an enormous vocabulary for a two year old." She was practically in tears.

"Karen?" She can hear the concern in the rabbi's voice.

"Do you know what's wrong?"

"I don't," the rabbi said.

She hung up feeling frantic and so anxious she had to take in large gulps of air. The apartment that she had chosen for its feeling of openness, the limited amount of clean lined modern furniture she had bought when she took her job in the museum gift shop crowded in on her. She had not intended her leaving to cause her son harm. She left in order to protect him. The next thing she knew she was calling the airline to reserve a flight to Boston. She went to her boss the next day and asked for a leave of absence, citing a family emergency. Now she wishes she had stayed where she was. Things are not working out at all the way she had planned. On the plane, when she was finally able to calm down, she envisioned her reunion with Jacob. He would be so happy to see her, so relieved she had come back. "Mommy! Mommy!" he would cry and throw himself into her arms. No doubt Simon would be happy to see her as well. But Simon treats her as if she is an intruder and Jacob pulls away every time she comes near him.

She prepares meals even though cooking is not her forte' dusts the furniture, scrubs floors, puts fresh flowers around. She feels more like a cleaning woman than a wife or mother.

After his bath Karen offers to read to Jacob, but he shakes his head no and points to his dad. While Simon puts Jacob to sleep she rinses the dishes in the sink with hot water and transfers them to the dishwasher. The porcelain sculpture of father and son with their violins sits on the kitchen counter exactly where she had placed it. She had specifically chosen that piece, although there had been a sculpture of a mother and child and one of two parents and a child, as if she had known even then what the future would hold.

By the time Simon comes back, the kitchen is clean. He opens a bottle of merlot from the wine rack that sits on the counter next to the father and son sculpture and pours himself a glass. He will take it into his study and begin his usual after dinner practice. When he turns from the counter to excuse himself, Karen asks him to pour her a glass as well.

Simon stands in the kitchen doorway staring at Karen just as he stared at the alluring stranger the night of his concert rehearsal. He had thought her a sign that one day he would have a woman in his life again. Only he had not expected that woman to be Karen.

Now that she has his attention, Karen is uncertain what she wants to tell him. An explanation as to why she has come back, her need to know that her son is all right, a question as to why silence has plagued both her son and her husband since her return. But tonight, because Simon is sitting with her, as he often used to, things seem, if not normal, at least easier for this one moment.

Simon drinks his wine quickly. He had intended to hand Karen the requested glass and leave the room, but seated across from her now, he is struck by the fact that despite all that has happened, she seems exactly the same, exactly as she had when they were music students together at Julliard and the unexpected power of her contralto voice, in stark contrast to her almost ethereal presence, had entranced him. Something in him had responded to her fragility. When he described her to his parents, he told them he had met the woman with whom he wanted to share his life. His mother had been quiet for a few minutes before offering the suggestion he should wait a while until becoming more deeply involved. Simon could not bring himself to heed her advice. Karen's voice, like the utterances of Homer's Sirens, attracted him beyond any other considerations. Unlike Homer, he had no crew to lash him to the mast.

Karen made it clear that she preferred a career to motherhood. When a berth in the Houston Opera Company was offered to her, Simon accepted a seat in the first violin section of the Houston Symphony Orchestra and proposed marriage. Unfortunately, Karen soon found herself experiencing such intense stage fright she was unable to perform.

"There are many singers who are better than I am," she finally told him. "I know now I would be perfectly content to be a mother. I can give voice lessons in the house while our baby sleeps." But of course she had not been perfectly content. She had left.

"I thought you would be happy to see me," Karen is saying. "It's obvious you're not."

Simon does not respond to this.

"The rabbi told me Jacob wasn't talking. Why didn't you let me know?"

"There seemed to be no reason. You left one day as if you had better things to do with your life than be here."

"I left because I didn't know what else to do. I tried to explain that to you when you came to Chicago. Jacob was speaking then. I care about my son."

"Your leaving indicated the opposite to me."

"I love Jacob. I intend to stay until he is talking again."

"It's been two years."

"Did you have him tested?"

"Of course. The doctor said he was fine. Nothing physically wrong and that I shouldn't push him to speak. So, I haven't. I've been taking good care of our son, Karen."

"I can see that, Simon. I wasn't implying anything more than that I had no idea about this until the rabbi called."

"You have every right to see your son," Simon tells her, "but tell me, how much do you really want to be with him. You keep Aviva with you all day."

Karen shrugs, then smiles tentatively. "I can't go from nothing to everything so quickly. He doesn't want to be alone with me. Surely you can see that."

"I see that. You're like a stranger to him."

"And to you."

Simon gets up from the table and begins pacing back and forth in the small kitchen.

"When you left, I told Jacob something must have happened, that I would find you and bring you back. I promised him."

"How could you have promised that?" Karen grabs Simon's arm. "I told you when you came to Chicago that I left because I couldn't take care of Jacob. You would come home and find him in his pajamas from the night before and think he was ready for bed early. You would pick him up from his crib, rock him, talk to him, sing, point out that the pajamas were a little dirty, take them off him, change his diaper. I held him in my arms most of the day, but I didn't feel anything. He started crawling, then walking. He was into everything all day long. Don't you remember, Simon? Lots of days I left him with Tasha and wandered around Coolidge Corner, praying I could go back and take care of him. There was never any dinner. I would go to bed when you came home. You thought I was tired from my day. I was tired from my life."

"From your life? What life were you tired from? You had a beautiful, wonderful little boy. You didn't even think it worth your while to tell me you were having trouble taking care of him so we could have done something about it?"

"You could have guessed. You could have asked. But you had to be 'Simon the good, Simon the awesome,' stepping in to take care of our baby, imagining I was perfectly fine. You wanted everything to be the way it was supposed to be, so you pretended it was." Karen is trembling.

"How do you have the nerve to walk back into this house without even bothering to tell me you were coming? How do you have the nerve to talk to me as if you never left?"

"It's very difficult for me to talk to you. I didn't know you hated me."

"I didn't know that either." Simon walks out of the kitchen.

He grabs his running shoes and opens the front door. Karen rushes down the hall to catch him. "What will I do if Jacob wakes up?"

He hesitates. He does not want his son to be alarmed. He does not want Jacob to think his father has suddenly left him. But of course Jacob won't think that. Jacob knows he would never leave him.

"Just tell him I'll be right back," he says.

Karen goes into the living room to wait for Simon. She stares at her wedding portrait, then at the photo of herself with Jacob. She had been so uncomfortable that day. Jacob was squirming in her arms. Simon had to jump up and down like a monkey to get him to smile.

He hadn't changed a thing in the house. Surely that must mean something. The entire time she lived here, the entire time she had known Simon, he had never been as angry with her as he had been tonight. When he comes back she will tell him she is sorry she left the way she did. She should have tried to explain. She should have called to see how Jacob was. "I thought I was doing the right thing for Jacob," she will say. "I never thought I'd come back."

As Simon runs, he pictures Ruchamah's enraptured face the night of the concert rehearsal. He misses her; he misses their easy conversations which do not induce feelings of guilt or pain.

He never should have told the rabbi he could call Karen. If only he had been more clear that day, but he hadn't known his own mind then. Everything had fallen into place once he met Ruchamah.

He runs past her house and stops for a minute. Just doing that eases his heart.

TWENTY-SEVEN

"Ruchamah?"

Her window is open this hot August night. Unable to sleep she has come back to the dining room table to the glass of wine she poured earlier but did not drink. She stares at the open manuscript before her. Miriam is counting on her to finish these translations for the Hebrew-English reading of her poems at the 92nd Street Y in Manhattan but since Karen's return she has her lost perspective and obsesses over each word, the way she did when she first became a translator.

"Ruchamah?" The voice travels up in a hoarse whisper. When she goes to the window, she sees Simon, pacing back and forth on the empty sidewalk in jogging shorts cooling down from a run.

Earlier that evening she had gone downstairs and out through the front door, as if at any moment someone was expected, but no one had been there, not even that crone. Karen has been here for two weeks and there still have been no visits from Simon, not even a call. *Tisha B'Av,* a time that commemorates the destruction of the ancient temple in Jerusalem, a time commemorating abject suffering and loss, has just passed. When she looks down at Simon this is exactly what she feels. This mixed with a longing so strong she is not sure she should let him in. Nonetheless, she presses the buzzer and waits for him at the top of the stairs.

Unshaven and disheveled, Simon looks as if he has gone to bed with his clothes on and forgotten to change before going out. Perhaps, he too, is unable to sleep. It's almost midnight. For one moment she thinks he has come to tell her that Karen is gone, but then she realizes this can't be. He would not have left Jacob alone.

Short of reaching the landing, Simon stops. "I know it's late," he says.

When she doesn't answer he says, "I'm sorry, I shouldn't have just dropped in like this," and turns to leave.

"No, it's all right, Simon. Come in." Ruchamah walks towards the dining room table. Still sweating from his run, Simon picks up a paper napkin to wipe his forehead and tosses it in the wastebasket she keeps under the table for discarded drafts, full of her wasted efforts today

She sits across from Simon still wearing the oversized tee-shirt and shorts she put on after swimming this evening, her usual meditative laps unable to calm her. Ruchamah felt abandoned by his absence and tried to tell herself they had found only a possibility for love. Theirs had not become a full-blown relationship. That would have broken her heart, but her heart felt broken nonetheless. Enough of this, she instructed herself, to no avail, as her hands following quickly, one after the other, propelling her through the water. There had been laughter and music the night of the rehearsal concert. There had been hope. She finished a few laps, stopped, floating aimlessly. If the crone in the wool suit, who had interrupted her swim the night of the *Rosh Hodesh* group, jumped into her lane that moment, she would have welcomed her rude distraction. Yet when Ruchamah left the pool, it was the woman who had danced naked in her yard, the one with the promise of love, she found herself seeking.

And Simon has come. Perhaps her dancing stranger had been swimming alongside her tonight after all and had chosen not to reveal herself.

Simon, as always, is unable to sit quietly. He picks up a pen and flips it over and over in his strong hands, then sets it down and looks around the room for a minute before finally meeting her eyes.

"Ruchamah, I've been thinking about you. I've been thinking about us." He hesitates.

"I've been thinking about Karen," she says before she can stop herself.

He reaches for her hand.

She looks at his outstretched hand and is afraid to take it, afraid she will not be able to let go. She sips her untouched wine. She wants to fill a glass for Simon with the sparkling wine from Israel she keeps for special occasions. But she does nothing. She will wait to hear what he has come to say.

"I miss you," he tells her. "I had no idea Karen was coming. She told me it was because she had just learned that Jacob had stopped talking. She thinks her presence might help him."

"It might." Ruchamah is trembling. She clasps her hands to prevent Simon from noticing. He seems to be telling her that Karen is back solely because of Jacob. But if that is the case, why hasn't he come to tell her this sooner?

"I thought she would be here a few days," Simon says. "But two weeks have passed and Jacob hasn't spoken. He doesn't want to be alone with his mother. I wish I could ask her to leave, but I have no right to keep her away from her son."

"Of course not," Ruchamah says. This must be Simon's way of telling her they cannot be more than friends. Perhaps the feelings he once had for Karen have returned. Knowing this would be unbearable.

"It's all right, Simon," she says. "It's been so long since anyone has been in my life in a romantic way, friendship is all that seems normal to me." Her voice cracks despite her effort to hide her feelings.

"No, Ruchamah. Please. I didn't ask Karen to come back. I don't want her here." And suddenly Simon is standing next to her. He draws her out of her seat. "Let me hold you. Let me show you that you that are not supposed to be alone." He rains kisses on her face. He kisses her mouth. His hands are in her hair. She presses her body so close to his there is no distance between them. She blocks out all thoughts of Karen and kisses him back, filled with desire. Her body tingles. Her heart is racing. She cannot let go of him and then they are lying on her living room couch. Impelled by desire, Simon slips his hand under her shirt. She pulls it up to ease his way. Distracted by the lumps in the sofa, she whispers his name. Simon?" Her voice is a question. "Aviva is down the hall." He nods and sets her slightly away.

Ruchamah takes a deep breath and laughs a little, forcing herself to stand.

In the kitchen, she pours a glass for Simon from the bottled water she keeps in the refrigerator and sets it on the counter. She pours another for herself and closes the refrigerator door.

Simon is sitting at the table once again. Putting her arms around him, she sets his water glass in front of him. He pulls her onto his lap. "I've wanted to be with you since the day I asked you to watch Jacob.

Ruchamah nods. "I felt that, too, but I was afraid. The good thing is that Jacob has his mother back, whether or not she stays."

"She's not going to stay," Simon says.

"Even if she does, she can find a place of her own. She can take all the time in the world to get to know Jacob again. We'll keep busy until this is settled. You have your concert; I have my work. I'm so late with my translations for Miriam's book at this point. Time will pass quickly. Won't it? Before we know it we'll be together. I would like that, Simon. I wasn't sure what you were going to tell me when you came, tonight. I almost thought," she hesitates, "I almost thought you came to tell me you and Karen were going to get back together."

"I only want to be with you, Ruchamah. I called the rabbi and told him to go ahead with the *Get* the night of concert rehearsal. All I could think of was you, was us. And I plan to officially file for a divorce as soon as the get comes through.

"Officially file for divorce?" Ruchamah pulls away from Simon. "What are you talking about? I knew you wanted a *Get*. Marcia couldn't help but tell me that but I assumed it was for religious reasons, after the fact of your civil divorce."

"I stopped wearing my wedding ring about a year after Karen left. I considered our marriage to be over. I just didn't take care of the paperwork." He takes both her hands in his. Ruchamah shakes her head no, stands up and stares at Simon.

"Paperwork?" She has paperwork, papers she has never filed. Drafts of poems, letters from poets, condolence cards she never threw away, not divorce decrees. I never even checked to see if Simon was divorced. How could I not have done that? She pulls her hands away, crosses her arms over her chest attempting in that gesture to isolate herself from him.

"You're still married, Simon. You never really let go of Karen."

"I let her go, Ruchamah. I had no life other than my music and Jacob. Because of you my life has begun again. Surely you must see that. The paperwork means nothing."

"To you perhaps, but not to me. You would be divorcing Karen now because of me. I would be your reason."

He stands for a moment regarding her. "I let her go, Ruchamah. I had no life other than my music and Jacob. I put all thoughts of Karen aside. I never expected to be happy again, except for Jacob, until I met you. Surely you can see that. I'll call my lawyer tomorrow.

She wants to accept this, but an image of Daniel lying so still in her arms pushes Simon's words away. Daniel didn't mean to die and leave. Simon didn't mean to trick her, but the joy she felt when he told her he only wanted to be with her has turned into despair. If only she could pretend that Karen had not come back. But she has never been good at such pretense. Karen is here. Simon is not free to be with her.

"Please, Simon," she says.

One look at her intractable face tells him any argument he can make is of no avail. He walks across her living room and closes the door behind him. She hears him run down the steps and open the outer door. It slams shut behind him.

She crosses the room, goes to the window and watches him walk away, exactly as Daniel had walked away from her in her dream. That crone who has been haunting her must be lurking just around the corner. She picks up her glass of wine.

Someone should finish this she thinks. Someone should do something. File papers. Put papers on file.

Simon could have done that. Perhaps he did file those papers after all and is on his way back to her right now, laughing in relief as stands beneath her window again and calls up to her, "I can't believe I forgot," he will shout from the street. "I just forget. Everything is all right. I have a copy of those papers right here in my pocket." Her heart leaps at this thought. But, of course, this is not going to happen

They have kissed each other. That is all. She presses her hands to her lips. Such passionate kisses. No one has kissed me since Daniel died, she thinks. Fourteen years is a long time to go without a kiss; I must have set some sort of record.

She gathers the glasses from the table and trips over the wastebasket Simon had pulled out. "Damn it," she swears, and sets the glasses back on the table in order to pick up the scattered papers. "Damn you, Simon."

TWENTY-EIGHT

A viva's house smells like oranges from the environmentally friendly cleaning solution Ruchamah has been using. Her mother has been frantically cleaning ever since Simon's visit. It's the middle of the week and their house is immaculate. All her papers, usually in a state of disarray on the dining room table, are stacked in neat piles.

"Mom?" Aviva calls as she returns from babysitting. Ruchamah is in the bathroom scrubbing the sink.

"Hi honey. How did it go today?" She wrings out the sponge and throws it back in the pail filled with perfectly clean water.

"Like every other day. Jacob either sits on my lap, jumps on me for a piggy-back ride or refuses to let go of my hand. He still completely ignores his mother." She hesitates. Her mother has no idea that she is aware of Simon's visit, that she lay in bed crying after he left. All she could think was that central casting had totally screwed up this lifetime movie. The writer had created a plot that had fallen short. A man with a young child falls in love with the mother of his child's babysitter. The children love each other as well. Then, the man's ex-wife comes back. Movie over! No sequel.

Her mother has said nothing about that visit. As usual they both are pretending that nothing remarkable has happened. "How long do you think Karen is going to stay?" Aviva asks. This is a test to see if her mother will confide in her, if she realizes this situation affects them both.

"I don't know." Ruchamah shrugs and changes the subject. "Are you hungry?" She's stopped scrubbing the sink and leans against it, a look Aviva can't quite read on her face.

"I'll make us some soup. Gazpacho. It's so hot." Aviva injects a note of brightness she doesn't feel into her voice. She will sit through dinner like the good daughter she has always been, a role she is fast tiring of.

"Sounds good. I'll make the salad. I bought a wonderful sourdough." Ruchamah tries for a bright note as well. She doesn't tell Aviva that she had gone for a walk earlier thinking she might pass Simon's house and catch a glimpse of Karen, without Aviva seeing her. Why she wanted to do that, she's not sure. Perhaps to see if she looks happy, although she won't know whether to attribute that to her being with Simon again or because of

Jacob. Ashamed of wanting to spy on Simon's wife, his wife, she reminded herself, she turned in the opposite direction and went to the bakery instead.

She follows Aviva into the kitchen now and watches as she chops tomatoes and peppers for the gazpacho.

"Do you think Karen wants Simon back?" Aviva asks, without looking up.

And there it is, the question Ruchamah has studiously avoided asking herself since his visit; afraid of the answer. Simon told her he would file for divorce. If he changes his mind, there is little she can do. There will be no more "tastes of Coolidge Corner". She will not have to worry about taking down the laundry that she hung out a line to dry in the summer air. Simon won't be there to see her under-things.

"We're just friends," she tells Aviva.

"Don't you think of Simon as more than a friend?" Aviva almost begs her.

"What's wrong with friendship?" Ruchamah walks into the dining room to set the table.

"Jacob doesn't want to be alone with Karen," Aviva says as she carries in the soup. She can't bring herself to tell her mother how confused she feels, how much she had been counting on having a little brother and a father in her life. She can't tell her that she actually has come to like Simon's wife. Jacob's mother appreciates her company, she talks to her more than Ruchamah does, she has even confided why she left in the first place.

"He needs a chance to get to know her again," Ruchamah is saying. "She's his mother." She ladles some soup into each bowl and takes some of the salad Aviva offers. "Nice dressing," she says.

"Oil and vinegar with some spices I threw in." They eat in silence for a while. "Simon is so uncomfortable," Aviva offers. "I think he wishes Karen would just leave." This is another test to see if her mother will admit that she, too, wants Karen to leave.

"I forgot the bread." Ruchamah gets up so quickly she almost knocks over her chair.

Nothing changes, Aviva thinks. Her mother has been this way for as long as she can remember, which is ever since she realized she didn't have a father. Whenever something goes wrong, her mother acts as if everything is all right. Aviva does the same so as not to upset her.

"I'll be at Lori's," she tells Ruchamah, as soon dinner is over.

"Have a good time," her mother says in a distracted manner. Aviva stares at her for a second. Her mother doesn't seem to be aware that even though things are not changing for herself, they are changing for Aviva. I have a boyfriend, Mom, she wants to tell her. Lori's cousin. That's really why I go there. We might have sex. What do you think of that? Maybe she'll tell her they are already having sex, but she can't bring herself to say something that isn't true only to shock her mother. The restraint she has practiced in their relationship is too ingrained.

Aviva hurries her steps. Lori answers the door as soon as she rings the bell. Ari's sitting in the living room. He stands up as soon as he sees her, a broad smile on his handsome face. Aviva waves slightly. She and Lori will go into Lori's bedroom and talk for a while and then she and Ari will take a walk towards the outskirts of the neighborhood.

At the moment, he seems to be regarding Aviva more as a friend than a girlfriend. He hasn't kissed her again, and has even apologized for doing so the night of the retreat. He has also admitted to having an Israeli girlfriend but says things aren't working out between them. He's not sure when he's returning to Israel and she's not inclined to wait. His parents are Zionists. They are proud of him in a way they never had been since he decided to make *aliyah.*

Aviva has not shared her own feelings. She has not told him she doesn't want him to return to Israel for any reason, that she is torn about her relationship with her mother, with Karen, her relationship with him. Mostly she would like him to kiss her again.

Tonight, as soon as they start on their walk, she takes his arm and wraps it around her waist. Suddenly, she stops, turns her body, her lips seeking his. He begins to kiss her, a deeper and deeper kiss. He lifts her, pulls her tight against his body leaning on the window of the Awesome Ten Nail salon. It's almost 9 o'clock. The store has been closed for hours. Inside a light shines dimly. Aviva closes her eyes.

TWENTY-NINE

Marcia has begun to make a friend of the refrigerator. She opens the door for the third time this morning after breakfast, staring, before she alights on something that attracts her, the last piece of chocolate silk pie. Caloric, of course but the sweat suits she is wearing lately will hide any evidence of the weight she is gaining. She probably won't be able to fit into her wardrobe when she gets called back to work, but then again, the phone has not rung, even with Shoshanah out of commission due to her fall, as her friend from the Sisterhood had informed her. This can only mean the rabbi is now relying totally on Sara, which irks her no end.

Jack has found neither her suggestions nor her insights helpful and has asked her not to come back to the store after the incident with a customer.

This when she hadn't even had a chance to make his operation more efficient. She would have tried before, but on Saturdays she had been at the synagogue checking that arrangements for a *Bar* or *Bat Mitzvah* ran properly. And although she had been tempted to go to the store Saturday afternoons, she didn't think it would look right for a temple administrator to be seen selling liquor on *Shabbat.* She had been so busy then. Now, with nothing to do, every day seems like *Shabbat.*

"I know you meant well," Jack told her as he put his arm around her, "but whatever possessed you to suggest that this customer should be drinking a better quality of wine? Marcia, you don't know my stock or my customers. You asked my best salesperson to take inventory so you could wait on trade. One customer was so irate he stayed until I came back to tell me I should fire my new helper, which is you, Marcia. Please. Please, find another way to spend your time. Volunteer for something. Go visit someone."

She still has Debby and Jeff's key on her key ring from the time she waited at their apartment for their bedroom set delivery while they were on their honeymoon. She could bring over the blouse she picked up for her daughter, a marvelous find from the Basement, but the last time she let herself into their apartment when they weren't supposed to be home, they had taken the day off and came racing from the bedroom suspecting an intruder. Debby told her in no uncertain words to call before dropping in. She can't go there.

She closes the refrigerator and sits down at the table with her piece of chocolate silk pie. It seems to her that her job has been lifted from her as easily as she's lifting this cake fork. She might not have quit. She might actually have been fired! No one has called to offer sympathy, no one had spoken up for her, nor told the rabbi she was invaluable. Not even Ruchamah, whom she has always considered one of her closest friends. After Daniel died, Marcia made all the calls to the congregation and the funeral home for her. She organized the *shiva,* while Ruchamah's parents were en-route from California. Then, she had invited her to come in to the office on the pretext that she could use some help. Sometimes Ruchamah just sat there, her hands in her lap, Aviva in a little carrier at her side. Marcia would practically have to wave a paper in front of her eyes to get her attention. Ruchamah had found it comforting to be around her then. She even said so. In retrospect Marcia recalls that what she actually had said was she found it comforting to be in a place where there was a lot was going on.

Marcia licks the remaining crumbs from her fingers. She had always been pressed for time in the office. Ruchamah, on the other hand, had nothing to do but listen to congregants' worries and complaints. After a while people called the office to see when she was coming in. Even if they took Marcia's advice they gave Ruchamah credit. Rabbi Kramer and Beth depend on her as well. Besides that, she's Beth's best friend. This, Marcia is quite certain, is the source of her trouble. Beth must have told her the rabbi thought she was trying to sabotage his efforts to make Kehillat Shalom a more inclusive community and Ruchamah had taken their side against her since she has not spoken up on her behalf.

Well she doesn't need Ruchamah, or anyone. And in spite of the rabbi's ridiculous idea that she call Rabbi Isaacs, she might just do that. If he were here, she would be in the office right now instead of searching through her desk for her address book so she can dial his number in Florida.

As soon as he answers, Marcia blurts out her story without even asking how he is doing. "I told Rabbi Kramer I wished you were still here," she adds. "Is there any way you would be willing to come back?"

"Leaving Kehillat Shalom might be a blessing for you," he says in response. "It has been for me."

"A blessing?" Marcia is appalled. There is no way losing her job can be anything but a catastrophe.

"When I resigned I had mixed feelings." Rabbi Isaacs continues. "I was no longer the rabbi that Kehillat Shalom needed; the congregants were ready for something new. So, as it turns out, was I."

"But, Rabbi, you and I were a team. The congregants loved you."

"Still, it was the right time for me to go. Didn't you ever think about leaving?"

She hesitates. "I did leave," she admits without going into detail, "but I'm going crazy with boredom waiting until everyone realizes how much they need me. Won't you try to come back?"

"I'm having too much fun. Believe it or not I've taken up golf. I study *Torah* with a group of retired rabbis down here. I can even enjoy a real *Shabbat* now, sitting next to my wife no less. We're going to Israel for the High Holidays. I know that Jack always wanted to travel. You'll be able to do that now. If you ever come to Florida, be sure and stop by to say hello."

When they hang up, Marcia shakes her head. Even Rabbi Isaacs does not understand. Her entire life, except for Debby and Jack, revolves around Kehillat Shalom. The Sisterhood, the book club, the fund-raisers, the couples she and Jack socialized with. She doesn't want to go to Israel. She doesn't want to visit Rabbi Isaacs in Florida.

She heads for the refrigerator again. Where is that piece of banana cream pie? She searches thoroughly, going through every shelf. It's gone. The way her job is gone, the way her friends seem to have deserted her. But there might be some people who don't even know she has been let go. Her old friend, Ida, for instance, whose husband has just been moved into the Hebrew Rehab.

She could warn her not to count on Ruchamah. Aviva would not still be babysitting unless Ruchamah had contrived to remain part of Simon's life. "She's not the goody-goody we all thought she was," she will tell Ida.

She changes out of her housecoat and leaves a note for Jack. "Visiting someone, just as you suggested." She checks Ruchamah's windows as she passes her apartment, craning her neck to see if Simon is visible. No sign of him, but he could still be there.

Ida is slow to come to the door, and opens it only slightly. Her hair is unkempt, her dress looks as if she has slept in it. Marcia's words of greeting die on her lips. She pushes the door open further and barges in. There is work to be done here. Marcia settles herself on the living room sofa. The room is a mess, magazines all over, empty or half-empty tea cups everywhere. Ida must be sick, but no, Ida says. "I'm not sick. A little tired. That's all."

Instead of sitting down with Marcia for a little chat, Ida begins picking up cups and saucers. Marcia helps her carry them into the kitchen and adds them to the pile in the sink. Ida has lost weight as well; that dress is hanging on her. Marcia lifts her eyebrows in disapproval. She might have come just in time to save her old friend, who seems to have perked up now that Marcia is there. Marcia shakes some liquid soap out of its container and begins washing the teacups by hand. Ida dries and puts them away. Into the silence that accompanies their working together Marcia pours an empty chatter about the weather, it's been hotter than usual this August and the way the neighborhood keeps changing so rapidly. She mentions some new stores and restaurants, and then she begins to talk about Nathan. At her husband's name Ida flinches, but Marcia is on a roll here. She goes on for a while about how Nathan never liked change, something she has in common with him, even though, as a member of the synagogue board, she often disagreed with him. She tells Ida that she regrets the arguments she had with him in the past, now that he is so incapacitated. When the dishes are finished Marcia puts the teapot on the stove to boil, almost as if Ida's house is now hers. She is doing a good job of taking Ida's mind off Nathan. Suddenly she notices that Ida's movements have slowed down.

"Sit," she says to Ida. "Sit. We'll have tea." Ida sits.

"Have you seen Ruchamah lately?"

Ida shakes her head.

"I thought she might be too busy to stop by now that she has another interest in her life." She waits for Ida to ask what Ruchamah's interest is, but Ida says nothing. She doesn't even look directly at Marcia.

Marcia ignores her lack of response. "She's busy trying to steal someone else's husband," she says. "You know Simon. Of course you know Simon." And without waiting for an answer, Marcia begins her tale, which expands to the point where it seems that Ruchamah has caused her to be fired and then, as if that wasn't enough, taken advantage of Marcia's matchmaking abilities to try and break up Simon and Karen's marriage now that Karen is back. As she says this aloud she feels certain that this is the truth, even though there is a niggle of doubt in the back of her mind.

"Everyone knows I am the neighborhood matchmaker; people will blame me if this happens. They might even think I've been fired because of it," she says to Ida. "If only you would talk to Ruchamah."

Ida takes a sip of tea. Now she looks at Marcia with interest. Encouraged, Marcia continues. "What we need is a plan," she says. "You have always have such a good effect on her."

Ida puts her teacup down and covers her mouth. Marcia is afraid she has made her ill with this information about Ruchamah, but no. Ida is laughing.

"I had no idea you were so entertaining, Marcia," she says. "Or such a good storyteller." She is up on her feet and removing Marcia's teacup from her. "I wish you could stay and tell me more stories, but I have an appointment." She makes a sound that resembles a chuckle or a stifled cough. Marcia can't quite tell which.

"Oh," Marcia says, a little surprised at the suddenness in which she finds herself at Ida's door. She isn't sure that Ida isn't throwing her out of her house in a polite way, but then Ida probably does have an appointment, probably with one of Nathan's doctors. Perhaps she should have said a bit more about the rabbi, tell her that she had called Rabbi Isaacs. She could ask Ida, who she's sure isn't so pleased with Rabbi Kramer's performance either, if she thinks they should do something, about him, such as hire a new rabbi. Yes, that's more in line with what she should have said to Ida. Well, she'll mention it to a few others. In fact, she'll start with the next Sisterhood meeting and see where it goes from there.

THIRTY

Karen sits next to Jacob on the floor of his room, leafing through a book of boats. Beside her is a selection of tempera paints and brushes. She breathes a sigh of relief when Aviva arrives.

"I was thinking of painting a mural on Jacob's walls. Look, I have pictures of boats and children playing on a beach. What do you think?" She hands Aviva the book.

Aviva shows the pictures to Jacob and he shakes his head no. "What would you like, Jacob?" He shrugs his shoulders and lifts his hands, palms up. He doesn't know.

"This is his favorite book." Aviva gets *Mike Mulligan and his Steam Shovel* from Jacob's shelf and hands it to Karen.

"Okay," Karen says, "Jacob, do you want trucks and construction equipment on your walls?" Jacob looks at Aviva and gives a huge smile.

"I think that's a yes," Aviva says.

"A construction theme it is then," Karen says. "And Jacob, one of your puzzles might do as a model."

Jacob stares at his mother as she speaks. He makes no response except to move closer to Aviva when she tells him his room is going to be beautiful. Jacob is always so happy to be with Aviva. His face lights up as soon as she walks into their house. If only he felt that way towards her, Karen thinks, but he still pulls away when she tries to hug him, he refuses to let her bathe him, and if it weren't for Simon's insistence, he would never let her read him a bed time story. Even so, Simon has to read him another as soon as she finishes.

"Why don't you take Jacob to the playground," she tells Aviva. "I'll have all the Mike Mulligan equipment drawn by the time you come back. And tomorrow, I'll paint them in."

"Jacob and I can paint with you."

"That's okay. It will go faster if I do it myself."

She doesn't catch Aviva's look of dismay, doesn't realize that Aviva's suggestion would help Jacob feel closer to her.

Karen and Aviva watch as he runs to get his sneakers, sits down and puts them on his feet by himself. He begins trying to tie the laces and gets as far as making two knots. He makes a face and lifts his feet. Karen bends to help him but he twists his body away from her towards Aviva.

"Look, now all you need to do is make two loops like this." Aviva makes two loops on one of the sneakers and shows him how to hold the loops so they don't fall apart. She finishes tying them. As he stands up the phone rings.

"Marcia?" Karen says into the phone. "Yes I do know who you are. Today? I could. "Thank you for asking me," Karen says, getting her pocketbook and handing Aviva some money so she and Jacob can buy some pizza on their way back from the playground. "I'll leave Mrs. Katz's number on the refrigerator. And later this afternoon, maybe the three of us can make cookies. I'll pick up the ingredients on my way back from lunch."

She hums a little as she draws Jacob's trucks on the wall of his room. Still humming, she steps into the shower. It will be wonderful to have someone to talk to. She knows Marcia slightly, having spoken with her in the office just before Jacob's *bris,* although she never set foot in the synagogue after that.

Marcia heaps potato salad onto Karen's plate, adds a roast beef sandwich topped with coleslaw and Russian dressing and watches as Karen pushes the food around on her plate. Such a skinny thing. She probably eats rabbit food. Marcia has decided to broach the subject of Ruchamah and Simon by filling her in on synagogue events throughout lunch, touting the benefits of the Sisterhood over that fringy *Rosh Hodesh* group, of which Aviva's mother is a member. She begins *kvelling* about Simon's musicianship, the way he has been taking care of Jacob during Karen's unfortunate absence, how good it is that she has come back and what a shame Jacob isn't talking. Karen cringes, but manages a smile. She is determined to make a friend of Marcia even though she finds her lack of delicacy and tact offensive.

Karen would like to contribute something to their conversation, but Marcia seems determined to do all the talking. After a while she finds herself murmuring a kind of "uh-huh" to show she's listening. She stops blanking out, however when the subject turns to, "Someone who is taking Simon's attentions personally."

Karen sets her coffee cup down. "Personally?" she asks.

"Ruchamah, Aviva's mother, the woman from the *Rosh Hodesh* group I mentioned before. Have you met her?"

Karen shakes her head.

"Aviva's mother. She's a widow who has set her sight on Simon like a newly focused telescope. Before you returned she spent a lot of time with Jacob when Aviva couldn't be there and he seems to have really taken to her. It's a good thing you've returned to fight for what belongs to you," Marcia continues, noting with satisfaction that ~~that~~ Karen has blanched at her words. "I don't want to interfere, but I wouldn't want you to be hurt now that you have come back to work things out with Simon." She leaves out the fact that she has played matchmaker and encouraged Simon and Ruchamah as she sets a slice of Debby's wedding cake that she defrosted earlier in front of Karen. "I'm sentimental," she adds. "I think marriage is

231

a blessing, my marriage to Jack, especially, and if there's anything I can do, talk to Ruchamah or whatever, I will be only too happy to do it."

Karen's headache begins as soon as Marcia started talking and it doesn't go away on her way home. She feels contaminated by the information Marcia has given her. Had there been a chance to respond, she would have told Marcia she had not come back to fight another woman for her husband. When she passes Ruchamah's apartment she stops. What Marcia said has no validity. Simon couldn't be interested in another woman. He's not even interested in being with her. He still sleeps in that little studio room, even though sleeping together was something they had both enjoyed. The next minute she is walking up the steps of Ruchamah's building and ringing her apartment from the foyer.

"Karen?" Ruchamah repeats, obviously taken aback. "Is something wrong?" Has something happened to Aviva or Jacob?"

"No. Not at all. I didn't mean to alarm you." Ruchamah is silent and Karen is at a loss to explain her presence. She can't tell her that Marcia has implied they are enemies, two women fighting over the same man. "I just wanted to stop by and tell you what a wonderful daughter you have," she improvises quickly.

"Thank you." Ruchamah answers. She doesn't invite Karen in.

Despite her disbelief, Karen decides she should check to see for herself if what Marcia told her could possibly be true. "Would you mind if I came up for a minute? I'm thinking of getting Aviva a present but I have no idea what she might like." There is a momentary silence before Ruchamah buzzes her in.

As she approaches a turn in the stairway Karen sees Ruchamah standing outside her open door. Ruchamah is nothing like what she imagined from Marcia's description. She's almost as tall as Simon, she is not wearing makeup and has done nothing to enhance her appearance by that loose fitting tee shirt that doesn't emphasize her figure. Besides, she appears to be several years older than Simon, though Karen is not sure, that could be due to her lack of make-up. He could not possibly find her appealing. Although that's not exactly what Marcia said. She implied that Ruchamah was interested in him.

"Are you sure everything is okay?" Ruchamah asks.

"Absolutely," Karen says. They stand in the doorway regarding each other. Ruchamah recovers first and asks Karen if she would like some coffee or tea to drink.

"Tea, thank you." Karen sits alone on the living room sofa while Ruchamah goes into the kitchen. Ruchamah's apartment is dark, the furniture heavy with a stateliness Karen admires, though she herself prefers a more sleek and contemporary style. The décor, Victorian, seems fitting. The furnishings mirror Ruchamah's obvious solidity. Nothing chic about them.

Ruchamah reappears with a tray and places it on the marble-topped table with brass filigree edging. All talk is centered on choices, "sugar, lemon, milk, scones," which suits Karen just fine as it buys her time to think about what she should say.

"Jacob is having so much fun with Aviva," Karen begins. "I just want to express my gratitude." And you, she thinks, you must be a wonderful mother to have such a daughter. Unlike me, who can't take care of my own son and who can't do without Aviva, even for one day."

"I'm sure she'd appreciate anything you give her," Ruchamah says. "The two of us have different tastes. I usually have to ask."

"I have the feeling that if I ask her, she will say she doesn't need anything, and I'm sure she doesn't."

"She enjoys music," Ruchamah offers.

"Then I'll get her a few CD's."

Ruchamah nods. Karen is as ethereal looking in person as she is in her photographs. And gentle, not at all like a person who would walk out on her child. She is struck by the irony of Karen dropping in like this, a repetition of Simon's visit a few nights before, but with a completely different agenda. Perhaps Simon said something to her. She doesn't believe Karen is here solely for the reason she claims.

"These scones are so buttery." Karen brushes aside the feeling she should leave now. She has an answer to her question about a gift for Aviva and has no other stated purpose for being here.

"Aviva made them. Baking is not my forte."

"I'm not a great baker either. Actualy, it turns out my only gift seems to be for drawing. I like color and design."

"Is that your field?"

"I don't actually have a field. Simon is the one who's gifted. When we were music students I sang, but I have terrible stage fright."

"I can understand that. I find it hard to get up in front of an audience," Ruchamah admits. Karen looks puzzled. "When I read my translations."

"We have that in common," Karen says. She's certain now that Marcia was wrong. If Ruchamah had set her sights on Simon she would be able to tell by her demeanor. Ruchamah would be hostile, serving up barbed comments instead of scones.

She sets her teacup down. "Thank you so much for your hospitality. I should leave. I promised Jacob I would pick up the ingredients for baking cookies."

Karen goes immediately to The Musicsmith and enlists the sales girl's help.

"Is she anything like me?" the teenager asks, indicating her pierced eyebrows and tongue.

Karen shakes her head.

"Not everyone likes the same groups even if they are in the same genre. How about a gift certificate?

"That's a good idea," Karen tells her. "She can pick out what she likes herself." Impulsively she makes the value of gift certificate almost twice as much as the cost of a few CD's. After all, she would never be able to take care of Jacob by herself. And besides, she told Ruchamah she wanted to get a gift for Aviva. Why not make it a really nice one?

She's almost home when she realizes she has forgotten to stop at the market. She has no idea that Aviva and Jacob had returned to the house almost as soon as she left because Jacob dropped a piece of pizza on his lap. Aviva had to put the left over pizza in a box and carry it home so he could change his clothes.

She could not have predicted that Jacob would be mesmerized by the trucks, backhoes and cranes on his wall. They are all different sizes, some drawn low enough he can trace them with his hand. His construction puzzle lies on the floor. He keeps taking the pieces out and matching them to the drawings on his wall.

Nor does she know that Simon has returned home early from work. Jacob grabbed his hand and pulled him into the room to see his mural, executed so carefully and with so much loving detail. A sliver of hope had ignited in Simon's chest and was quickly gone as he remembered how happy he had been at the thought of his beautiful wife becoming their child's beautiful mother and how devastated he was when she left. He is not ready to believe her latest incarnation. But he intends to tell her he appreciates the efforts she is making when she gets home.

Ever since Karen came back, his heart had been divided between his son's needs and his own. He has avoided Ruchamah since the night of his visit but it is she who consumes his thoughts. He ignores Karen, as she lies in the next room although the night he kissed Ruchamah he felt such a stirring of desire he almost wandered into the bedroom to reach for her.

So after putting Jacob to bed that night, he feels ready to have the conversation with Karen that he's been avoiding.

When he goes into the living room, she turns a bright and smiling face towards him. She doesn't mention visiting either Marcia or Ruchamah. Although she doesn't believe Marcia's allegations against Ruchamah, she can see how Simon might be intrigued by her calm and comforting presence. This has made Simon newly precious to her. While he puts Jacob to bed, her thoughts turn to how loving he has always been in the past, how supportive of her endeavors, though none have been successful. There is no one else in her life who loves her unconditionally. Simon is a rare person. Someone worth keeping.

She tells him that Jacob will soon be in school full time and that she intends to get a part-time job. It was only having to be alone with Jacob for hours and hours when he was a baby, when he cried all the time and she couldn't comfort him. She thought she was losing her mind. And she was ashamed. She doesn't know if other women feel this way. She was always afraid. She touches his arm as she talks to him. When Simon asks her what she was afraid of, she says she doesn't know. She has always been that way. She takes his hand.

"What did you do when I left?" she asks. "Was there another woman? Is there another woman?"

THIRTY-ONE

Nathan is walking in a straight line, holding his body as erectly as possible. He is on the lookout for his wife whose name he has been trying desperately to recall. She looks something like this blonde woman who has been trailing him ever since he left what he is quite sure is a hotel room, but it has no phone and he is clear that the woman at his side was not in the room with him when he closed the door. He thinks he might have been in the wrong room since he can recall a man lying in the next bed. This is unusual and also he has never stayed in a room with twin beds. He sleeps in a large bed with his wife.

He searches in his pocket. Now he can't find his room key. Lately he has been losing things. There is something very wrong with this situation;

something he needs to figure out. He thinks he is on a business trip of some kind but doesn't recall how he traveled here. Did he fly or take a train? Perhaps he drove. He is probably in New York.

Someone takes his arm, the woman who has been trailing him. He stiffens. "It's all right, Nathan," she says and smiles. "Shall we walk together?"

Maybe she is his wife. He's not quite sure, and if she is, then he is not lost. And she is holding the keys. Good. His room key is probably there, too.

"Nathan," the woman with the keys addresses him now. "In a few minutes your wife will be here. Your friend, Simon, is giving a concert in your honor today."

But Nathan is concerned about his room key and he reaches for the loop of keys she has in her hand.

"We need this one," she says reassuringly and opens the door to the section for Alzheimer's residents.

Ida hasn't slept alone since they were married; she has to pull Nathan's pillow over to her side of the bed where she embraces it and holds it to her heart. It is an inadequate reminder of how good it felt to sleep next to him each night. In the past few years it was just to cuddle as their lovemaking evolved from the fiery passion of their younger years to a more romantic pleasure. Honestly, she wouldn't mind sleeping at the Rehab with him, but there's not an empty bed in the place, the demand is so high. Now he shares quarters with a gentleman, also afflicted with Alzheimer's. The men ignore each other, taking care not to bump when they cross the room, waiting for the other to come out of the bathroom. Their mannerly selves have persevered, vestiges of their former personas.

Sometimes when Ida visits, Nathan ignores her, busying himself reading and rereading the same section of the newspaper. It is then that the exhaustion, which is always with her these days, assails her. She is tired of having to visit Nathan, tired of being alone at night. Tired. After the day center told her they could no longer guarantee Nathan's safety and recommended round-the-clock placement, she had tried with even greater diligence to care for him at home. Occasionally Nathan would get up in the middle of the night to make himself a cup of warm milk and forget to turn off the stove. One morning he dropped a towel over the burner. When she saw the corner of the towel catching fire, she began to scream at him and found she couldn't stop. The next morning Nathan swung at her as she tried to help him lace his shoes. Martin, who had come early to work on their finances, witnessed this and stepped in between his father and her.

Nothing has been the same since. Sometimes, before she goes to the Rehab she takes long walks in the neighborhood and stops to buy supper on the way back, but the Butcherie only has food packaged for two or more. Often she just buys bread and soup. Lately, Ida has begun to feel more and more angry, even though Nathan is the one who is suffering. He is the one who had to leave their home. She resents him even though she knows he can't help it. She told Shoshanah this the other day, hoping to be talked out of feeling so negative. Shoshanah, still lying on her living room floor several hours a day, discouraged because her back was taking so long to heal, got up to put both arms around her. "I love you," she said. "Your resentment and anger will fade in their own time."

Ida can't imagine how long that might take. Susan keeps calling with suggestions of things to do. Maybe her mother could volunteer somewhere, take classes, do art projects. After the scene they had the other day it is even hard for Ida to want to spend time with her daughter. Susan had brought her some fresh flowers to cheer her up. Ida was cheered. "Your father always brought me flowers," she said. "Every Friday night, for birthdays and anniversaries, often for no reason and at all."

"I know, Mom. Dad was great that way."

"Please, don't say 'was', Susan."

"You don't seem to want to know that Dad is only going to get worse. You have to face that. Everyone says it's best to be aware of what's going to happen."

"I don't know who 'everyone' is. They didn't ask me."

"Mom you continue to live in your dreams. You sit in the house as if you're waiting for dad to come home and be just fine once again. You must know that can't happen. This disease does not reverse itself. I hate seeing you so upset, hoping for the impossible."

"And why aren't you upset, Susan? This is your father."

241

"I am upset, but I'm prepared. You should be too. You'll be able to cope better."

"Isn't it enough that I know in my heart where the future lies? It's no secret, what's happening with your father." Ida threw up her hands and ran into the bedroom.

She didn't hear Susan leave. Nor did she know that Susan had gone straight to the Rehab to wait until Jan could squeeze her in to her hectic schedule.

"You've heard this before?" Susan says after recounting what had just passed with her mother.

"Most experts think that information will help, but your mom clearly doesn't want to know the details. Susan, your mother is no ostrich. She's fully aware, but she doesn't want to talk about it. The future is far too bleak."

"My brother won't even discuss this; he hardly comes to see our father." Susan burst into tears, crying so hard she had trouble catching her breath. Jan suggested that another family conference might help and told Susan she would call Martin herself to set something up. Only then could Susan bring herself to leave the office. She put a bright, if forced, smile on her face and went upstairs to see her father.

Ida selects her pink chiffon dress and places her anniversary pearls around her neck. Simon is dedicating a special performance for Nathan at the Rehab today. Everyone is doing so much. Too much. Ruchamah comes to visit Nathan with her. The *Rosh Hodesh* group constantly checks in.

Even Marcia callls her. But nothing anyone does relieves her anguish.

In the car, she turns to Simon, setting down the strudel she's baked for later on her lap. "I hope you know how much Nathan will appreciate this, even though he might not realize that you're doing it especially for him.

"I'm happy to do it. The Alzheimer's has not affected his love of music. Did you know he was always telling me, after Karen left, that I should find someone like you?"

Ida laughs and some of the pressure in her chest eases. "Nathan loved to give advice," she says, "free or otherwise."

"I should have gotten divorced," Simon says. "He told me that, too, you know."

"No, I didn't know that," Ida says.

As they pull into the parking lot, he says, "I'll get my violin and music and begin setting up while you get Nathan." He opens Ida's door.

She leans over and kisses him on the cheek before climbing out. "I hope you always have the best in life, Simon. Nobody deserves that more than you." She gives him a brief wave as she enters the building, her package of strudel grasped in her hands.

When she reaches Nathan's room she finds him struggling to put on the clip-on bow tie she bought to replace his hand-tied ones.

"What is this contraption," he yells as soon as he sees her. Ida is taken aback until she remembers Nathan is always irritated with her before he seems to recognize her, although her name never leaves his lips.

"A bow tie. I thought you would like something new for Simon's concert." She avoids telling him that he can't knot the real bow ties anymore, nor can the nurses and aides who are not used to them.

She takes the bow tie from him and clips it on. "You look very handsome."

"Thank you." He touches her pearls and smiles. Tears come to her eyes.

"Simon has a surprise for you," she says as they walk out the door.

"Wait," Nathan says. Where are my keys?"

"Don't worry. I have them," she holds onto his arm as they walk to the elevator. It's one-thirty, but she wants to be sure they can get front row seats for the concert which will start at two. Nathan has always insisted upon being early.

Within the half-hour the large auditorium fills with residents and staff seated in the chairs provided, with numerous wheelchairs wedged in between. Devorah, the activity director, makes a few announcements and then introduces Simon, citing, among his accomplishments, his acclaimed concert at Jordan Hall.

"I came today to honor my friend and fellow music lover, Nathan Tenenbaum," he says, and adds a slight bow, "Nathan, this concert is dedicated to you."

Ida touches his arm and points to Simon; Nathan nods his head.

Ida reaches for his hand.

Simon introduces his students. They are dressed, as Simon has requested, in white shirts and black pants. The men wear black clip-on bow ties. "Look, Ida says. "They're wearing ties, just like yours Nathan."

"Our first piece is Mozart's Clarinet Quintet in A, featuring Jonah Greene on clarinet," Simon announces. "We'll play the first and last movements. Listen for strains of East Side, West Side in the opening bars. Mozart thought of the clarinet as the instrument most like the human voice, and you can hear it sing its way through the quintet."

When the music stops, he waits for the applause to subside before introducing Schon Rosmarin by Fritz Kreisler as he brings on Han Chin, a piano major who will accompany him. "Originally this piece was accredited it to an obscure composer, but years later Kreisler owned up to having written it himself. A pompous music critic accused him of unethical conduct. In a display of chutzpah, Kreisler challenged him to write something this good if he thought it was so simple. Listen to his musical description of a beautiful young girl. Kreisler paints the portrait in only two minutes."

Simon picks up his violin and Ida finds herself traveling back in time to the first date she had with Nathan. They waited in line for an hour before the Boston Symphony Orchestra box office opened, having been immediately drawn to each other at the wedding of mutual friends only a few days earlier. Far too shy to embrace in order to ward off the wind and cold, they shivered as they stood in line. "This must be our lucky night," Nathan said when they finally made it inside the lobby. "The BSO sets aside 100 'rush seats' for each concert, and two have been left just for us." That's how they came to hear Fritz Kreisler in person, far above the stage in the last row of the balcony. For a moment Ida almost forgets where they are. Today, Simon is their Fritz Kreisler.

The concert winds up with a medley of Klezmer music. Simon places his violin under his chin and begins to solo in the opening strains. The notes circle around and around, making curlicues like smoke in the air until he moves into the familiar strains of Romania, Romania, Romania with Jonah's clarinet sharing the lead. Nathan's face is alive with delight; his foot begins to tap to this spirited jazz-like music of Yiddish speaking Eastern-Europe so often played at weddings. Nathan's cousin, also from Germany, used to be embarrassed by Nathan's love of this low-brow style. It was one of the few times Nathan could not have cared less about falling off the cultural high road. Near the end of the concert when the music moves into a delirious tempo, Nathan raises his fist and shouts "Setz" before each repetition of "aye diga didi dum."

Following a standing ovation, for those who could stand, the audience files out to a rousing reprise of Romania, leaving only the musicians, Ida and Nathan behind. Simon hops off the stage to embrace Nathan. "So, how did you like your concert?"

"Good," Nathan says, patting Simon on the arm. "Very good."

"I hear there's something for us in the next room. Come," Simon says as he and Ida walk with Nathan between them into a small dining room to a celebratory dessert table, complete with Ida's home-baked apple strudel.

"Simon, you sounded like Mickey Katz today." Nathan surprises everyone with his comment after a bite of the strudel. "Ida, remember when I insisted you join me to go hear Mickey Katz sing Yiddish songs at the Opera House? He takes a second bite of strudel and just as inexplicably gets lost in his thoughts. A slight smile never leaves his lips.

Soon, Simon packs up his violin and begins to say goodbye to his students. "Ida, I'm ready to go whenever you are. He walks over to Nathan to hug him goodbye.

Nathan takes Ida's arm. "We have reservations at Schrafft's. Simon will you join us?" Ida is taken aback. The Coolidge Corner Schrafft's has been closed for years. But after this lovely concert she can't bring herself to tell this to Nathan. Nor does she know how to explain they are not eating dinner together tonight. He will go back to his floor and she will go home. Ida looks around helplessly. Devorah comes over and puts her arm around Nathan.

"Mr. Tenenbaum, why don't you come with me."

Nathan pushes her away. "I'm going to Schrafft's with my wife and friend."

Simon crosses the room to Nathan. "I have to go home to Jacob soon, but first let me tell you a funny story about Fritz Kreisler's wife and her conversation with the impresario, Boris Godolvsky."

"Fritz Kreisler. How is he?" Nathan asks as Simon steers him towards the elevator as Simon looks over his shoulder at Ida and signals her to wait.

As soon as Simon brings her home, she calls Devorah who assures her that Nathan is okay.

She puts down the phone and wipes her eyes with one of Nathan's old handkerchiefs. She wads it into a ball and throws it across the room, then retrieves it. Being this angry won't help, she tells herself. But at least if you're going to throw something, find something heavier than a handkerchief.

THIRTY-TWO

D ear Elijah,
       The adoption forum is in a few hours. I feel like celebrating already but I'll wait until it's over. I came to the office early and found myself alone with Rabbi Kramer, except for the few congregants who were wandering in and out. I took calls about the forum, then looked over the latest Bulletin, which I had helped prepare. It was quite sparse, filled mostly with mention of the holidays. Beginning with *Rosh HaShanah*, almost every day until *Simchat Torah* is filled with some kind of ritual observance. There were many calls for tickets; I referred them to the announcement in the Bulletin: "Tickets will be mailed out a week before *Rosh Ha Shannah*. I wonder who will mail them.

At lunchtime I went out to the garden to pick a small bouquet of flowers to put into the vase on my desk, actually Marcia's desk. I was filling a little paper cup from the large bottle of spring water that occupies a small space in back of the office, when the rabbi came in to pick up a copy of the Bulletin. When he sat down in the chair at the side of Marcia's desk to read it I filled a cup for him.

"Thank you," he said, setting the Bulletin aside. He drank quickly. "You do so much, Sara. Frankly I don't know how we could manage without you. You have become an integral part of the Kehillat Shalom community. You must find us overwhelming." He has no idea. His face was lined with fatigue, his shoulders slumped. He has come to the main office every day since Shoshanah's accident to respond to congregants, without much success as he has had to listen to their questions about his "almost absence," as they call it. "I haven't been myself lately," he said. I stopped myself from admitting that I hadn't been my true self lately, either.

"I'm sorry," I said. "I hope things get better for you soon." I almost felt guilty knowing that soon I would be abandoning him. I was tempted to reassure him that things were going to improve. Shoshanah would be back tomorrow and, after tonight his anxiety would disappear, his marriage would be restored to the way it once was. I wanted him to know that it was his office volunteer, Sara, a.k.a Serach, who had engineered his future happiness, but, of course, I could not tell him that. "Since I've began volunteering," I said instead, "I've come to appreciate how inclusive Kehillat Shalom is." I bit my lip to keep from blurting out that it even harbored a spirit. His face lit up. This might be my best intervention yet, a bit of conversation, a lot of praise.

I extolled everything from the new prayer book that the congregants had created to Shoshanah's cantillation class. I told him I was impressed that so many congregants besides me volunteered and that I had taken it upon myself to plant a few rose bushes in the garden. "I hope no one minds," I said, "even though I'm not a member of the garden club." Whatever entered my mind, left my lips. I listed the various and sundry social action endeavors I had seen first hand, ending with, "You even have an adoption forum tonight."

His entire demeanor changed. "You know," he said standing up, "I think I should return to my office and get rid of that paper pile on my desk."

As you have often told me, Elijah, "Less is more" but unfortunately I seem unable to remember that.

Later that afternoon, Beth came to the office. "What a lovely bouquet" she said, noting the flowers on my desk. "Are they from the garden?" I nodded

"Tonight's the adoption forum," she told me. "Hillel and I are going."

"There's been a lot of interest," I said. "Attendance should be good."

"I could help out for a while I'm waiting for Hillel." Beth took calls, some about the forum, some about holiday tickets, added paper to the Xerox machine, found a library book someone had dropped off and, instead of returning it to the library, sat down to read. I looked at the clock. Almost five. The

251

forum was at seven. The office would close soon. Beth told me she was going to freshen up a bit and that perhaps she and the rabbi would go for a walk before the meeting. A few minutes later she was back clutching a note and looking very upset. "Hillel left this. He said he'd meet me later. Do you know where he went?"

I felt myself blanch. "No," I said, as calmly as possible. "I'm sure he'll be back soon. He always pops in to say goodbye. But since you're waiting for him, could you keep an eye on things for a few minutes? I have to run an errand." And with that I grabbed my satchel and flew out of the office.

I should have been paying closer attention. And I should have been faster. Hillel was sitting in his car, which had been parked outside the synagogue, and pulled away just as I ran down steps. He drove around the block, returned to the synagogue, stopped the car, but did not get out. I threw on my traveling cloak and slipped in. Perhaps he'll change his mind, I thought. We could both just sit here for a minute so he can gather himself together before we go back inside.

Instead, he started the car again, drove to the highway this time and followed a route I knew well. It was still early, however. He would have about fifteen minutes to visit, although why he had chosen to do so at this time, I had no idea.

He parked in the Rehab parking lot and went in to the reception desk. I was right behind him. He asked for Nathan and took the elevator to his room. Nathan was sitting on the edge of his bed staring at the television set overhead. When the rabbi greeted him, he seemed surprised.

"I'm Rabbi Kramer from Kehillat Shalom." The synagogue name didn't register either. "Your synagogue," Hillel said. Nathan nodded. "I'm your rabbi."

Nathan frowned.

"I thought we might say a few prayers together. I brought a *siddur.* The old one. The one you were used to. I remember that you don't much like the new one."

"No." Nathan said. But he shook his head yes, which both the rabbi and I interpreted to mean he didn't like the new *siddur* but he didn't mind listening to a prayer from the old one. The rabbi sat down on the bed next to Nathan and opened to the *Sh'ma. "Sh'ma Yisrael.*..."Hear Oh Israel. The Lord is my God. The Lord is One." Nathan recited each word along with him. I sat in the back of the room checking the clock on the wall. After the recitation of the *sh'ma,* other prayers followed, some in Hebrew, some in English, all of which Nathan knew. The clock's hands pointed towards six. If we didn't leave soon, Hillel would be late. But he didn't seem to be in a hurry. He seemed relaxed, content, peaceful, as if he was supposed to be here saying prayers with Nathan. And although I was desperate for him to leave, at the same time I was without a sense of urgency. This was the first time the rabbi had visited Nathan. If he could do this, he could do anything, I was certain. We had all the time in the world although we had no time at all. Nathan stopped reading.

"Martin?" he asked, looking carefully at Hillel.

"Hillel," the rabbi told him. Nathan repeated his name.

"It's a simple thing after all, isn't it?" Hillel said, more to himself than to Nathan. "All I had to do is show up."

"Simple," Nathan nodded agreement. Hillel stood up. He would be late, but we could still get there.

We pulled out of the parking lot, past the Rehab and drove down the highway in the opposite direction of the synagogue. I tried to read his thoughts. His mind was blank, open to receive whatever would enter. Adoption Forum. I concentrated. Adoption Forum. He turned on the radio and pressed his foot down on the accelerator and all was lost at that moment, Elijah. All was lost.

Hillel drove away from the synagogue for hours. I could not influence him to come back until the forum was well over and he had almost run out of gas. It was after midnight before he finally went home.

I've been sitting in the synagogue garden all night wondering what to do. It's clear I have lacked your kindness and compassion, Elijah. Sometimes I see you looking down at earth with tears in your eyes. Each time a baby is born, you're happy for the new life yet sad because the world is in such dire straits you're afraid for the child. It always seemed to me that you suffered from being sentimental.

You accused me of being heartless as well as mindless. Perhaps you were right. After you left I was determined to prove that my "messing around in the congregants' lives" as you so succinctly put it, hadn't harmed anyone. I decided to find a way to send Karen home. My loyalty lay with Ruchamah and Aviva. I didn't expect to like her. I happened to be at her house the day Simon was so furious with her, both for leaving and for coming back. And I found myself wanting to defend her. "She couldn't help it," I whispered, knowing that if I had ever had a child, I would not have had to leave her because I couldn't care for her. In my time there were always women who would have come to my aid. The women of Kehillat Shalom would have helped Karen, too, but obviously she hadn't been able to ask anyone. Now she has a chance to make things right with her son. Even my heartless self couldn't interfere with that. And as soon as I realized I was unable to rely on an act of will to carry out my plans, my self-confidence left me. Oh, I tried. I went to everyone's house with one idea or another.

When Ruchamah sent Simon away, I stood outside thinking, no. Simon, go back. Ruchamah, call him back. I concentrated all my energy, but my plan for the two of them disintegrated before my eyes. When Marcia threatened to have Hillel fired, I went to the Sisterhood intending to speak up for him, if only as the office volunteer. It wasn't necessary. Shoshanah spoke in his defense. I was furious at Marcia, who had gone to Ida's for the sole purpose of badmouthing Ruchamah, but I thought her desire for revenge might have been my fault. I should have curbed my impulse to compete with her although I would not have minded had she left of her own volition. Wasn't Ida magnificent? The way she "guided" Marcia out of the house? Still, that didn't change the fact that she was suffering. It no longer mattered that I had intended no harm. And I thought about how angels bend over each blade of grass. Did you mean to imply that angels bend with care to keep their balance so the grass is never crushed? I think that's what you must have meant, Elijah.

When you came to the baby naming, and I declared that my plans would work, I already had half an idea that this might not be so. My life used to be predictable. You would send me out to a synagogue, I would come back in three days, having accomplished some kind of repair. I knew exactly what to do and how to do it. I know I should accept the fact that I have not been able to accomplish this at Kehillat Shalom and return to the Garden, but Elijah, I feel as if I belong here. As Serach, I may have ruined things, but as Sara, I have an impeccable reputation. I'm a caring, helpful, industrious, even interesting person, everything I'm not when I'm in the Garden. There are things I can still do, like keep an eye on Aviva. I worry when she's with Ari. I would feel better if she could talk to her mother about him. And there's Ida. I want to do a few things to help her. Water her plants. Keep the sink clear. Make her a little soup. This is what I've learned. Small things like soup, are a whisper of a blessing and sometimes huge in a person's life.

If I stay, I can keep working in the office. At the very least I can send out the holiday tickets, although Marcia hasn't told anyone where they are.

The me that is both Serach and Sara would like to be here for the High Holidays to hear the sound of the *Shofar* and imagine becoming a legitimate member of this community. Though I've constantly interfered in the congregants' lives, even Serach has a place here. A rabbi, in a synagogue I swept through once, told his congregation there was room for everyone in a community. "Even the most annoying person provides an opportunity for others to complain." If anyone knew who I really was, I'm sure I could fulfill that role.

Kehillat Shalom sent the old pews in my hideout to a synagogue that serves as a shelter in New Orleans after Katrina struck. For now they're being used as temporary beds, just as I used them. The rabbi may continue to be distracted, but the social action committee is raising money to help the hurricane victims. I don't mind sleeping on a few of the extra stacking chairs they keep here. There's always plenty of food and enough donated pieces of clothing to make it worth my while. Besides, Kehillat Shalom has a garden. Not as large as ours, but there are more people to tend it. Shoshanah often eats her lunch here.

She's coming into the garden now. She waves, I wave back. She bends to smell the roses that I planted. Shoshanah, I find myself whispering, perhaps you can get through to the rabbi. Perhaps you will find a way to comfort Beth. She looks up startled, almost as if she has heard. I take a deep breath. A breeze envelops the garden.

Serach

THIRTY-TI IREE

"Shoshanah? What are you doing here on your first day back to work?" Beth opens her door, her consternation evident.

"You called in sick. I was worried." Shoshanah steps into the house and hands her a small bouquet of roses. Beth looks exhausted; her face is drawn and colorless.

"Thank you." Beth holds them up to her nose as she takes them. "These smell so sweet. Let me get a vase."

"They're from the synagogue garden," Shoshanah calls, as she sits down on the mauve love seat in the living room. "I'm not sure I should have picked them but when I went out to the garden they looked so inviting. Sara was there, too, sitting on a bench, writing a letter, I think. When I reached down to cut the roses, a light breeze started up. The letter Sara was writing didn't stir, but her skirt lifted. I could have sworn I heard her say your name. The breeze got stronger. I felt impelled towards your house."

"I've been worried about you as well," Beth calls back as she open a cupboard in the kitchen. "Your injury was pretty serious. It's just like you to check up on me, Shoshanah." In truth, she wishes Shoshanah had not come. She feels a kind of desperation and hopelessness today that she doesn't want anyone to observe.

"I don't quite feel like myself though," Shoshanah says, more to herself than to Beth. Her accident has affected her in ways she could not have predicted. This morning, for example, she came to work early, completed vocalizing and intended to plunge into her usual activities. The rabbi had also come in early to welcome her back. "Don't do too much, today," he said. She assumed he was being polite but when she passed the main office, she noted Hillel already deeply involved in conversations with several congregants and didn't stop. She went to her own office and closed the door thinking she was probably not completely ready to have returned. Sitting in her chair she began to drift, to dream, as she had when she was incapacitated. Melodies she had never heard before came tumbling into her mind and she found herself singing them aloud, taking notes, as if this was her only work, to create beautiful *nigunim* for the congregation. When she finally told her mother about her fall, she did not offer to come. "All my presence will do is encourage you to return to Kehillat Shalom more quickly than you should so you can resume the rabbi's work as well as your own. No, my darling, I will stay where I am for the time being and come to see you once you have recovered and please, take your time."

"I like your sculpture of women dancing together," she says as Beth reenters the living room holding a clear glass vase in which the bouquet nestles. She sets it on the marble coffee table.

"One of the mother's from the pre-school is in the *Rosh Hodesh* group. She gave it to me last week," Beth says.

"I've been wanting to come, but....."

"You should, Shoshanah. The women are supportive and no tales are told outside the group. Sometimes I wish I weren't the rabbi's wife so I could speak freely. Can I get you anything?"

"Just some water, thanks." Shoshanah follows her into the kitchen. "Is there anything I can do for you?"

You could go back to the synagogue and take care of the preschool, Beth thinks; she can't bear to look at everyone else's children today. "You do too much already," she says instead. "Even flat on your back, you've managed to talk to almost every congregant while my husband and I tried to resolve our personal problems. That is ridiculous if you think about it."

"It's probably not ridiculous."

"Just a little inconvenient?" Beth shakes her head. "You don't have to be polite, Shoshanah."

"All right. A little inconvenient." She grins. And yawns.

"Working at Kehillat Shalom should be exhilarating, not exhausting. Maybe that's why you got hurt. You have to talk to Hillel before you burn yourself out. That's why I'm home today. Taking time to rest." Not really resting; just obsessing, Beth is inclined to tell her. Only Ruchamah knows how discouraged she has become. "I feel as if I've caught something from Hillel," she told her. "A malady that renders me incapable of getting past my own thoughts."

"We would all get more rest if Hillel hires Marcia back for the holidays," Shoshanah says. "Sara and I ransacked every drawer and couldn't find the tickets."

"And hiring her back might stop her from trying to get Hillel fired," Beth says.

Shoshanah is taken aback. She had done everything she can to keep this information to herself.

"Nancy told me you defended Hillel so eloquently no one even voted to begin a search. For which I thank you, Shoshanah. Come." She hands her a glass of water, heats up the tea she had been drinking in the microwave before Shoshanah arrived and walks ahead of her back to the living room.

"No one voted," Shoshanah says, as she sits down. "At the meeting some people said the synagogue was supposed to empower congregants and they were happy to run study groups and organize conferences and workshops.

But afterwards, several women called me to say they want Marcia to come back and they're gathering names for a petition to take to the Board."

"Did you mention this to Hillel?"

"I thought maybe you might tell him."

"I see." Beth sips a little tea and sets the cup down on the coffee table. She places her hand on its cold surface. This is how she feels. Cold as stone. When she looks at Hillel she sees a man she doesn't recognize, a stranger who has decided to live with her for the sole purpose of disappointing her. Ordinarily she is able to reach deep inside herself for understanding and compassion, but after last night, she has no compassion for Hillel. She thinks she might have to leave him.

"I don't know that he would listen to me," she tells Shoshanah.

"I feel somewhat responsible. I don't think Marcia wanted to leave. And when she did, I didn't even ask what happened."

"She might have hidden the tickets to remind us she's a necessary presence in the synagogue. Hillel tried to talk to me the day she left. He wanted my advice, but that afternoon his problems with Marcia weren't at the top of my list."

Shoshanah sets her glass on the coffee table. She'll speak to Hillel herself about hiring Marcia back on a temporary basis. After the holidays she won't be able to continue doing as much. She barely made it to the last make up class to finish her bracelet; she had forced herself to go. Mostly because she wanted to see Noah.

"I'm seeing someone," she tells Beth. A classmate from the DeCordova. At first I only went out with him to prove to my mother that I had a date. Now, with the holidays coming up, I don't have much time to be with him. However, Noah said he would join me at services if that's the only way he can spend more time with me."

"That's wonderful, Shoshanah. One of the best reasons for coming to synagogue that I can imagine." Beth can't keep herself from enjoying Shoshanah's obvious pleasure. "Maybe Noah could keep you busy after the holidays so my husband will pay attention to the congregants again. I haven't been able to motivate him."

"He's trying now," Shoshanah says.

"Very trying, as far as I'm concerned," Beth laughs and suddenly the bitter lump in her throat begins to ease.

"You look a little better then when I came," Shoshanah says. "Your face has more color." She picks up her glass and carries it into the kitchen.

"I'll walk back with you," Beth says. "I could use some fresh air. I'll help you and Sara look for the tickets. And if I can calm down, we can talk to Hillel together. It will certainly be a change from the lack of conversation the two of us have been having lately."

On the way back to the Kehillat Shalom, Beth tucks her arm through Shoshanah's. "I'm glad you were 'impelled' to rush over."

"It might have been the roses. No one knows who planted them, but they seem to be having a powerful effect."

THIRTY FOUR

When Marcia opens the front door, she can hear Jack talking to someone on the phone.

"I'll tell her. I'm sure she will be happy to hear this." There's a pause, then Jack adds, "Yes, to help out."

"Help out where?" Marcia drops a bag filled with gels and mousse from the beauty shop onto the kitchen table. "I can't help anywhere. I'm busy with the house." Fabric swatches are draped all over the living room furniture.

"That was the rabbi," Jack says, trying not to stare at Marcia's hair, which is now a bright red. He stops himself before he tells her he thinks she is getting to be a nut job. She has been so out of control lately she is beginning to resemble a caricature of herself.

He is afraid to tell her he doesn't like her hair this way and he does not like her this way. He has had to stop asking her to refrain from changing the entire house around the minute he leaves for work. Marcia follows him around all evening, lamenting that no one appreciates her efforts and if he would only contribute his decorating ideas, she will put things exactly where he wants them.

"Leave the house the way it was," is all he told her. "I like everything the way it used to be."

Now the entire household is in disarray, as if Marcia had decided to placate Jack and had begun to rearrange things back to the way they were, but had forgotten where everything belongs. The bed is half-made, the house half-cleaned. She leaves various post-it notes, not only on her desk in their bedroom where she has always left them, but stuck on tables, adhered to door posts, even plastered on the window of his car. Her latest arrangement has his favorite chair in the middle of the living room next to the sofa even though he has long appreciated having it in the corner close to his reading lamp where he turns the pages of his newspaper while she talks. He can't bring himself to tell her that he likes his life at home to be on automatic, knowing that whenever he lowers himself into his favorite chair at the end of the day it will be there to catch him.

Any suggestion that she is not doing the right thing leads to a tirade followed by tears. Is she a non-entity now that Debby is married and she is no longer working? Why can't she be a woman of leisure? She has never been able to do what she wants all day. Now that she can, she generously offered to help him out at the store, but no, that is his domain.

Jack has had to back off. He recommended that she not visit Ida for a while after Susan called to say Marcia had upset Ida with some kind of story about Ruchamah. Marcia told him she was doing a friend a kindness and would visit anyone any time she wished. Jack is not her father, who, by the way, was the only man she would let tell her what to do.

"Rabbi Kramer," he tells her now in an overly cheerful voice, "wants you to come back to the office for a while. He needs you. Your help with the High Holidays," he qualifies. He doesn't dare imply she has her job back. The rabbi has made that clear, repeating that this is a temporary problem the office is having, emphasizing the word "help".

"I'm not going," Marcia says and walks into the bedroom. "I'll be right out to fix dinner."

Jack groans. Marcia has been so unfocused lately that she leaves out key ingredients when she cooks.

"I told him you would be there. He's expecting you," Jack says in front of the closed door. He will get her to the synagogue office if he has to carry her.

"They're calling me to come back because they can't find the tickets I stored in the bottom of one of utility closets, in a locked box. Let them figure it out for themselves. Anyway, I've been thinking we should change temples. We could try Beth Tzeddek a few blocks away."

"We've been going to Kehillat Shalom for over thirty years." Jack forces himself to take a deep breath, more than alarmed now. "Maybe the rabbi wants to apologize."

"I won't accept."

"It's only right. Before *Yom Kippur,* you have to forgive him."

"I don't have to. There's nothing that says I have to. The person who did something wrong is the one who has to ask forgiveness. The person who is wronged is free to forgive or not."

But later that day Marcia goes through the pile of suits she has set aside for the Hadassah Bargain Spot and hangs them all back in her closet. She picks out the blue one she bought just before Debby's wedding. She will call the rabbi back to make an appointment and she will dress regally. Perhaps she will show him some mercy. After all anyone can make a mistake.

"I appreciate your coming in," the rabbi begins. "We can't seem to find the list for the High Holidays and I was hoping, if you have some time, you might help us straighten things out. Unless you've taken another job?"

This does not sound much like an apology to Marcia, but who can tell what the rabbi's intentions are. He has always been somewhat obscure to her.

"So he didn't apologize but he needs me," Marcia says to Jack that night. "I told him I would think about it. I don't want him to take me for granted. But it would give me a certain pleasure to make sure Sara isn't sitting at my desk."

"But you're going?"

"I'm going. It's something to do until I decide what to do."

"Good," Jack says hiding his absolute pleasure. He continues skimming through the newspaper. If Marcia goes in tomorrow, it will be the first time he would have alone in weeks. He'll take the day off and try to come up with a plan so that the rabbi keeps her permanently.

He will move his chair back into the corner of the room where it has always been so he can sit and read in peace and quiet for a day. He will make sure to put it back in the middle of the room before Marcia comes home. Things already seem better. Jack can hear Marcia humming.

Marcia rummages through her shoe collection searching for her highest pair of heels. They are at least 3 inches. That will raise her above Beth and that volunteer. Not that she's begging to have her job back, but she isn't planning to make it easy for anyone to let her go.

THIRTY-FIVE

"These look delicious," Ruchamah says, peering into the containers of *glatt kosher* food that Beth has brought for Miriam's visit. "You made so much, there'll be leftovers after Miriam leaves."

"Did I tell you we had to ask Marcia to come back? Beth hesitates. "I hate to tell you this because...."

"I know she was badmouthing me," Ruchamah says. "Ida called to warn me. I plan on speaking to Marcia. I just have to wait until I'm not so angry."

"Maybe when she sees you she'll apologize." Beth closes the containers, opens the refrigerator door so Ruchamah can put the food away.

"I don't want her apology. I don't want to have to forgive her."

"I know how you feel. I don't want to have to forgive Hillel either. My mother thinks I should begin the adoption process without him. She can't wait until we have a child because then I'll know what she went through when she raised me."

Ruchamah laughs. "What were you like?"

"Stubborn." Beth laughs. "When do you have to be at the airport?"

"In an hour. Miriam's flight comes in at ten."

She can't bring herself to ask Beth about Simon's concert. She doesn't want to know whether or not Karen was there. When she cut out the Boston Globe review, she could see Simon at Jordan Hall, lifting his violin. She could hear every note. She can't seem to stop herself from reliving their moments at the café.

When she gets to the airport, she parks in the garage and goes to the waiting area. Miriam's flight has not arrived. Ruchamah takes the review out of her pocketbook. "It is not only the music that intrigued this reviewer, but the soloist himself... Like an animated Al Hirschfeld drawing, the soloist possesses an uncommon fluidity. His movements alone reveal the music." She reads on. "In his role as coach as well as soloist, it is obvious that Levitt, along with the conductor, Stephen Larsen, has enabled this student orchestra to achieve a performance worthy of professionals."

She looks up in time to see a group of people descend the escalator to the baggage area. As soon as she spots Miriam, she feels a sense of profound relief. At least these few days until *Selichot* will not be filled with thoughts of Simon. She folds up the review, puts it back into her pocketbook and calls to her friend, on her way to welcome her.

Ruchamah's dining room table is littered with pages of paper and empty teacups. She and Miriam have been working for a few hours now and have finalized four translations. Miriam stands up to stretch and hands Ruchamah a sheet of paper. "This is my newest poem. I want to include it in this book, especially since it is my first to be published in Israel."

JERUSALEM

Y'rushalayim

city of Shalom
city of wholeness
holy city of

Jews
Muslims
Christians

warring factions
territorial claims
conflicts
proposed solutions

carve up this
ir shalom
city of wholeness
no longer one piece

how to find peace

"I hope I can do this poem justice," Ruchamah says after reading it. "It's poignancy depends so much on English word play. Homophones like whole and holy, peace and piece."

"Then there's Jerusalem," Miriam says. "Literally two words in Hebrew, *ir* for city and *shalom,* peace coming from the same root as *shalame* which means whole, all of one piece. That is what peace is, a feeling of completion. Everything as it should be."

"Everything as it should be," Ruchamah shrugs. "Sometimes that's hard."

"I didn't intend for this to be political," Miriam continues. "For me, it's an outcry. How much can this city take without damaging its very soul?"

"Will you read this for *Selichot?*"

"No, I wrote something else for the service that I'm hoping to add to the new book as well."

"I'll try and find my way into the Jerusalem poem as quickly as I can. I'm sorry I've taken so long with these." Ruchamah hands Miriam the folder with the completed translations. "I haven't been as focused as I like."

"Your translations are worth waiting for," Miriam says. "But I think we've done enough for today. I'm looking forward to spending *Shabbat* with you."

A few autumn leaves are falling as they walk in a nearby park *Shabbat* afternoon. Their bright colors gleam on the still green lawns.

"I just received the latest copy of Abacus," Miriam says as they walk. "There's a review of a poetry book that Edie Garon translated. The reviewer commented that her translations were so off the mark the poet's intention was unclear. When I gave her my *Sukkot* poems, they came back totally robotic. It was sheer luck that I was at the 92nd. Street Y the night Nehemiah Siegal introduced you as his translator. Our collaboration was *bashert*."

"Just like our friendship. Meant to be."

Ruchamah is as pensive today as she had been that night. Miriam links her arms through her friend's. "You have to know that I didn't come all this way just for the reading or even to look at your translations." She slows her steps and turns to look at Ruchamah. "Something is bothering you."

"You're right."

"Is it Daniel?"

"There's always Daniel. But there's someone else or there was. Before I knew it, we were declaring our feelings for each other." She shrugs. "Things didn't work out."

"Is it over?"

"I think so. I wish it wasn't. And there's something else. Probably more your thing than mine. All summer I have been seeing this woman, who shows up in different guises. First she appeared in a dream where she blocked my view of Daniel. That terrified me. Then she showed up in the pool during my meditative swim. And after I met Simon, she danced naked in my yard, shedding the skins of her years as she unveiled herself."

"Very interesting," Miriam says. "Not very modest, but intriguing. I haven't yet written crones or naked strangers into my poems. Perhaps I should try."

Ruchamah laughs. "Only you would think this is inspiring. But never mind. I haven't seen her since."

"Maybe she'll come back. I'd love to meet her."

"If you do, please let her know I'd like a word with her. 'What are you doing in my life?' I would ask or rather, 'What are you doing to my life?'"

"I'll be glad to ask her, if I see her. My life has also changed. Ever since my poems were published, David and I have been struggling. I had to start traveling for book tours. He's had to learn how to cook for himself and be more available to our children. All of this creates a lot of tension. We're not used to arguing. I never had to defend myself before. But now I think David looks forward to my going away occasionally. I know he was happy I was coming to be with you."

"That makes at least two people happy you're here." Ruchamah hugs her as they leave the park.

Rabbi Kramer welcomes the congregation to the *Selichot* service and introduces Miriam. "You will hear her work in English, but since Ruchamah is translating these poems into Hebrew, they will soon find an Israeli audience."

Miriam approaches the *bimah.* "Thank you for inviting me. I feel like an honorary member of Kehillat Shalom. I have written this poem in your name.

SELICHOT

This night we dress
our beloved Torah in white
garb of holiness and cleansing
as we chant the niggun
song without words
haunting melody

Avinu Malkeinu
we have sinned before You

Avinu Malkeinu
forgive us and pardon us
liturgy of Rosh HaShanah
Selichot of Yom Kippur

This night we gather
in the holy sanctuary
foretaste of the days of awe

Open our hearts
our lives
to forgive
to love
to hope

Miriam's poem strikes a blow to Ruchamah's heart. Open herself to love, open her heart? Oh no. Close my heart, as you did when Daniel died. Form a protective seal that cannot be broken this time. Shoshanah reads from the words of Rabbi Moses ben Nachman, best known as Nachmanides, who wrote six centuries before Freud. "If you bring forth what is within you, what is within you will save you. If you do not bring forth what is within you, what is within you will destroy you." Ruchamah does not want to bring forth what is within her. Even Miriam's presence has not dispelled her distress. Not only is she angry with Simon, she is once again consumed with thoughts of Daniel.

Time collapses as she turns the pages of her *Siddur.* It is six weeks after Aviva's birth. Ruchamah rains kisses on Daniel's back. Daniel refuses to turn over. He's teasing her, joking, but no, not joking. Dead. The joke is on her. She has been left alone, bereft, a widow with a child, vulnerable to the first man she allows to come close. A cry escapes her lips. Aviva, sitting next to her, takes hold of her hand.

"Mom, are you alright?"

"I'm fine, Aviva," but she does not let go of her daughter's hand.

The rabbi addresses the congregation. Rabbi Nachman's words echo in Ruchamah's mind. "If you don't bring forth what is within, what is within will destroy you,"

All I wanted was to live again, she says silently. Why didn't You, God, give that to me? You sent a stranger to warn me, then you sent Simon with his broken promise. You gave me hope and took it from me. Now it's *Selichot,* a night of forgiveness and I still cannot forgive Daniel for leaving me. And I cannot forgive Simon.

Shoshanah's voice, almost of another world, spins out the soothing strains of *Avinu Malkenu.*

"Our Father, our Mother, be gracious to us and answer us, even when we have little merit: treat us generously and with kindness, and be our Help."

Avinu Malkeinu, this prayer is communal. If someone is unable to pray, cannot formulate the words, the community stands as one to utter this prayer. Perhaps tonight someone in the congregation will pray on her behalf.

THIRTY-SIX

Ruchamah and Aviva leave for *Rosh HaShanna* services together. She hasn't told her mother about Ari yet. It's the New Year and she is about to do some very new things, most of which she is not sure of. Ruchamah puts her arm around her daughter and in spite of Aviva's uncertainty of what lies ahead, she puts her arm around his mother's waist so they are walking almost in step.

Karen has not made any preparations for dinner; after Simon finishes cooking, he lets Jacob decorate the gefilte fish with carrots, making faces on each of them. For the mouths, he places the strips of carrots in straight lines. "No smiles tonight? Not even for the New Year?" Simon asks.

Jacob shakes his head no. No smiles.

Susan and Martin have reluctantly agreed to have dinner with their father. Ida can't seem to make them understand that even though their father is living at the Rehab now, they are still a family. The fact that Nathan's Alzheimer's is no longer just an intellectual possibility is particularly hard for Martin to accept. He is appalled by his father's mental deterioration. "I can't believe this has happened, and so fast," he says over and over. Sometimes he peers deeply into Nathan's eyes, seeking the father he had always known, the one who had never found him acceptable, which would be far more preferable than the stranger who peers back at him, smiling faintly, as if he is not sure who he is looking at.

Attired in Nathan's favorite silk dress, blue with white flowers and a mandarin collar, Ida waits for her children. She has succeeded in applying enough makeup to cover the dark circles under her eyes. After their dinner, she will tell her children that some days Nathan greets her with a kiss filled with abandon, as if he has no cares in the world, and for that precise moment, on those days, neither does she.

Jack cooks dinner early so Marcia can get back to the synagogue to open up for services. Well aware her happiness might be short-lived, she savors it none-the-less. After all, she is the "Wonder Woman" who got all of the High Holiday tickets out on time, despite the late start. Hopefully the rabbi will bear this in mind and let her stay on as though nothing unusual had ever happened. She had reluctantly given that volunteer, Sara, a ticket after both Shoshanah and the rabbi asked to do so. Sara had thanked her profusely and Marcia found herself wondering whether or not she had misjudged her.

Beth cannot bring herself to forgive Hillel. Yesterday was his birthday. She had forced herself to behave as if everything was normal, baking him the chocolate black out cake from his mother's recipe. He was late getting home. He glanced at the cake, kissed her quickly on the cheek and put a shopping bag in the closet in his study. She can hardly bring herself to speak to him as she gets dressed for services. She has no idea that Hillel walked around Coolidge Corner for hours, having left the synagogue suddenly, without a word to anyone as to where he was going. He hadn't known himself. He was passing a toy store when he caught sight of an erector set in the window. An erector set was the only kind of toy he had been allowed as a child. His father always thought he should build something, make something, constantly be productive.

He would have so much preferred to receive something like this little wooden dog sitting on the shelf in front of him for birthday. He set it down on the floor, mesmerized by the quirky way its haunches went round and round as he pulled it. When a slight breeze on the back of his neck caused him to look up, he caught a glimpse of the woman he had seen the night of *Erev Shavuot*. She was holding a small child by the hand, older than the child in his vision. The boy laughed with delight as he pulled the same kind of wooden dog Hillel was holding. When he followed her to the check-out line, he found himself standing alone, toy dog in hand. Without conscious thought, he handed his credit card to the cashier. Any child would love this little dog he thought as he carried it home, although if Beth sees it she might come to the conclusion he has changed his mind about adoption. Why else would he bring a toy home? Why else, he wonders as he goes to the closet now and takes out the shopping bag.

"Are you ready?" Beth asks, as she comes into his study. "What do you have there?"

He takes the dog out of the shopping bag. "Just something I bought yesterday."

"Oh, a toy dog for the preschool," Beth says. "It's adorable. The children will love it.

THIRTY-SEVEN

It's four in the morning. Karen has already called the airport to reserve a ticket on the noon flight to Chicago and packed her suitcase. She's sitting on the edge of the white coverlet on the bed she and Simon used to share, waiting until she can wake her husband and son. She wishes she were the kind of person who could go to Kehillat Shalom and offer up a personal prayer for things to work out, but she chose not to attend services for *Rosh Hashanah*. She won't be here for *Yom Kippur*. In spite of her efforts, neither Jacob nor Simon have accepted her back into their lives. She would have liked to come to the conclusion that her leaving had been a mistake, one she deeply regrets. Instead she feels as if she is suffocating. She loves Jacob, but she loves him as if he is someone else's child, a little boy she sees once or twice a year at holidays and birthday parties. As for Simon, it was only the thought that he could be interested in another woman that had inspired purchases of delicate underwear and the desire to sit in his study while he prepared for his concert. In spite of that, he asked her to stay home with Jacob that night. Nothing she has done had evoked his desire, just as nothing has brought Jacob willingly to her.

She gets up to look around the room again. Somehow she missed that blue silk scarf under the bed. She picks it up and reopens her suitcase. Then, she takes a notepad from the bedside table, puts it back. She can't leave her husband and her son a note, the way she did the last time. She has to tell them; this time she has to make sure they understand why she is leaving.

In the kitchen Karen prepares an elaborate breakfast; a houseguest surprising her hosts. She wakes Simon. Then she goes into Jacob's room. She bends down and kisses his forehead. "Wake up Jacob," she says. He is instantly awake looking at her, her little mute son. She could gather him in her arms, despite his protests. She could tell him she is sorry she left him before, that she intends to stay and although she isn't very good at taking care of children yet, she's learning. She'll never give up. She'll never stop trying. "Come," she says instead. "Breakfast is ready." Jacob yawns sleepily, follows her into the kitchen, finds his father's lap and leans against Simon's chest.

"I made this for you," Karen says, unnecessarily. She wants them to drink the juice or coffee, eat the

283

French toast, the slice of cantaloupe sitting like a quarter moon on their plates, but neither lifts a spoon or picks up a cup. Karen brings her coffee to her lips. It has a bitter taste. She should have left a note. It would have been so much easier. She would have been gone by now. At the very least she could have told Simon her decision last night, because whatever she has to say to him cannot be said in front of Jacob.

"Jacob," Simon says, as if intuiting her intention, "How would you like to take your breakfast into the living room and watch Clifford?" Jacob grins. He lifts his plate carefully and without spilling a thing, begins to carry it out of the kitchen. "Good job, Jacob," both Simon and Karen call.

"I need to talk to you," Karen says

There's something I have to tell you as well," Simon says.

"Go ahead."

"You first."

"Remember the night I asked you if there was another woman in your life?"

Simon nods.

Karen hesitates. Her words are as clearly etched in her mind as if she had written them down. "That was the night I realized you were no longer in love with me. I was shocked when the rabbi called to tell me you wanted a *Get*. I assumed our marriage was over the day I left. I kept waiting for you to realize this and send me papers from your lawyer, which never came."

"I couldn't accept your leaving."

"But you can accept it now. Am I right?"

Simon nods.

"For a brief moment, I thought we might have a chance. I waited for you to come to me at night, but you never did. I waited for you to want to spend time with me, but you can hardly tolerate my presence." Karen places her key on the table. It sits among the coffee cups and juice glasses, close to Simon's plate, almost touching the moon shaped cantaloupe which has not been eaten. She takes a breath and her words rush ahead of her thoughts now. "I was going to leave a note, like the last time, but that time, I wanted to run away. This time I want to be able to come back and spend time with Jacob." She looks down at her plate and then forces herself to look at him. "I will certainly give you a *Get,* Simon. We should be divorced." She takes a deep breath. This feels right even if the breakfast she had gone to so much trouble to prepare is a waste. "What did you want to tell me?" He leans over and kisses her cheek.

"My version of what you just told me."

Jacob comes into the kitchen and sets his empty plate on the table.

"You ate everything," Simon says. He picks him up and sets him on his lap. Karen gets up from her chair and kneels down next to him. "I love you, Jacob. I want you to be happy. You are my remarkable boy. I wish I could stay here all the time with you, but I can't. I want to come back and see you. I want you to come to Chicago and see me and your grandma and grandpa. They miss you. Just like I did."

Jacob buries his head in his father's chest.

"Jacob, please look at me." He shakes his head no. He doesn't move. "Please,"

Slowly he turns his head and she looks into his bright blue eyes brimming with tears. He has understood her every word. "I want to be able to read to you and play with you and hold you whenever I can. All you have to say is 'okay.' Please, Jacob," Karen says. "You can talk. Talk to me. I love you. See." She takes the paper she was going to write her note on and writes, "Dear Jacob. I love you." She points to herself and draws an eye. She points to her heart and says "Love," and she puts her hand over Jacob's heart. "You," she says. "I love you."Jacob?"

When he doesn't respond, she stands up and tells Simon she will have her lawyer contact him, and runs from the room. Simon closes his eyes and rocks Jacob in his arms. Jacob puts his arms around his father's neck. "Okay," Jacob says. "Okay. Okay. Okay." His voice is loud and carries into the bedroom where Karen is standing pressed against the door, her fist in her mouth to block her sobs.

Before the congregants step foot into the sanctuary for the *Kol Nidre* service, the ushers remind them to take a seat in silence to preserve the sanctity of this time. The rabbi and cantor stand before the open ark to say their proscribed penitential prayers before the *Torahs,* still dressed in the white garments of *Selichot.*

Hillel asks to have the sanctuary lights dimmed, "to remind us of how the Jews of 15th Century Spain had been forced to convert to Catholicism and hide their practice of Judaism during the Inquisition. All year long they had gone through the motion of participating in church services. But each *Erev Yom Kippur* they would gather secretly in cellars, keeping the lights dim, chanting *Kol Nidre*, this haunting 8th century melody from Iraq, to ask forgiveness for vows they made counter to Judaism, those vows they could not keep. Young boys kept watch outside lest strangers or soldiers pass by. They were to toss pebbles against the basement windows as a sign of warning."

Simon is seated alone on the *bimah*. The only light emanates from the open ark. He draws his bow downward on his violin to create the first note. *Kol,* he intones *kol* for all. *Kol Nidrei,* all my vows.

"All vows and oaths, all promises we make and the obligations we incur to You, O, God, between this *Yom Kippur* and the next, let them be null and void should we, after honest effort, find ourselves unable to fulfill them. Then may we be absolved of them."

All vows, Simon thinks as he continues to bow the haunting strains of the Max Bruch arrangement of this ancient melody. *Kol Nidre.* Let his wedding vows, the most sacred he has ever made, now be null and void.

Continuing to bow, his arm feels heavy. As the notes build one upon the other, the tone lightens and the tension leaves his face. When he finishes the last note, he joins Jacob in the first row and puts his arm around him. And, as Shoshanah begins to chant the opening words of "*Kol Nidre*", a wave of acceptance washes over him.

THIRTY-EIGHT

M arcia goes to work every day. It's late September. No one says anything; the paychecks keep coming. Jack is so grateful she's been given a second chance, he has donated cases of his finest kosher wine, enough to carry Kehillat Shalom through many *Oneg Shabbats*.

"Remember," he tells Marcia each morning, "try and keep your opinions to yourself. Above all be tactful, Marcia. Tact is everything. That's how I built my business."

Marcia does not remind Jack that her hard work helped build his business; she doesn't tell him she is still upset that he did not want her in his store. She has bigger fish to fry. She is intent on keeping her job for a long, long time. Don't make waves and the boat won't rock, she tells herself as she leaves the house. She has decided on a course of behavior that is working extremely well. When people come in to the office to use the copy machine she thanks them for helping her. She answers the phone in what she considers to be a phony, almost gushy tone of voice, but no one is complaining. The pre-school has started. Beth, with little time to spend on administrative issues, races in during her almost non-existent lunch break to see if Marcia needs anything and sighs with relief when Marcia tells her everything is under control.

To her amazement, she finds she no longer resents Sara, who seems content to work in the back of the office on any task Marcia assigns her. Sometimes her friends from the Sisterhood come in to see if she can have lunch and she goes out with them, happy the office is in Sara's capable hands.

She has enhanced her computer skills and now e-mails members courteous responses to their questions. The rabbi seems friendlier once again, as well. He probably assumes she has become more accommodating. And, if this illusion is what it takes to keep her job, so be it.

The office is busy with the seasonal start-up of the religious school and adult education program "The Shekhinah and the Role of Feminism in the Mystical World of Judaism," is one of the classes on the rabbi's fall schedule. Marcia can just imagine what that will be about. But it's none of her concern. All she has to do is run off his handouts on the copy machine, and she does.

Yesterday Ruchamah sent Marcia an e-mail listing the full year's dates for the *Rosh Hodesh* group for the Master Calendar. When she noticed that the November date conflicted with the B'nai B'rith meeting, she automatically began her reply to Ruchamah informing her there would be no room for the women that month. Then, she remembered Jack's daily warnings, and gave the *Rosh Hodesh* group the Social Hall, scheduling the library for the smaller B'nai B'rith meeting. This accomplished, she deleted her original message to Ruchamah and tells her that *Rosh Hodesh* is set for the year.

Today a call came in from a gay member who wants to discuss a Jewish marriage ceremony with the rabbi. "What!" Marcia started to blurt out and imagines Jack scowling at her from across the desk, so she managed to add a courteous "else would you like me to add to the message?" and was rewarded when Jack's image nodded approval.

At noon she slips a birthday card out of her pocketbook, signs it and leaves it on the center of the rabbi's desk. Then, she removes a gift bag from her file drawer and leaves the synagogue, taking advantage of her lunch break to walk to Ruchamah's apartment and presses the buzzer.

"Ruchamah, it's Marcia. Could I come in?" She waits for a minute and when there's no answer buzzes again.

"Ruchamah? I have something for you." She looks into the inner lobby towards the stairs to see if Ruchamah is on her way down but no one's there. A few minutes later someone exits the building. Marcia catches the door before it closes and mounts the stairs to Ruchamah's apartment. She knocks and raises her voice. "A little something I picked up the other day. I thought of you when I saw it."

Ruchamah opens the door.

"I know I'm interrupting you," Marcia says, "but I didn't think this could wait." She follows Ruchamah inside. "I've been thinking...." She waits for Ruchamah to ask her what she has been thinking and plunges ahead when Ruchamah is silent. "When I lost my job, I thought you had gone to the rabbi to complain about me, but now that I'm back, I think I might have been wrong." She walks past Ruchamah into the dining room and deposits the gift bag on top of a pile of papers.

"What are you doing?" Ruchamah is incensed that Marcia has had the nerve to barge into her house uninvited like this after spreading rumors about her relationship with Simon. She has managed to ignore her the few times she has seen her over the summer. And even avoided sitting anywhere near her on *Rosh HaShanah*.

"This is a peace offering," Marcia says. "Aren't you going to open it?"

"I didn't know we were at war." Ruchamah makes no attempt to look in the bag.

"No one believed what I said about you anyway," Marcia says. "So no harm was done."

"Our friendship was harmed," Ruchamah says.

"Oh." Marcia sits down at the table across from Ruchamah. This is going to be much harder than she assumed. She had spent ages at Filene's, not in the Basement, upstairs in the regular store, looking for just the right thing, but Ruchamah doesn't seem to appreciate the effort she is making to apologize. "I was angry and hurt," she says by way of explanation. "On *Rosh HaShanah* when the rabbi said we had to ask those we wronged to forgive us, I realized that I had wronged you, I had bad-mouthed you, committed a *"lashen horah"* and that I had to make things right. So here I am. Cutting out my evil tongue so to speak." She waits for Ruchamah's response.

"You're not saying anything." Marcia is breathing heavily, clearly upset now. She can't believe that Ruchamah doesn't seem to want to forgive her. "Well," she brightens. "You could at least look at my present. I'll take it back to Filene's if you don't like it."

"I don't want a present Marcia. My heart's not into accepting one."

"I'll leave it here anyway." Ruchamah is being most unreasonable. Marcia gets up from the table, gathers her handbag and heads for the door. "When your heart gets into the right feeling, you can open it." She walks out of Ruchamah's apartment without bothering to close the door behind her and bounds down the staircase, narrowly missing a collision with Aviva in the outer lobby. Standing on the front stoop a moment, she catches her breath. Marcia shakes her head at how sometimes things just don't work out for her and is about to leave when she hears Aviva's excited voice through the open window asking her mother what was in the bag.

"I have no idea," Ruchamah says.

"Did Marcia leave it?"

"She did."

"Should I take it back to her house?"

"She left it for me."

"Why don't you open it?"

"Please, Aviva."

"Is it a present?"

"Probably. Alright," she finally says. "I'll open it so we can both forget about it."

Marcia turns around and peers up at the window. She imagines Ruchamah lifting her gift from the layers of white tissue paper.

"Look at this shawl, Mom. It has fringes. And it's every color of the rainbow. It's gorgeous. Let me wrap it around you. This is your taste, Mom. It doesn't look like anything that Marcia would wear. And here's a note. 'This is something to let you know I was thinking of you and I wish I had been thinking of you before I jumped to the wrong conclusion.'"

"What does that mean, Mom?"

"I think Marcia's trying to tell me that she made a mistake; she forgot we were friends."

THIRTY-NINE

It's almost dusk when Ida gets out of her daughter's car. No, she does not want Susan to come in. She has spent most of the day with her daughter and Nathan. She doesn't want to hear Susan's lectures about how Ida should occupy herself in her spare time. She wants to be alone in the privacy of her own home, looking at old photographs and dreaming of the way things used to be.

She waves good-bye to her daughter and inserts her key in the door and stops as soon as she enters the house. Someone is on her deck! She takes a step forward, listens. There is that noise again. Something is being dragged across the deck flooring. Slowly, she walks through the kitchen, opens the back door and stands open mouthed to see a group of her friends from Kehillat

Shalom running around with slats of wood and cornstalks, arguing as to which panel fits next to which. Voices are rising.

"What are you doing?" she asks.

"Making a *Sukkah* for you," Jacob shouts and rushes to throw his arms around her waist. "Hi, Grandma Ida."

"This is not necessary," Ida says to all of them, as she wraps her arms around Jacob. Her dismay at the crowd subsides immediately as she realizes what she has just heard. Ida hugs him hard. "You're talking!" Jacob nods and grins. He has called her Grandma Ida, the name he had given her when he first started speaking, just before Karen left. She wants to take him into the house, sit him on her lap and let him chatter away. This would be such pleasure. Her greatest pleasure since Nathan became ill.

She does not want this *Sukkah.* This year she wants to eat by herself, read a book, disappear inside the pages of someone else's life.

"We're going to eat with you tonight," Jacob tells her, taking her hand and tugging her onto the deck. "Daddy says we're not having our own *Sukkah* this year."

Ida lifts her eyebrows. "So that's how it is," she says. "Shall I assume no one else built a *Sukkah* as well?"

"We thought we'd surprise you," Aviva gives her a hug. "Besides, we have ulterior motives. You have the best setting. A *Sukkah* never really works in the back of our apartment building."

"Jack helped schlep the wood panels of our pre-fab *Sukkah* over to your house today while you were visiting Nathan," Ruchamah says gently.

Ida stares at her. "So your *Sukkah* is now my *Sukkah?*" She sits down on her rocking chair, which has been moved off to the side.

"If I had known earlier, I could have helped Jack bring the panels over," Simon says to Ruchamah. He puts his hands on his son's shoulders and smiles at her but she seems not to have heard as she makes no response.

Jack, who is organizing the panels, hands them off one at a time to Nancy. He waves at Ida. "Marcia wanted to come but she's busy making sure everything is ready for the service tonight." He says this cheerfully but glances uneasily at Ruchamah.

"She probably thinks the *Rosh Hodesh* group is going to perform magical incantations inside the *Sukkah,*" Beth whispers to Ruchamah, as she crosses the porch to Ida. "Ida, can I get you some tea or some water?"

"No," Ida says. "Thanks. I'm fine." She is annoyed that Beth feels she has to offer her something in her own home. Only that cleaning woman, who's been showing up recently, can get away with that. She doesn't know where she came from and she doesn't care. She arrives early most mornings with a cup of tea, tidies up and shakes her head. Ida has been shaking her head right back, stubbornly drinking coffee, even though it gives her heartburn. She makes it just the way Nathan loves it. The other night her visitor brought dinner, which looked remarkably like the usual leftovers after a ceremony at Kehillat Shalom, and sat down to eat with her. And just as she's thinking about her, her cleaning woman enters the porch. Holding a glass of water, and looking directly at Ida, she sets the glass down as she walks around touching the sides of the *Sukkah,* which is now up and stabilized. She finds a pumpkin someone has left and adds it to the pile of cornstalks and brightly colored leaves that lie in the corner of Ida's porch. No one else seems to have noticed her.

"We can line the top of the frame with these," Simon says, picking up the cornstalks and showing Ruchamah. "Donnie and Stan dropped them off earlier from a cornfield in Framingham."

Ruchamah doesn't know what these overtures from Simon are meant to convey. Karen left a few days ago, but as far as she's concerned, nothing else has changed. She moves a few steps away and offers to hold the ladder for Nancy, who takes the cornstalks from Simon and starts up the ladder to Jack.

"Wait a minute Nancy. Let Simon bring the rest."

"What's the matter, Jack. Can't a woman climb a ladder around here? How do you think we manage when you guys aren't home?"

"Be my guest," Jack tells her. Nonetheless, he holds the top of the ladder as she climbs.

"Remember to leave plenty of room between the stalks," Beth says as Jack lays them over the trellised roof. "We have to be able to see the moon and stars. At least this year we're guaranteed one clear night. The forecast is for heavy showers later this week."

Ida watches as Pam hangs several strings of cranberries along the *Sukkah's* inner walls.

"Look, Ida, Judy strung these beads in preschool." She holds up a huge string of multi-colored stars and moons.

"Very nice." Ida nods as she gets up from her chair and disappears into the house, closing the door emphatically behind her. She stands in her kitchen feeling a combination of loss and anger. Nathan should be here. Not synagogue members without him. I am too tired for all this company. I'll lie down on my bed and close my eyes for a few minutes. Then I'll go out and thank them for coming. At least that way I'll be in control of something.

When Ida gets up she walks back into the kitchen and stands at the window to watch as more decorations are added and people stand back to look at their handiwork. Carole glances at the now empty chair where Ida had been sitting. "I think this might be too much for her," she hears her say.

"I'll tell her we would like to be with her, but we can leave if she prefers." Ruchamah heads towards Ida's back door.

"Shall I go with you?" Simon asks gently.

Ruchamah stops. "Why don't you go?"

"You're right," he says. "Two of us might overwhelm her. Ida, can I come in?" Ida opens the door.

"Interesting shells." Simon points to the seashells lining her windowsill.

"My grandchildren 'borrowed' them from Maine, as they like to say, and painted them with those brightly colored birds."

"They would look wonderful in the *Sukkah.*"

"I was just wondering about that myself," Ida says. She gathers them and places them in Simon's hands. "Why don't you add them to the other decorations."

"How about you?" Simon says. "I think you would look wonderful in the *Sukkah,* too."

"I look better inside my house," Ida says stubbornly, "but you go out and have a good time."

"It's not really such a good time."

"Well, for a holiday that is all about joy, I feel like I'm a kill joy right now. You don't need me out there."

"But I could use your company," Simon holds out his arm. "Not everyone is happy to see me."

Ida looks at him knowingly. "If you weren't such a good friend I wouldn't be doing this," she tells him. She takes his arm and steps out to the porch with him.

"We were worried we were overwhelming you," Beth says, more a question than a statement, giving her a hug.

"I don't want anyone to make a fuss," Ida tells her. "It's hard for me to be with people these days. But I am pleased to have such a beautiful *Sukkah.* Nathan would be happy about it, too." She has tears in her eyes as she returns Beth's hug. So, I won't be alone tonight, she tells herself. Maybe that's a good thing.

The sun is about to set by the time the *Sukkah* is finished. Jack packs up his tools. Simon tells Ida that he and Jacob will go shopping and be back later to eat in the *Sukkah,* if that's all right?

"We're also eating here, tonight," Aviva says. "We brought tons of food."

Ida nods assent, but Simon takes one look at Ruchamah's constricted face and reluctantly says that he forgot that they were supposed to go to another neighbor's for tonight. "We'll come tomorrow night, Ida. We'll bring dinner."

"Grandma Ida will you make me chocolate pudding?"

"Since it's your favorite, Jacob," Ida says, "I'll make it."

Simon touches Ruchamah's shoulder briefly as he leaves the porch. Ruchamah reaches her hand up to contain the warmth his touch has left behind. Jacob dances along beside his father. "See you tomorrow, Grandma Ida," he calls. Only the *Rosh Hodesh* group and Aviva remain.

"It's such a miracle that Jacob is talking again," Ida says to everyone left on her porch. And she considers if there is one miracle, there might be more.

"Would you like us to bless your *Sukkah?*" Beth asks.

"A blessing would be good," Ida responds. Nathan and I could use a legion of blessings. They invite Aviva to join them as they enter the *Sukkah.* An *etrog,* large cousin to the lemon, and a *lulav,* along with candles, a Kiddush cup for wine and a challah to sanctify *Sukkot* await them on the table, which is covered with a beautiful cloth embroidered with the phrase, "To every thing there is a season…." from *Kohelet,* Ecclesiastes, the traditional text for this holiday. Each woman takes a turn holding the *etrog* in the left hand, and the *lulav* formed by binding palm, willow and myrtle branches in the right, and says the prayer, *"Baruch ata Adonoy, Elo-heinu Melech ha'olam, asher kid'shanu bi'mitzvo-tav, vi'tzivanu al ni-tilaat lulav.* Blessed are You, our God, Sovereign of the Universe, who sanctified us with *mitzvot,* and instructed us to raise up the *lulav."* They shake the *lulav* to the north, the south, the east and west, ending with a shake up to the sky above and down to the earth below. As they finish, they put their arms around each other. Beth gazes at all around her and says, "Our *Rosh Hodesh* group has provided us with shelter throughout the year, a place where we can feel safe, just as the *Sukkah* gives us shelter at this time of the harvest. May we continue to reap the richness of the friendship between us and bring the fruits of our lives to each other." Tonight they do not need to hold a *tallit* above them to create their sacred space. They have the *Sukkah* itself, with the partially open roof giving access to a sky rich in stars and unlike their usual new moon *Rosh Hodesh* gatherings, a full moon.

"Ida, we bless this *Sukkah,* this beautiful but temporary shelter, and your place in it. "Come. Please light the candles."

Carole divides the challah into two parts, one for each side of the table. Everyone pulls off a portion to eat following making *hamotzee,* the blessing for bread. When Ida reaches out her hand for a piece of challah, her mysterious cleaning woman hands it to her. She must have managed to sneak in between Ruchamah and herself. "Amen," Ida joins in before biting into the challah, taking note of its sweetness.

As they sit down together for the meal, the full moon rises illuminating her stranger, who is walking away.

FORTY

In the synagogue, 54 chairs encircle the sanctuary. As Ruchamah enters, Marcia hands her a card with her seat number written on it. "Nice scarf," Marcia says and smiles tentatively.

"I think so, too. It resembles a *tallit* because of the fringes."

Fringes? Isn't that just like Ruchamah these days, to be entranced with the fringes? But she seems to have forgiven her and that's a good thing, Marcia tells herself as she greets Ida.

"Number 18," Ida sighs as she looks at her card. This is her first time at Kehillat Shalom without Nathan. She had said no to Ruchamah's appeal and no to Simon, but when he put Jacob on the phone she could not refuse.

Just as she was walking up the steps to Kehillat Shalom, her now almost expected companion appeared at her side. "I was beginning to think you lived in my house," she said laughing. "If you're coming to *shul* with me, shouldn't I at least know your name?"

"Hi, Ida. Where are you sitting?" Ruchamah asks.

"Section 18. And you?"

"I'm in section 51. Right next to Aviva. She came earlier with Lori and her cousin, Ari."

"I've never seen her looking so animated."

"She and Ari are going out. It seems my daughter is growing up."

Ida looks around to see where her friend is, but she seems to have disappeared.

The door opens. Jacob runs ahead of Simon, straight to Ida and hugs her.

He crosses over to Ruchamah and hugs her as well. As soon as he spots Aviva he plunks himself down on the empty chair next to her.

"I see Jacob found our section," Simon says as he approaches Ida and Ruchamah, "Even though he didn't wait for our card." He holds up his number, "51." Ruchamah doesn't know whether to relate this coincidence to the gentle hand of fate or the not so gentle hand of Marcia. She's unaware that ever since Karen left, Simon has received a daily visitor, the alluring stranger who came to him the night of the concert rehearsal. She stands in the doorway listening as he tunes his violin. And every night she appears at his kitchen table after dinner with a glass of wine in her hand. Simon believes her constant appearance means that he and Ruchamah are meant to have a future together, but Ruchamah has not returned any of his phone calls. He has had no indication that her anger towards him has dissipated or that her dreams of Daniel have changed.

Daniel still walks away from her, but ever since *Selichot,* the stranger no longer obstructs her view. And just before waking this morning, the crone put her arm around Daniel's waist. As the two of them walked off together Daniel looked back as if to say, "Things are all right now, Ruchamah. See. I have not been left alone." When she woke, her heart was light, her sorrow gone. She considers telling Simon this, but he's heading towards his seat.

"Ruchamah, remember when you made cookies with me?" Jacob asks as she sits down. "Can we do that again? Can you come to my house?" He leans across his father's lap to hear her reply just as Rabbi Kramer and Shoshanah greet everyone from the center of the circle.

"We gathered on *Shavuot* when the *Torah* was given," Hillel begins. "Tonight we will present the entire *Torah, Parasha* by *Parasha.* We will sing, dance and move from an ending to a new beginning. You are sitting in the order of the *Parashot* that we have been studying each *Shabbat.* Please read the copy on your seat to remind yourself of what is within it. While the adults are busy doing this, there's fun to be had in the activity room for the children."

"Could we take Jacob?" Aviva asks.

"Of course," Simon says and watches the teenagers depart with his son.

Ruchamah has begun reading her copy of *Parasha Nitzavim.* Simon is anxious to tell her that he has filed the paperwork for his divorce. He wants to hear her laugh as he paints a picture of how Jacob has been running around the house shouting as if his words have been locked up so long they escape in huge rushes. But instead, he forces himself to read the *Parasha.*

Marcia has dressed carefully in the bold red suit she found at Filene's Basement. She has been scanning the crowded synagogue as she waits for latecomers to arrive. Now that it's the end of the holidays, she feels she's on borrowed time. Obsessed with proving her worth, she's determined to greet everyone personally.

Jack turns around several times to look at his *zaftig* wife. She's no wisp in the wind and he'll take her any way he can get her, but he's relieved she's dyed her hair its usual deep auburn that accentuates her tailored suits and matching shoes. Things are almost back to normal. As long as she continues to take his advice, he's pretty sure things will stay that way.

"We begin again and we begin anew," Rabbi Kramer says, when the congregants have finished their preparation. His slimly held hope for a child of his own is gone. Tonight he will tell Beth that he is ready to begin the adoption process. He never brought the little toy dog to the preschool. He's saving it for their new son or daughter. He will say a special prayer to thank God for giving him the wisdom to change his mind and he will tell his father he will honor the family members who died in the Holocaust by naming his adopted children after them. He will bring them up to honor themselves and each other, to have compassion and to regard every life as sacred.

If only he felt more joyful, but he knows that as soon as he tells Beth, his heart will follow. Hopefully, *Simchat Torah* marks the end of his holding onto what he cannot have. Beth, sitting with Ida, looks at her husband, a slight smile beginning at the corners of her mouth. We begin again and we begin anew, she thinks. For the past few days Hillel has seemed more like himself. He makes a concerted effort to listen. And the other day Shoshanah called to say that he'd taken at least half of the workload off her shoulders. "Noah feels like sending him a thank you note," she told her. Hillel returns her smile and makes a mental note to remember to give her the flowers he has saved for later in the synagogue refrigerator. He should have said something to Marcia. Given her over-zealous efforts of late, she might open the refrigerator and assume they belong on the dessert table. He still has work to do as far as his administrative assistant is concerned.

The congregation looks at him expectantly. "Each year," he continues now, "brings both joy and sorrow, not unlike most of these Torah portions. Your job tonight is to search for the joy in your portion and present it as a few lines of a song. For example, the first *parashah, B'reishit,* speaks of the creation of the world. For that we might sing, and he belts out, "Oh what a beautiful morning."

"Thank God we have our cantor," Manny calls out. Everyone laughs, especially Hillel.

"I will unfurl the entire scroll so each congregant can stand behind his or her designated *Parasha* and literally 'uphold the *Torah'* as you give, I mean sing, your synopsis. The opportunity to start over, to learn new things, to understand more than we understood before is indeed something to celebrate."

Simon glances at the Torah portion. "Now that we have our assignment, what do you think we should sing?" he asks Ruchamah.

"Nitzavim comes almost at the end of the Torah," she says, "when Moses has to tell the Israelites that after leading them through the desert for forty years, he is not allowed to cross over into the promised land."

"He could only look from afar," Simon says. "I understand how he felt Ruchamah. I have hurt you. It's the last thing I would have wanted. I placed barriers in our path. I can't seem to cross over them to you. Is there anything I can do to make this right?"

"It's true that Moses cannot go into Israel, though everyone else can." She glances at Simon. He looks so forlorn. "There is immense joy in our *Parasha,* Simon. Right here in this verse God says, 'I have put before you life and death, blessing and curse. Choose life.' I think that is what Moses is telling us. It is the only choice. Worth the risk." But," she adds, quickly, "we only have one minute left to choose a song."

"That's easy. You'll know this one."

When the rabbi calls the children back, they follow him up to the *bimah* where he takes the Torah from the ark. Bearing their newly made Israeli peace flags, courtesy of Aviva, who has written a review of "Billboard from Bethehem" for the Bulletin, a documentary featuring Israeli and Palestinian soldiers who have laid down their weapons and are traveling together across the United States to work for peace, they form a line behind him and begin to sing loudly and with spirit, "*Torah, Torah, Torah siba lanu Moshe.*" After they descend the steps, they circle the congregants who hold out their prayer books to touch the *Torah,* returning them to their lips to indirectly kiss the sanctified book. When the chanting ends, the children sit on the floor in the center of the room. Shoshanah removes the cover and ornaments and unfastens the wimple that binds the scroll. As Hillel begins to unfurl the Torah, he hands the first dowel, *Eitz Chaim,* to Jack in the first section. Jack signals Marcia to join him. "I don't want to hold the *Torah* now," she says as she takes the chair he saved for her, "but later, I'll go up on the *bimah* to dress it." Marcia places her hand on his shoulder.

Rabbi Kramer reaches the 18th *Parasha,* directly in front of Ida. She stands, remembering how reluctant Nathan had been to touch the *Torah* and how she had encouraged him to do so when the rabbi created this ritual last year. Tonight, she moves carefully to take hold of its top edge and just like her fellow congregants around the room, her fingers, like clothespins, suspend the parchment. *Torah* secured, she takes a deep breath. She holds history in her hands, the beginning of the Jewish People. She is part of this story, now a fortunate part, she tells herself remembering Germany and the armband she used to wear. Tomorrow she will go to Nathan, take his hand and say, "This is the hand that touched the *Torah.* Now you are touching the *Torah* through me."

The entire scroll is almost unfurled by the time the rabbi reaches Simon and Ruchamah. Simon helps Jacob, who left his place in the center of the circle, to hold onto the bottom of the delicate parchment from below. She smiles at Simon. He lifts the hand that is not holding Jacob's and gently touches her cheek.

The rabbi begins to circle the room, using the silver *yad* that *Shoshanah* crafted to indicate each portion.

"Now we will come to know the true meaning of *Simchat Torah,*" he says. "*Parasha* by *Parasha* we'll go through the entire five books of Moses--Genesis, Exodus, Leviticus, Numbers, and Deuteronomy. So, sing out your song."

With a nod to Cole Porter and a wink at Marcia, Jack evokes the begat scenes of the first *Parasha* in his tenor voice. "Birds do it, bees do it, even ed-u cat-ed fleas do it, let's do it, let's fall in love."

Shoshanah and the rabbi join in the laughter then move along. Congregants sing out verses from Rodgers and Hart to the Beatles, Sondheim to Joan Baez. "*Parasha* 51," Shoshanah calls out.

Simon bursts into song. "To life, to life, *l'chaim*.' Choose life. *L'chaim Ruchamah*," he whispers as the rabbi moves on.

"*L'chaim*, Simon," she whispers back.

"*L'chaim*," Jacob says. "*L'chaim*, Aviva."

"*L'chaim*, Jacob," Aviva answers. "I like your Hebrew pronunciation."

"My mother's going to come back soon and draw some more murals," he tells her. "Save your blue paint for me, okay, Aviva?"

When they finish the final *Parasha,* Rabbi Kramer says, "Tonight we have come to know the full *Torah. Simchat Torah.* Literally, the joy of *Torah.* We only have one more thing to do. "And that is," he pauses, "to celebrate." He looks at Beth as he speaks. "We have only to celebrate," he repeats, and this time his words are meant only for her.

With that, Jack helps rewind the Torah. Hillel calls Marcia up to dress it once again in its year-round colors not displayed since *Selichot.* The congregants stack the chairs against the wall. Hillel empties the ark of three other Torahs along with each of the ornaments: *yads,* breastplates, and crowns and hands them to the waiting congregants. "It is time for our seven *hakafot.*"

Simon picks up his violin and joins his Klezmer band, the *Simchatim* on the bimah. He lifts Jacob onto his shoulders and begins to play. The first procession begins.

Congregants of all ages, many of them carrying *Torahs* and ornaments, form lines and slowly twist and turn, zip and unzip into formations resembling the process of mitosis, replications of the very DNA of which they are created.

Jack pulls Marcia into the dance. At first she shakes her head and tries to move away. She has always stood on the sidelines checking that things proceed properly, and tonight, things are going well. Surely the rabbi will want to keep her. She relaxes her hand in Jack's. If she gets to stay, she will indeed have something to celebrate. And so will Jack.

Ruchamah and Aviva look for Ida. As they take her hands to draw her into the procession. She resists at first, but moves in when they remind her that this will be the slow one and she can do it. As the next *hakafah* is called, all *Torahs* and their ornaments are exchanged. Ida hands off the crown that Beth has captured for her to Aviva and steps aside; each of the six *hakafot* to follow will increase in rapidity and length.

When they get to the fourth *hakafah,* only women are invited to dance. Simon returns Jacob to his shoulders so he can see Ruchamah carrying one of the Torahs. She is surrounded by other women, demonstrating their joy in the Sephardic fashion by ululating in shrill tones. The men take over the next dance and Shoshanah hands her Torah to Stan who immediately passes it to Hillel with a grin. "Don't worry, Rabbi. I've got your back." Stomping feet and accented huzzahs hold sway. For the sixth *hakkafah,* Simon plays his violin while he dances in the center of the largest circle. Shoshanah hands the Torah to Aviva, reaches for Noah's hand. Beth runs into the circle, takes Shoshanah's hand and gives it a little squeeze. "I like him" she whispers.

"Me, too," Shoshanah whispers back.

"Me, three," Noah adds.

Jacob runs over to the band during the seventh *hakafah* to grab his father's bowing arm; Simon attempts to set his violin down with care as he follows his excited son into the fray. "You be the lead daddy and I will be the whip, like when we roller skate." Simon weaves them through the crowd. Jacob grabs Aviva from her conversation with Lori and Ari on the sidelines. Aviva, not to be the tail for long, spots her mother leaning against the wall to catch her breath and pulls her into the dance. Simon makes a sudden turn and takes Ruchamah's hand. The four of them become a circle. Hand in hand, then arm in arm they spin, in the hub of the community wheel.

The band ends the breathless dance with a few slow measures to make way for the *Torah* service. Exhausted, the congregation sits on the floor as the scrolls are brought up to the *bimah* to be read. Ruchamah and Simon, sitting side by side, listen to the last verses of Deuteronomy. "Oh happy Israel! Who is like you, a people delivered by the Lord...." followed immediately by *Bereishit* – the beginning – the story of creation ending with the words stating God's response. "*Kee Tov.* It is good."

EPILOGUE

Serach sits on the steps of Kehillat Shalom. A half-moon floats in the night sky. She opens her satchel, cataloguing her souvenirs, touchstones of her summer at Kehillat Shalom: one of Miriam's poems translated by Ruchamah, the swanboat pin from Ida's jewelry box, a wine glass from Simon's cupboard, an extra button from the new red suit Marcia was wearing, a citron Shoshanah never used for her bracelet and a ribbon from the bouquet the rabbi intended for Beth.

She closes her satchel. Her journey will provide what she needs. You can come back, she tells herself. Everything is okay now, at least for a little while. You'll stop on your way to other synagogues and check up on everyone. Go now, before you are unable to leave.

In the garden, she picks a late blooming rose before lifting a light breeze to carry high Kehillat Shalom's songs of celebration.

"Shalom L'hitraot," she says softly.

"So it took a little longer than three days," she'll tell Elijah. "But who's counting."

GLOSSARY

Aliyah -- to go up -- 1. to the ark in the synagogue
2. to go to Israel to live

Avinu malkeinu -- Our father, our King -- Hebrew
prayer

Bar Mitzvah/Bat Mitzvah -- religious celebration of
a 13 year old

Bashert -- meant to be

Balik -- Chaim Nachmun Bialik -- Hebrew poet

Bikkurim -- first fruits of the harvest

Rhoda Kaplan Pierce & Sandie Bernstein

Bruch -- Max Bruch, a German Romantic composer and conductor

Challah -- Jewish egg bread often braided

Cholent -- meal prepared before Shabbat starts on friday night and warmed in the oven till use the next day

Davenning - praying

Ess, ess, mein kind -- eat, eat, my child -- Yiddish

Fresser -- big eater -- Yiddish

Fritz Kreissler -- violinist known for creating his own melodies

Frum -- very religious

Gabbai -- sexton at a Jewish religious service

Get -- religious divorce

Gut Shabbas -- Good Sabbath -- Yiddish

Hakkafah -- processional with the Torah on Simchat Torah

Halacha -- Jewish law

Hevra Mipacha --Healing group

Kehillat -- community

Kibitzing -- conversing -- Yiddish

Kiddish -- Hebrew prayer to sanctify the wine

Klezmer -- KLEZMER -- Jewish Eastern European music

L'chaim -- to life

L'hitra'ot -- see you soon

Midrash --a process of interpretion by which scholars filled in the gaps within the Old Testament.

Mitzrayim -- Egypt -- Hebrew

Mitzvah -- a commandment, a good deed, a celebration

Niggun -- melody

Oneg Shabbat -- refreshments following the Friday night Shabbat service

Parashah -- Torah portion of the week

Rachmones -- deep empathy

Rechem -- womb

Rosh Hodesh -- head of the month

Schlep -- carry -- Yiddish

Selichot -- Saturday night service before Rosh Hashanah

Shabbat -- the Jewish sabbath

Shabbaton --Shabat retreat

Shalom -- peace, hello, goodbye

Yiddish -- historical language of the Ashkenazic Jews -- Germanic and Hebraic

base written Hebrew script

Shivah -- week of mourning

Shofar -- ram's horn

Siddur -- prayerbook

Simchat Torah --

Sukkah -- shelter in the harvest fields,

Tammuz -- Jewish month

Tikkun Olam -- acts of loving kindness

Torah -- the five books of Moses

Tzeddakah -- charitable giving

Tzimmis -- dish if roasted root vegetables

Yad -- pointer used when reading the Torah -- Hebrew meaning hand

Yahrzeit -- yearly memorial date

Yehudah Amichai -- shelter in the harvest fields

Yiddish- historical language of the Ashkenazi Jews

Yom Kippur -- Day of Atonement

ABOUT THE AUTHOR

Sandie Bernstein is a poet turned novelist co-authoring her second novel with Rhoda Kaplan Pierce. Literature aficionado forever, creating her own has enhanced her joy and understanding of the media as have all the endeavors of others that illuminate her life who create art, music, theatre and cinema. Sandie enjoys life as a voyager, swimmer, Jewish woman and humanist in the cradle of her family -- beloved husband Neil, daughters Phyllis and Vicki, their husbands, Dave and Herschel, and grandchildren, Justin, Ilana, Lev and Hadi.

Rhoda Kaplan Pierce is a writer, poet and mixed media artist. She is the author of: a play, *Fade to Black* with Carolyn Pogue, *The Apple That Wanted*

Rhoda Kaplan Pierce & Sandie Bernstein

To Be Famous, New Rivers Press, co-author of Leah's Blessing with Sandie Bernstein, Kehillat Press and previously, a poet in the New York CIty Schools Poets in the Schools Program.